LIKE TREES, WALKING

LIKE TREES, WALKING

Ravi Howard

Amistad *An Imprint of HarperCollinsPublishers*

A hardcover edition of this book was published in 2007 by Amistad, an imprint of HarperCollins Publishers.

First Amistad paperback edition published 2008.

Designed by Janet M. Evans

The Library of Congress has cataloged the hardcover edition as follows:

Howard, Ravi.
    Like trees, walking: a novel / Ravi Howard.—1st ed.
        p. cm.
    ISBN: 978-0-06-052959-8
    ISBN-10: 0-06-052959-8
    1. Donald, Michael, 1961–1981—Fiction. 2. African Americans—Crimes against—Fiction. 3. Mobile (Ala.)—Fiction.

    PS3608.O93 L55 2007
    813'.622

                                                        2006048442

ISBN 978-0-06-052960-4 (pbk.)

08 09 10 11 12 BVG/RRD 10 9 8 7 6 5 4 3 2 1

For Laura

For Mom, Dad, R. Jai, and Mama Clara

And he looked up and said,

"I see men like trees, walking."

—MARK 8:24

Acknowledgments

The early financial support and encouragement of Marita Golden and Clyde McElvene of the Hurston/Wright Foundation allowed me to call myself a writer. Also, this novel benefited greatly from sessions led by Patricia Elam and Danzy Senna at the annual Hurston/Wright Writers' Week.

Over the last five years, the stewardship and notes from my agent, Dorian Karchmar, and my editor, Claire Wachtel, have been appreciated beyond words. To Dawn Davis and Rockelle Henderson: I am honored to be a member of the Amistad family.

Also, the completion of this work was aided by generous grant funding from the New Jersey State Council on the Arts.

Prologue

Those of us already gathered along the beach check the wind. With matches cupped in our hands, we watch the smoke rise into the breeze that comes off the water. The conditions have to be right. The wind has to be blowing east. Rising tide and an overcast sky. Nights like these, when conditions are right along the Eastern Shore of Mobile Bay, the salt water from the gulf mixes with the fresh water from the rivers. The fish and blue crabs stop swimming then. Why it happens, I'm not exactly certain—something about the oxygen, the water temperature, and the currents no longer running true. The fish and the blue crabs are stunned, traumatized. At the place where the waters meet, they just float on the surface like they're dead.

When the tide rises in the early-morning hours, the silver sides of the flounder shine as they wash up on the shore.

The crabs collect in the soft sand just below the surface of the water. We wait for them here. Some gather them with scoop nets and stakes while others pick them up in their bare hands and carry them home in washtubs and baskets. Nights like these are called Jubilee.

At night, Mobile is brightened by the shipyard beacons and the battleship lights, but on this side of the bay it's dark just like it should be. It took a few minutes for my eyes to get acclimated, but now I can see details in the darkness, the outlines that separate the water, the tree line, and the moonless sky. The only lights that connect the east and west shores are those scattered along the causeway and the ones on the bridge.

When my brother Paul and I were young, riding in the back of our father's truck, we lay on our backs and counted them, 240 each way. Once we turned off Highway 98 and left the bright spread of the bridge lights, only a few dim lampposts lit the waterside woods. There was more to hear than there was to see. The Edgewater Beach road was covered with oyster shells bleached by the salt water and sun, and the only sound I heard above the engine drone was the crush of our tires grinding the road shells into dust.

I make my way to the spot I like to claim, a rocky stretch at the south end where it's never too crowded. As I walk farther down, it's difficult to see who's speaking as folks say hello when they pass. Some I recognize, others just know me through my family. Most people in Mobile either know us or know of us. Strangers would come up to me all the time saying that they remembered a kind word my father or my grandfather offered when burying their loved one. They had seen our family photo on the church fans parishioners waved on hot days, trying to cool down the humidity or the Holy Ghost.

Among the black funeral homes in Mobile, ours is one of the oldest and considered among the best. In the picture, my grandfather, my parents, my brother, Paul, and I stand on the front steps of the funeral home. In black script beneath our feet—"Deacon Memorial: Seven Generations in the Service." In some of the old churches we work in, I still see those fans, creased and faded, with the same picture that still hangs on the wall in the mortuary office. It was the last picture we all took together. I was seventeen then.

People tell me how much I look like my father, even though I know it's not true. In that photo, my brother, Paul, was a carbon copy of Daddy as they stood together on that bottom step. The lines of their faces were identical like their pinstripes. As I stood on the second step behind my father, I had the rare chance to tower above him. People only say we look alike because I stood beside him in church vestibules saying the consoling words that I had heard him say for years. Once my parents retired, I was left to say the words alone.

I carry my basin in one hand and my stake in the other. I carry tucked under my arm a grocery bag that contains, among other things, a Crown Royal sack. When Paul arrives, I can pour a little liquor like I always do.

It's 11:45 P.M., and the date on my watch is stuck in the space between fourteen and fifteen in anticipation of midnight. A few minutes from now, I'll be forty. Forty is supposed to be a milestone, a "big one," as they say. A party has been planned in my honor. My wife, my kids, and my parents have been up to something. They have that obvious silence about them of people trying too hard to keep a secret. I'm sure they've gone to a lot of trouble to get everyone together, so I'll act surprised.

I'll have a good time like I always do. July means family

reunions, the Fourth, fireworks, and picnics. Most of all, July is a month I've always shared with my brother. He was born 362 days before me. We were, as my father would sometime call us, the damn-near twins. For three days every July, we were the same age.

"Old man Roy Deacon."

It takes my eyes a minute to adjust so that I can see him. I can only hear his voice at first. When I see Paul, I am reminded of how the years have treated me. I am much rounder at the middle even when I suck in my gut, and my hairline has gone its own way. Paul hasn't changed. Seeing us there together, it might be hard to imagine that we were born so close together.

"How's forty feel?"

"Wouldn't know yet. Got fifteen minutes left. Let me enjoy it."

"How does it feel to be on the verge of a grand transcendental moment?" he says. He likes to talk shit. "On the cusp of something greater than yourself."

"I'll tell you in fifteen minutes."

He seems satisfied enough to give me a moment's peace. I drop everything, and I'm lucky not to break the bottle when everything hits the sand.

"What'd you bring?"

I don't have to say it, just open the grocery bag to show him the purple Crown Royal sack.

"You always come through, Roy. Always did."

His face turns to a frown as soon as he sees what I have rattling around in my washtub, the other contraband my wife doesn't let me eat at home, a big bag of Funyuns, peanut brittle, and a can of sardines.

"If your stomach could talk," he tells me.

I am ashamed to say I haven't changed all that much. The habits I made when I was young I still carry, especially the ones that started on this stretch of beach. Our favorite part about summers on the bay was Jubilee time, and Paul looked forward to them more than his birthday. Of course, you always know when your birthday is coming, so it's never a surprise. Jubilee nights are different. They only happen in the summer months, twice, maybe three times a season. Every few years one would fall somewhere between our birthdays, and we would celebrate here.

I miss those days. My father told me when I was young that things change between brothers when they get older. My father's not as healthy as he used to be, and he sees his only brother once, maybe twice a year. He always says there's not enough time to catch up on all the days you miss. I didn't understand it when I was younger, but now it's clear.

Paul and I started coming to the Jubilee when we were children, but it was more fun when we were old enough to come alone. After we claimed our spot, Paul would catch an hour or two of sleep until the surf came in. I would wake him, and then we'd talk and drink whatever we'd stolen from the liquor cabinet. We listened to WBLX on Paul's transistor radio while we made our stakes, setting ten-penny nails into the ends of old broom handles and filing them down to a point. These we used to pierce the shells of the blue crab and drop them into the washtub.

I would always scoop the crabs while Paul collected the fish. He ran a lanyard through the mouths and gills of the gathered flounder, bunching them like bananas on the end of a string. The other end of the rope carried a steel spike that he drove into the sand. As the fish lay in the shallows, their sides expanded and contracted as the surf washed over them, keeping them alive until we were ready to take them home.

When he pulled the fish from the water for good, they flapped their heads from one side to the other, waiting for the gulf tide to pass across their gills once more. Instead, they found the air that choked them. When I was a child, I stared into the buckets and watched the wide, staring eyes of the fish as they grew weary of trying. In the end, they just went still.

I still have some of those same tin basins. I keep them stacked beneath the worktable in the corner of my garage until nights like these when I walk across the sand, stake in one hand and washtub in the other. Once it's filled I'll need two trips to get everything back to the truck, but I don't mind the walking.

A constellation of matches, lighters, and flashlights peppers the dark, flickering like a far-off city. For as long as there have been people here, these nights on the Eastern Shore have been mystic hours. Before the slaves and settlers, the Mobila Indians gathered what the waters left at their feet. The explorers who came here named this place the Bay of the Holy Spirit, trying to appease the shallow waters that endangered their vessels. The bay bottom is covered with the remains of ships that got battered to pieces.

The slaves called the waters sacred as well, but for different reasons. They believed these waters were spirited by slaves who died on the boats, their bodies thrown into the night waters. When the Jubilee nights came, the slaves called what the waters left their manna. They were said to have believed that the waves were God's hands pushing it to the shore. *Jubilee* was a word that meant everything to them, freedom or heaven—whichever came first. For some of the Africans that lived here, these nights were the only times when food was plentiful. All these years later, such nights have become recreation. For me they are an escape from the world on the quiet end of the beach. A night of solitude before a birthday with too many candles.

"What's on the menu for tomorrow?" Paul asks me.

"Same old same. Cake and ice cream. Gumbo, liquor."

"Not all at the same time, I hope," he said. "But with your greedy ass I guess it doesn't matter."

Paul has his shoes off. He has those high-arched feet that barely touch the ground, look like they're always ready to run. When he was a child, he would stand in the tide waiting for the Jubilee to brush against his feet.

On the north end of the shore, the procession of headlights is still coming around the corner from the beach road. They pass the signpost that carries the familiar greeting. "Welcome to Daphne, the Jubilee City." I've passed that sign on the road no telling how many times to swim, to fish, and to gather on birthday nights, Jubilee or not, even if it's just long enough to drink a little liquor and pour a little more onto the sand. Just a little something I do to mark another year's passing.

We all have our habits. My mother saves the newspapers from our birthdays. Tomorrow's early edition will come off the press soon. In the morning, she'll add it to the *Mobile Press-Register* stacks neatly arranged in the RC Cola crates she saves. She keeps them in the closet under the staircase, stored away from the sunlight.

It used to seem silly to me, but I suppose I should be thankful for forty years' worth of newspapers. Every week, I deal with the loved ones of people who'll never have another birthday. Many of the people are folks I had known. My father told me that times would come when the people who came across our table would be friends.

Near my mother's crates of front-page birthdays, she has a small filing cabinet where she stores her important papers. Among them, news clippings and mementos from watershed days. Facts to share with her fourth-graders. First black man elected to some office. First black woman to reach some milestone. Lest we forget, she still likes to say. Files and files of monumental days, each labeled in neat school-teacher handwriting.

Some of those days don't need mementos. It would be nice if forgetting could cancel them, show us how the world could have been if those days never happened at all. Forty years' worth of days and ones like those are what I remember the most.

Among the keepsakes in that cabinet, my mother kept the news clippings about Michael Donald, neatly trimmed and filed in chronology, as if putting them in order helped it all to make sense. The first of the lot was a story from the evening edition, March 21, 1981. That was a Saturday. That morning my brother found Michael's body hanging from a tree on Herndon Avenue. Michael Donald was a friend of ours. Forty years' worth of days, and ones like those are the ones I remember most, not because I want to but because I have no choice.

PART ONE

Early Saturday Morning | MARCH 21, 1981

Paul had always been a creature of the night. We both were. When we were children, our nocturnal habits were permissible only during Jubilees. We looked forward to staying up past midnight, and as the morning hours grew in number we watched the dim light collect itself at the edges of the sky. It was an innocent intoxication—that sleepless fatigue that comes while waiting for the tide. A strange disorientation took hold when I no longer had a night's sleep to separate one day from another.

We weren't the only ones awake. The cities were quiet on both sides, but the world along the water was a place of constant motion. Twelve hundred freighters passed through the narrow shipping channel every year on the way to the state docks up the Mobile River. The shipyards and factories, the gantries and cranes, the tall stacks that smoked up the sky day and night—these were our skyscrapers.

Even in those early hours, the lights at Gulf Land Paper were always burning, Easter and Christmas included. Even when I wasn't close enough to see the mill, sometimes I could smell it. As a child, I thought there was no stench worse than the sulfur fumes from the paper mill. The only people who couldn't smell it were those closest to it. All the mill workers had nasal fatigue, when the fumes were so overwhelming that the nose could no longer detect them. Paul said that after a while the odor didn't bother him, but I could still smell it on his work clothes whenever he walked through the door.

My brother started working in the paper mill when he turned fifteen. Mr. Davie from across the street had worked for the mill for twenty years, and he was one of the first black supervisors. We had been in Mr. Davie's Boy Scout troop when we were young. I think some guys only joined because they knew he gave summer jobs to neighborhood boys he thought would make good workers. Most everybody wanted a plant position where they could make double or three times what they could get flipping burgers at McDonald's or stocking shelves at TG&Y. Paul liked his pay better than the $3.35 minimum wage my father paid me. I had asked for an even $4—would have settled for $3.50—but he said no.

"You need to understand how hard some folks have to work for a dollar," Daddy had said. He liked to lecture me on the big picture. Claimed that I'd appreciate all I stood to gain. All this would be mine, he had said once, standing in a room full of caskets.

I had never received a paycheck with a signature other than my father's, but Paul had never had to rely on him for money. He'd always known how to hustle for a dollar—paper routes, mowing lawns, cleaning gutters—or any of the itemized tasks listed on the "Paul Deacon Enterprises" flyers he stuffed in the neighborhood mailboxes. "Anything that you won't do, I can do for a dollar or two."

Before he even started working at Gulf Land, Paul already had plans for his wages. Our uncle Parnell had a Mercury pickup, something like the one Lamonte drove on *Sanford & Son*. For ten years, it had been sitting in his backyard, where the paint had oxidized and the tires had rotted. Paul offered him $300 for it, way too much, considering.

Mr. Davie had already promised Paul a job when he turned fifteen, but getting Mr. Davie's approval was only the half of it. He still needed our parents to say okay and sign the work permit. Paul tried Mama first.

"Your father and I'll have to talk about it," she told him.

Most times that meant no, especially since Daddy thought that the paper mill was somewhere other people's children worked, those without the benefit of a good education, middle-class upbringing, or a family business that was over a century old. He wasn't the kind of man who looked down on people, but he didn't make a habit of looking up to folks either.

"People talk about blue-collar work like it's an absolute virtue," he had said. "Some people do it because they have no choice. Either by their own doing or by the world being what it is. There's more to working hard than sweating for somebody's wage."

At that time, the sign in front of the funeral home read "Six Generations in the Service." As far as Randall Deacon was concerned, the seventh generation was a done deal. Before he had even heard about Paul's career aspirations that summer, he had already signed us up for the certification classes at Bishop State College. He even taught the field study courses at the funeral home and hoped we'd be among his students as we prepared to run the funeral home one day. Since I was thirteen, I had worked with my father, running errands, typing death notices, and whatnot. As soon as I got a license, I was driving the family cars I'd spent years washing. There was never a moment when I said, This is what I want to do. By then, I was already doing it. More and more, I'd heard my parents speak of what they planned to do in their retirement. Trips they would take, hobbies they looked forward to. The expectation seemed clear that soon after college, Paul and I would be responsible for the business. My father thought those odd jobs would be good training for the back-office side of things, but Paul was buying time. It was more than a phase. My brother had already told me that he had no intention of joining the business.

"I'll be damned if I ever drain blood from a body," he said.

My father had hopes of seeing Paul and me work in the funeral home together. Sometimes while I was there working, Daddy would slip and call me by my brother's name. The firstborn had always worked in the business, and my father had no idea things would be any different. Eventually, it would all come to a head when Paul worked up the nerve to give him that work permit. Daddy didn't say anything at first; he just worked that stare into Paul, waiting for him to explain.

"I figured you had Roy around," Paul said, looking at me as if to apologize, "so I thought you could do without me."

"You need to start learning the business. I think I've been more than patient with your little projects."

They looked at each other and said nothing, maybe hoping the silence would be enough to make the other change his plan. Paul could have eased into it, tested the waters first, but that never was his style.

"I don't think— I know this isn't for me."

"There's nothing wrong with being a mortician."

"There's nothing wrong with the paper mill. It's good money."

"It's somebody else's money," my father said, staring at the blanks of the permit, all filled in except for his signature. "That mill doesn't have your name on the front."

Paul waited for a moment, gathering his response.

"Since I'm never going to be a mortician anyway, I don't see any point in starting something I won't finish."

I waited for the inevitable rant, the history lesson, my father's reassertion that he wasn't running a democracy. But it never came. That was more of a shock than anything my brother had said. Paul was as stubborn as my father was, but he wasn't arbitrary about anything. I guess Daddy realized that my brother wouldn't have walked into that office unless he intended to follow through. My father continued to sit there in silence, holding the work permit like it was something heavy.

"Your mother and I will have to talk about it."

The permit sat on my father's desk for two days. They finally had their Camp David meeting on the back porch. I couldn't hear what they said to each other, and Paul would never tell me, but that afternoon my father made his long, slow signature on the carbon form. *Randall Jacob Deacon.* When the certification classes started in June, I was the only Deacon on the roll.

Meanwhile, Paul started out in the Gulf Land office, making coffee, answering phones, getting lunches, and making better money than I ever had. By the end of summer, his pickup truck was sitting on steel-belted radials instead of cinder blocks in Uncle Parnell's yard. Paul stayed on at the mill working after school and on weekends during the fall, and Mr. Davie told my father about how hard he worked. Daddy hoped Paul would stay in the front office, working in management at least, but that would entail a jacket, a tie, and sitting in one place for the better part of eight hours, requirements that never appealed to my brother. Once he graduated high school, Paul got an apprentice position and started working the night shift. That fall Paul started college at South Alabama and spent three night shifts a week working one of the huge combines that chewed Alabama timber into pulp.

I got used to Paul coming home in his work clothes the morning after a shift. When I walked downstairs on most Saturdays, Paul and I would eat a couple of the doughnuts he'd picked up from the Krispy Kreme on his way home. Before I headed to our first funeral and he headed to bed, we'd talk for a while. I'd catch him up on the *Sanford & Son* reruns he missed even though he'd seen them all. Then he'd go to sleep, and I'd go to the first funeral of the day.

On the way into the house, Paul would bring in the newspaper off the front porch. When I woke up on March 21, 1981, the *Mobile Register* still lay on the doormat, hiding the woven letters that spelled out WELCOME. Paul should have been home by then, and I was starving.

My mother had already left to set up the flowers that were delivered early every morning. We were burying Nelson Whitfield at New Shiloh. His body was still in the mortuary chapel from the wake the night before. I followed the same schedule I adhered to every other Saturday. It always started with the five-minute drive from the house to the funeral home. From there I was supposed to drive Mr. Whitfield to the church at nine o'clock.

My last clean dress shirt was wrinkled, so I set up the ironing board in the washroom. From there I would be able to see Paul at the back door with the Krispy Kreme box in his hand. If I didn't get something to eat before Mr. Whitfield's service, I'd have to wait until the afternoon. By then it was going on seven o'clock, and I couldn't wait any longer. I dropped two slices of white bread in the toaster. Before the coils turned red, the phone rang.

When the phone rang so early in the morning, it oftentimes meant somebody was dead. An elderly person had passed in the night. A Friday-night traffic fatality. The families of deceased would set about the task of notifying family and friends, and somewhere among the sad litany of phone calls, they dialed our number.

As a child, I would answer the phone in the family room during my morning cartoons. Our parents had instructed us on the phone etiquette they expected at all times, especially when the caller could be a grieving family member. *Turn down the television or radio. Speak clearly and mannerly.* It had become a conditioned response, because there was no telling who was on the other end.

A second ring.

The sound echoed through the green plastic casing of the rotary phone mounted next to the laminated list of emergency numbers, just below the calendar that carried our picture.

The phone rang once more.

Eventually these calls would be mine alone. I had always listened to the reassuring tone my father took: earnest without condescension. Listening more than speaking.

Choosing the right words and knowing exactly when to say them. The proper timbre of the voice. By then I was a senior in high school, and I had worked more funerals than I cared to count. Had fielded just as many phone calls. Despite the preparation, I had not yet mastered the fortitude that my father exuded, the calm that his voice carried no matter who was the subject of the call.

"Nobody needs your grief on top of their own," he had said many times.

Just before the fourth ring, I answered.

"Deacon residence. Roy speaking."

It was Sergeant Kincaid, whose voice was familiar from our church choir, the smooth tenor that would lead songs. Although he had that rock-steady tone expected of police officers, on that morning his voice was shaking.

"Roy, I—I need to speak to your daddy."

"Just a second, I'll get him—"

"Roy," my father said.

I had assumed I was the only one awake. As though he had heard his name being called in his sleep, my father stood behind me clad in a bathrobe and pajamas, reaching for the phone. While he spoke to Sergeant Kincaid, I pretended not to listen while I sprayed the starch on my collar. Mr. Kincaid's voice spilled out of the phone, but the words were too distorted to make any sense of. As Daddy looked out the window, I tried to read his face but got nothing.

Out of habit, my father would run his fingers along the carvings in the gopher-wood table while he reassured the person on the phone, but this time his hands were still. He said nothing. The only sounds I heard were the cryptic hum of Sergeant Kincaid, and the whisper of the iron making its steam, water droplets sizzling against the steel before they turned to vapor. I rested the iron and pulled the left sleeve tight across the board.

"Is Paul all right?"

I heard my brother's name just as I reached for the iron. Instead of the plastic handle, my fingers touched the face, burning a red line clear across my palm. I swore in silence, waiting to find out what was happening.

"Where is he now?"

The toaster in the kitchen coughed up my slices, but my hunger was already gone. In its place came the resulting uneasiness of hearing my brother's name in the early-morning phone calls that in our house only meant one thing. After a heavy silence, my father's fingers loosened, and he mouthed a *Thank God* as he collected himself.

"We'll be there in ten minutes," he said, just before he hung up the phone. "We have to go see about your brother," he told me.

"What's wrong?"

"Michael Donald was lynched last night," he said. "Your brother found the body."

It didn't make sense. Michael went to Murphy High School, graduated with my brother. He played ball at the rec center. He went to school every day and church on Sundays. The shock of finding out somebody was dead was only magnified when you found out how. Of all the ways I'd heard of, seen. Lynched. People didn't get lynched in 1981. My questions came faster than I could find the words to ask them, and I tried to sort through it as the pain in my hand throbbed. Before my father ran up the stairs two at a time, he yelled back for me to get his keys.

"Yes, sir."

By the time I got his keys five minutes later, he was waiting for me at the car, fully dressed.

We made our way down Springhill Avenue, one of the tree-lined streets that had made our city famous. Mobile was called the City Under the Trees. The slogan didn't tell the whole story, because some of those trees had stories of their own. The last man lynched in Mobile was James Lewis, a name that was on our books because my great-grandfather buried him in Plateau. It had been sixty-some-odd years. My grandfather was my age when it happened, and he had shared some of the same kinds of stories my parents told Paul and me. They never tried to shield us from the ugliness of the world, but they must have assumed that certain things would stay in the past. Apparently, that was too much to ask for as my father's Lincoln sped toward Herndon Avenue. A lynching was just around the corner.

I didn't have to look for the street sign to know where we would turn. Blue and red police lights washed across the Krispy Kreme on the corner. Half a dozen apron-clad employees stood at the side entrance, staring down the street. Two patrolmen put up the blue wooden barricades that had probably been in storage since Mardi Gras. Another officer carried a roll of yellow police tape, an endless string of boldface cautions flapping against the concrete as he walked down the block.

Paul's truck idled on the curb with parking lights on and the door wide open. The radio was on. The weather report that came through the speakers told us what we could already feel, cool morning temperatures, low humidity, easterly wind gusts. I all of a sudden felt cold, as if hearing about the chill made it that much sharper.

My father and I split up to look for Paul among the crowd of people halfway down the street. I found Sergeant Kincaid standing in the middle of the street with his back to me. He held a large pair of hedge clippers, squeezing the handles slowly, cutting nothing but air.

"Mr. Kincaid, where is he?"

"He's still in the tree. They won't let me cut him down until the coroner gets here."

"I mean Paul. Where's Paul?"

"Oh, I'm sorry. He's right over there in my patrol car."

He had only looked at me briefly while we talked. His eyes kept blinking in twitches and darting around that tree.

"You all right?"

It took him a moment to answer.

"I won't be until they let me cut him down. Even then, I don't know. Go on and see about your brother."

"Yes, sir."

Sergeant Kincaid's patrol car was parked on the far side of the hanging tree. I didn't want to see Michael there. Just being that close made my sick. The Hot Doughnuts sign had clicked on in the Krispy Kreme window, and the smell nauseated me. My throat burned, and my stomach twisted. With the tree in my periphery, I keep my head toward the patrol car, where I saw the top of my brother's head as he slouched in the passenger seat.

When I opened the door, Paul sat with his hands folded in his lap, pressing hard on his knuckles. Mud covered the front of his coveralls, and patches of dried blood stained his windbreaker. He didn't even look up to see who had opened the door before he started talking.

"I'm sorry about your doughnuts."

"Don't worry about that, Paul."

"I'm sorry."

"It's all right."

"No, it's not. It can't be all right."

He rolled his head toward me with a heavy turn as if it took every muscle to look my way. The remains of tears stained the corners of his eyes.

"You saw it?"

"No, I didn't want to look."

"Yesterday, we played ball at the center. It was me, Mike, Earl Peters—you know Earl from around the corner—Pony Shade, and Tunk Turner. Some boys from Down the Bay tried to run us off the court, but Mike was on fire. Said we were going to all meet up there this afternoon."

He looked toward the tree, then down at his watch. "Couple hours from now."

When I sat down on the grass by his opened door, the dew soaked through my slacks. Paul kept working the knuckles, cracking them as many times as the joints would give.

"Mike told us he'd see us tomorrow."

I had no idea what to say. My mouth had gone dry, and I suppose my mind had, too.

"I'm sorry," I told him, more reflex than words.

Crowds had gathered on opposite ends of the street. Behind them, the traffic on Springhill and Old Shell crept by as the drivers strained to see the source of the commotion. A garbage truck sat behind the barricades, idling hard as the orange-clad trash men waited to empty the brimming steel cans.

Paul turned his head back at the tree beyond the driver's-side window, but sitting there on the ground, I couldn't see it. I didn't want to. I just stared at the radio that came to life every few seconds as the officers talked in codes I didn't understand.

"Don't look over there, Paul."

"I'm gonna see it anyway."

"Me and Daddy came to take you home."

"I couldn't do a thing for him," he said. "He was already cold."

"I know."

"Those shoes are the same ones he played ball in yesterday."

New tears rolled through the residue of old ones and disappeared into the goatee that had not yet grown in full. On the other side of my brother's face, there were two splotches of dried blood. He had no physical wounds, so it must have come from Michael's body. I folded my handkerchief to the clean inside and handed it to him.

"I kept yelling until somebody called an ambulance," he said, wiping his face. The first strokes only smudged the blood even more, but the tears helped to dampen the cloth so he could wipe his face clean. "Then the police came and made me let him go."

He stared down at the crimson streaks, then folded the handkerchief closed.

"I just want to go home."

My father stood with Sergeant Kincaid halfway down the street. We started walking that way, but a lanky white man in a navy windbreaker and khakis stopped us. He looked from me to Paul, and down to the scribbling on the pages of a small leather-bound writing pad with empty brand-new pages.

"Are one of you two Paul Deacon?" he said, his diction as official as one could have imagined.

"That's me."

His shiny badge looked as brand new as he did. He wore a wedding band that, too big for his finger, slid between his knuckles. His forehead was gathered as he stared at the half-empty page like he was waiting for something to appear. He smelled like Old Spice and looked not much older than we were. His eyebrows were the only hair on his face, and a small razor nick ran along his chin. The only indications of his age were the new bags that were forming below his eyes.

"I know this is a difficult morning for everybody, but I just need a bit more information."

"I already told everything to Sergeant Kincaid."

"Well, I appreciate Sergeant Kincaid doing that," he said. "I'm Detective Wilcox, and I'm assigned to the case, so I need to get some info directly. Just need a few minutes."

Detective Wilcox mustered a half smile, but his brow never straightened. Despite the chill in the air, the sweat had started to darken the baby blue cotton of his button-down. One hand held the notebook and a ballpoint pen from South-Trust Bank, and the other hand was shaking.

"I don't know what else I can tell you," Paul told him.

"Now," he said, "if a friend of mine died, I think I'd want to do everything I could to help him."

"I hope you never have to find out."

"I understand that it's a difficult time."

He employed the same empty language that I used to speak of death when I had nothing better to say, just hoping to get through the awkward moment and on to the next.

"How did you know the victim?"

"From Murphy."

"My wife went to Murphy," he said. He waited for a response as if we were supposed to say "That's nice. What year?" As he looked at us, his eyes darted toward the gathering crowd. He kept turning his wedding band, twisting it counterclockwise like it held magic that would make everything all right. After a pause that was too long to be comfortable, he returned to his questions.

"When was the last time you saw the victim alive?"

"I saw Mike yesterday afternoon. About five."

"Where was this?"

"At the King Rec Center."

"Was it normal for him to be out at night, alone?"

"No."

"Anybody have it in for him?"

"No."

"Did he have a girlfriend over here?" He didn't look us in the eye when he said it. Just stared down at the notes he scribbled. "You know, maybe one of these white girls round here took a liking to him."

He looked up then and kind of shrugged his shoulders as if somebody else had asked the question.

"No," Paul said.

"I'm not judging—but something like that might get an ex-boyfriend, you know, some other man worked up enough."

"Like I said, sir. He wasn't mixed up in anything like that."

"What was he doing all the way over here?"

"Why don't you go ask him?"

Detective Wilcox looked at me then, like I was supposed to apologize for my brother. My patience was just as thin as Paul's, and neither of us wanted to be there a minute more than we had to.

"I'd like to take him home now," I told him.

As Wilcox looked at us, the crowd down the block had grown bigger. Twice as many police officers littered the street. They were just different versions of the same. Light blue shirts and navy pants and hats. A few had sunglasses in their shirt pockets, ready for the sun to clear the trees. There were a few county sheriff's deputies there to boot. All of them, no matter what their stripes, went over to the tree to have their looks.

From where I stood, Michael's body was hidden in the shadows. Still, I couldn't help but see his face. Remember him sitting on our front porch with Paul. See him in the hallway at school. Paul's eyes kept returning to those branches, but in a way I suppose his eyes had never left. When I put my hand on Paul's shoulder and started to lead him away, I felt the weight of him against my hand, as if I was all that kept him from hitting the ground.

"One more thing," Detective Wilcox said, flipping to a blank page. "I figure both of you are nice young men, and your friend, too. But there's been some drug activity around here."

Paul's neck and back clenched up all at once. He moved away from my hand and turned around. His balance returned, bolstered by anger that pounded in his temples.

"How many times do I have to say it?"

"It's hard to be sure sometimes."

"I'm damn sure."

As little respect as my father had for the Mobile police, he always told us to be cool and answer their questions. Remember names and badge numbers. Wilcox. 214. Paul and I had lived by those rules to avoid conflict.

"I don't mean any disrespect to your buddy," Wilcox said. "I'm just considering all the angles."

I didn't see him walk over, but I was relieved to hear his voice. My father's hands were now on Paul's shoulders where mine had been.

"A black man in a tree," my father said. "How many angles do you need?"

My father was too pissed to be cordial. He didn't re spond when Wilcox introduced himself. Daddy spoke into Paul's ear, too loud to be a whisper.

"How are you holding up?"

Paul shrugged. Daddy always hated when we did that. He had always told us that a shrug was not an answer for anything, but on a day where answers were scarce, it seemed appropriate.

"Sergeant Kincaid said you-all found a cross burned in front of the courthouse this morning," my father asked him. "Do you have that in your notebook?"

"I don't assume anything until I have all the facts, sir," Wilcox said. By then he was as ready to leave as we were.

"Considering the circumstances, I'm going to take my son home now. The sooner we leave, the sooner you can get back to work."

Wilcox stared at the stains on Paul's clothes, then his eyes moved toward the tree and beyond to the news vans at the end of the street.

"He touched the body. I'll need his coveralls and his jacket for evidence."

My brother pulled his arms out of the jacket and let it fall back on the patrol car. Paul wore jeans and a T-shirt beneath the coveralls that he'd unzipped, let gather in a heap at his feet. Once Wilcox folded the clothes into trash bags, he scribbled something on his pad before he returned it to his pocket.

"I assure you, the Mobile Police Department is going to do all we can to figure this out."

The sad part was that he probably meant it. He stood tall, as though his posture made the assurance that much stronger. It didn't matter what he said, because the truth of it was playing out behind him, the Mobile police milling about the block in slow and steady chaos. The only crime scenes I'd seen were on the news and on cop shows. There was always a slew of police officers knocking on doors, canvassing the area, and pursuing the guilty parties with prime-time tenacity. Nothing of the like seemed to be happening on Herndon Avenue. The gathered authorities were taking their turns looking at Mobile's first lynching in sixty years. Before we left Detective Wilcox, my father made one request.

"Cut that boy down before his mother gets here."

My father led us away, but not in the direction of the commotion. We detoured onto Old Shell and circled the block to avoid the crime scene. It was amazing the difference a block could make. One street over from the madness, Hallett Street was as quiet as a neighborhood was supposed to be just after sunrise on a Saturday morning. A sloped field ran behind the Herndon Avenue properties, and the roofs of the wooden houses rose above the backyard fence line. We reached the middle of that block, where the crown of the hanging tree topped the pickets, and the strobes of police light bled between the slats. After we got in the truck, Daddy closed Paul's door and tried to muster a smile.

"It's going to be all right."

Paul didn't even look at him. "When?"

"Soon," my father told him, but Paul just stared straight ahead as if "soon" was some place beyond the windshield, some landmark we would pass on our way home.

WBLX had stopped playing music on "Saturday Soul Showcase" to take phone calls on the scene unfolding around us. The news of the hanging and the burnt cross had spread. Rumors and theories were already being hatched. Phone lines couldn't hold the anger as the loud voices cut through the distortion and static. Paul switched off the knob, and we were left with the street music of the passing cars as they rattled a loose manhole cover on Springhill Avenue.

My father had taken us the long way around, hoping that he could shield us from the body in the tree, but it turned out to be a noble gesture that was all for nothing. There was no room in the street for us to turn around, so we had no choice but to drive right by the heart of the crime scene. We drove toward the crushed box of Krispy Kremes in the gutter. A few starlings had gathered, picking over what was inside. The birds scattered as our car approached, came right back as soon as we passed.

"Sorry about your doughnuts."

"It's all right, Paul."

"I can get you some more."

"It'll be all right."

Sergeant Kincaid stepped aside and looked toward the tree, the hedge clippers dangling by his side. I had never had much use for praying, but at certain times, I would say a word or two just in case someone was on the other end of the line. I started praying then for Michael and for his family, but most of all I prayed that the coroner would come soon.

As we drove down Herndon toward the corner, Paul rested his head against the window. The circles of breath against the window matched the heavy falls of his chest. He looked exhausted, and I thought he had fallen asleep until he clapped his hands over his ears, with the veins rising along the back of his hands. He heard the sound of my unanswered prayer. The coroner's truck sped past us, but it was too late. I looked back and saw Michael's mother, her remaining children supporting her as she saw the tree. I can still hear her screaming.

By 11:15 Saturday morning, I was leading Nelson Whitfield's procession over the bay to Little Bethel Cemetery. Mr. Whitfield was ninety-three years old. From what I had gathered, the doctors told the family that they could do no more. Take him home and make him comfortable, they'd said. Everybody in the world who loved him had come together for farewells while Nelson was still able to hear them. He died in his sleep sometime Monday night. At his funeral, his friends and family didn't have much to say. Perhaps they had said it all to him before he died, so there was no need for the shouting and screaming.

Nelson Whitfield's loved ones rode in the family cars my father and Bertrand drove. Behind the long black Lincolns was the remaining procession, a dozen cars of all kinds, linked by the bloodshot glow their headlights gave in the daytime. Once we reached Little Bethel, the gathered mourners arranged themselves beneath the green-and-white tent that shaded the last bit of unoccupied ground in the family plot, littered with the dried-out remains of roses, knuckled magnolia twigs brought down by the storms. Some people left artificial flowers, thinking that the false colors would never fade. I knew different. I was the one who on occasion cleared the stained silk of the weather-beaten flowers that eventually fall to pieces just like everything else.

The Whitfield plot lay toward the back of the Little Bethel lawn. The oldest of the family headstones, discolored by the mud and the years, was as spotted as the hands and faces of the elderly kin gathered at the graveside. They waited, looking tired but patient, and listened to the reverend repeat the ashes-and-dust words they had all heard each time their ground was broken once again. They showered brother Whitfield with fistfuls of flowers and dirt before we lowered him into the ground. Once it was over, the pallbearers remained close to one another, as if they would be called upon to carry him one more time. The family members peppered us with the words that were flattering and eerie. A beautiful service. He looked good. If only it ended like that for everybody, a peacefulness that everyone couldn't help but see.

By the time the noon sunshine had breached the thick shade of Little Bethel, Nelson Whitfield's kin were going their ways, and I was going mine. The only benefit to driving a hearse was that it was a one-way trip. I didn't have to drive the families back home again, a two-way journey where the silence was as awkward as the conversation.

On the way across the bridge, it was just me and the empty hearse and no procession of people wondering why I was driving so fast. It took me twenty minutes to get back across the water. Once I came out of the tunnel onto Government Street, I passed the courthouse, where a circle of burned grass surrounded the charred remains of a cross. The ones pictured on television or in history books were tall and sturdy, dwarfing the men who stood around them. The one in front of the courthouse was just a mockery of a cross, two pieces of wood emaciated by fire. It was waist high to the sheriff's deputy who leaned on the nearby railing, smoking a cigarette. I couldn't help but wonder why the remains of the burned wood—like Michael Donald's body—had been left for so long for all the world to see. A two-ring circus a few blocks removed.

Traffic crawled on both sides of the avenue, and the deputy stamped out his cigarette and walked toward the street, reaching in his back pocket for his leather ticket book. "There's nothing more to see here" was what he might have said if he had bothered to say anything at all. He talked with a gesture, waving the scratched binder from one side to the other, shooing flies. The clock on the courthouse said 12:30. I had promised Lorraine a ride home from Dunbar High School. Her play practice was just about over, and she'd be waiting for me.

I dropped off the hearse, and drove my Datsun over to Dunbar. I pulled into one of the spaces beneath the statue of the school's namesake. Beneath the pewter statue, a thick piece of weathered oak had the name Paul Laurence Dunbar etched into the grain. Gift of the Class of 1956, my father's year. The school wasn't an art magnet back then, just one of the black high schools. Like the others after desegregation, Dunbar needed to justify its continued place in the world. Those that could not—Mobile County Training School, Central—had become empty shells, and a decade of thrown rocks had made black eyes of the windows. Dunbar survived, and its second coming had been that of a performing arts magnet. Lorraine was among the students from the other high schools who came to Dunbar for two hours a day to study music and drama.

At the far end of the parking lot, the doors to the wood-shop were open, and a student stood over a table saw, his hair topped with a crown of the same sawdust he sprayed into the air. It carried that damp, sweet smell that came from just-cut wood. A girl with hands splattered with three colors painted the sign that would sit in front of the school:

Dunbar School of the Performing Arts

· Presents ·

A RAISIN IN THE SUN
April 24–26, 1981

The shop teacher walked around them, favoring his left side, rubbing a piece of sandpaper between his fingers. He waved hello when he saw me. My freshman year I had taken Mr. Oaklyn's class, riding the bus over from Murphy two periods a day to build the sets for the spring and fall plays, building cities and rooms from donated scraps of lumber. Once I started working at the funeral home, all that came to an end.

I walked into the front door, with the auditorium double doors straight ahead. From a short length of chain a cardboard sign hung from the door: REHEARSAL IN PROGRESS—DO NOT ENTER. There were other signs along the walls and above the pay phone, mimeographed copies with the same three-lined warning:

NO RADIOS.
NO PHONE CALLS.
NO VISITORS.

They hadn't heard. Lorraine and the others had been sequestered in that auditorium since early that morning. They probably had no idea what had happened within walking distance of Dunbar. If they had, they'd want no part of rehearsing lines and blocking steps.

The stage doors were flanked by glass cases meant for championship trophies. The one on the right held the acting awards, yellowed reviews from the *Inner City News*, decades-old playbills pieced into a collage. In the other case, head shots of the cast had been arranged alphabetically on the bulletin board behind the glass. Near the bottom, "Lorraine Watters starring as Beneatha." She had used one of her senior pictures, an eight-by-ten that matched the wallet-size I had in my billfold.

On the display-case glass, the lit panel of the Coca-Cola machine behind me left its reflection, bright enough for me to see a shadow move across it. It was Marcus Olden, standing in front of the snack machine. He'd spent most of his time at Dunbar trying out for lead roles, only to end up in the booth working the lights. He stood there shaking his head like that was the first snack machine he'd ever seen.

"I want some Juicy Fruit, but my mama put green onions in my eggs this morning. I might need some Double-mint. That's life, I suppose, balancing needs and wants."

He held his right hand to his mouth and made a breathing sound that was something between Darth Vader and Bobby Blue Bland.

"Hey, Roy, can you smell my breath?"

"If I could smell your breath from way over here, I don't think Doublemint would do you any good."

"What would you do? Juicy Fruit or Doublemint?"

"How much is it?" I asked him.

"Fifteen cents."

"How much do you have?"

"Forty-five."

"Buy both."

"I can't. I need thirty-five cents for Cheetos."

"Cheetos are worse than green onions."

"Good point. Doublemint."

He slid a nickel and a dime into the machine, and the change rattled in the bottom of the empty coin box.

"I'm so indecisive. That's why Mrs. Cooley won't cast me in anything. She said I need to be more confident in my artistic decisions onstage."

He looked at me as he said this, and his fingers missed the mark and punched the button between the Doublemint and the Juicy Fruit. A pack of Big Red tumbled down.

"Shit," he said.

"Lorraine still inside?"

"She's onstage. Doing that scene where ol' boy tells her to put on some clothes and run a comb through her hair."

"Thanks."

The doors to the ground floor were still locked, so I walked up to the booth. The staircase leading up to it was so narrow that I could touch both walls at the same time. Halfway up, I could hear Lorraine's voice projecting those same lines she'd recited from memory while we were driving home from school.

She stood onstage in her homemade costume, with

some gold bracelets she'd found at the flea market. She had on the jeans that her mother said were too tight, the ones she would change into in the bathroom before homeroom. She had on her head a scarf covered in circles that she'd found in the attic along with the dashiki that smelled like mothballs no matter how many times she washed it. I told her I didn't think people were wearing dashikis in the 1950s.

"Bencatha was ahead of her time," she had told me. "Or better yet, the times were behind her."

"This is my last play in high school," she had said to me the day after auditions. "The next time I'm onstage, I'll be in college."

"High school will be over before we know it."

Everything in those final months of high school, no matter how trivial, was the last something or other. The last house party. The last time we'd go to the Krystal on Dauphin Island Parkway after a basketball game. The last time Lorraine and I might live in the same town, go to the same school. She had it all planned out. She was going to Howard, and after that to New York to act. I was going to Xavier, and after four years in New Orleans I would come back home to work in the family business, a future that I'd had no say in.

Marcus had taped the script to the wall. The margins were filled with his reminders—lighting changes, closing curtains, sound effects, and the like. My eyes went back and forth from the lines on those worn-out pages to Lorraine, as after weeks of practice, she said them by heart.

Beneatha: You are looking at what a well-dressed
          Nigerian woman wears. Isn't it beautiful?
          Enough of this assimilationist junk!

OCOMOGOSIAY! [The music comes up, a lovely Nigerian melody.]

On the script taped to the wall, CUE MUSIC had been printed in bold capitals, circled, and underlined twice. The entire cast turned around and looked up to where I was standing. Mrs. Cooley stood up and started yelling.

"A lovely Nigerian melody, Marcus! Watch for your cues!"

Mrs. Cooley was a low-slung woman with a rhinestone chain around her neck to hold her glasses, the kind with arms connected to the bottom of the frame so they looked upside down. She put them on and squinted like a sniper. Eartha Cooley was one of the nicest women in the world, but she also carried a gun in her purse.

"Marcus. I know you hear me."

I turned on the microphone.

"Mrs. Cooley, Marcus stepped out."

Mrs. Cooley held her glasses to her face, looking hard my way. "Who is that?"

"It's Jesus," somebody shouted. "He came back just like he said."

"It's Roy, Mrs. Cooley."

"Well, when you see Marcus, tell him I'm going to kill him."

Just then Marcus came stumbling over the top step. He grabbed my shoulder for balance, sending a bright smear of Cheetos dust on my shirt.

"Shit. Did I miss the cue? Goddamn it."

The echo of his voice came back to us just as Marcus realized the microphone was still on. Everyone downstairs stood with their mouths open just like Marcus did.

"Yes, you missed the cue. And I need to see you in my office to discuss that language. And your daddy's a deacon in the church."

"Ain't no damn church deacon," Marcus said to me. "He's a trustee." He forgot the microphone was still on.

"You better turn down the volume before you sass me." Mrs. Cooley didn't need a mike. Her voice carried. "Being mannish is not the same as being a man."

Marcus sank down into one of the creaky left-handed desks that lined the booth. He took his Big Red out of his pocket. When he folded a piece, it was so stale it snapped in two.

"Ain't that some shit."

With a look of horror, Marcus glanced over at the microphone, but by then I'd switched it off. The only voice echoing around the auditorium was Mrs. Cooley's.

"We'll take ten minutes," she said. "Come back here in your right mind."

By the time I got back downstairs, the cast and crew had gathered in the lobby outside the auditorium. The red-lettered sign that read REHEARSAL IN PROGRESS—DO NOT ENTER had been knocked to the floor. The auditorium was filled with loud talking and laughter. Often, too often, I heard bad news before every one else did. I watched people go about carefree in the comfort that comes from being oblivious.

Lorraine stood at the drinking fountain next to the girls' bathroom. She had taken off the scarf that had covered her head, letting her hair go its own way. Beneatha Younger decided to wear an Afro halfway through the play, so Lorraine had opted to do the same. She let her relaxer grow out and sported a short natural that she sprayed with strawberry Afro Sheen. In the big purse she carried around, Lorraine kept the wig she wore for the first half of the play.

"We started late," she said. "We have another hour or so."

She rinsed out her Tab can and filled it with water. As she took a drink, she stared at my shoulder.

"You have Cheeto dust all over your shirt."

"Marcus," I said.

"Everything he touches," she said as she dabbed her scarf under the water fountain and ran it along my shoulder. "He can't win for losing."

They had been rehearsing there for the last few Saturdays, and I had enjoyed sitting somewhere in the back, watching and listening. Since I'd been on the crew before, Mrs. Cooley made an exception to her no-visitor rule. It was a good way to get the morning's work out of my head. But the memories of that morning weren't even old enough to be memories. It was still happening. I wondered how long it had taken them to take down Michael's body. I wondered about his family, about everything.

"What's the matter? You look sick."

"You remember Michael Donald?"

"Yeah. Used to be with your brother sometimes. Why?"

"He got killed last night. They lynched him."

Lorraine raised her hand to her mouth, and the damp scarf hung limp at her side. She leaned back against the water fountain. She said nothing, but her eyes questioned what I said. All I could do was nod. I was again the voice of the worst kind of news. I didn't want to be the one to tell everybody. I hated that look on people's faces the first time they heard that somebody had died. Mrs. Cooley was standing twenty feet away, but she had heard every word.

"Lynched?" she said. "My Lord."

She said it loud enough for everyone to hear, to get quiet to find out what was going on. The cast, chosen for their projecting voices and extroversion, stood around me in silence. Mobile was a small place. A quarter of the kids in the play went to Murphy. The rest of them had more than likely seen Michael around, but it really didn't matter if they knew him or not.

Mrs. Cooley disappeared into the principal's office and reemerged with the television cart. The wheels squealed each time the cart hit the gutters and the grout between the tiles. When she turned on the set, the audio came on before the picture tube got warm, so everybody stared at the empty screen as the sound of bad news echoed off the bricks and tile. *"The body of the nineteen-year-old Mobile man was removed from a nearby tree hours ago. There is no word as of yet on a motive . . ."*

Mrs. Cooley turned her head away from the screen, staring into the case of photos and posters that had been there longer than she had. It didn't matter. The glass carried the TV's reflection, so she saw it all anyway.

"An unnamed police spokesman told us that there has been increased drug activity in this area. That is one of the leads they are following at this time."

Mrs. Cooley took her glasses off and let them fall to her chest. She dropped her head into her hands and rocked slowly in her chair.

"In nineteen hundred and eighty-one," Mrs. Cooley said. Her voice was low but her words clear.

"The police also found a burned cross on the courthouse lawn. Authorities have yet to confirm whether or not they believe the two incidents are related."

"That's enough," Mrs. Cooley said. She jumped up and shut off the television then. "You children need to get your things. We're going home."

Children. Any other time there might have been

some protest at Mrs. Cooley's words, but not then. They had called the serial killings in Atlanta the "child murders," even though some of the victims were in their early twenties. That didn't matter. When young people start dying—when their parents have to put them in the ground and wonder why—it's easy to see that we are all somebody's child.

"Nobody's walking home, and nobody's waiting for the city line. If you didn't drive, you're riding with me."

As everyone collected their bags, Mrs. Cooley unlocked the wheels and began to push the television toward the administration office. She moved quickly. Too quickly. When she realized the thick orange plug was still jammed into the outlet, it was too late. The force of the taut cord jerked the television off the shelf. When the top corner of the set slammed against the tiles, the explosion of glass and plastic was followed by startled screams. Then the room turned the empty kind of quiet as everyone froze and looked down at what was left of the console, the insides of the picture tube gone to pieces.

"You all need to be extra careful," Mrs. Cooley said.

Everyone took quick but cautious steps as they left the school, mindful of the upturned shards of glass that had slid across the waxed tiles. Booker Brown swept the big pieces into a pile with his foot as Mrs. Cooley took from the custodial closet the yellow Caution signs left on wet floors. Once she had arranged them in a circle around the mess, she fished out a key ring that held at least two dozen keys and her assorted charms—a rabbit's foot, a four-leaf clover of tarnished silver.

Henry Lumas and Booker Brown lived not too far from me, so they squeezed into the backseat of my car. The others piled into any seat they could find in the half dozen cars in the parking lot. Mrs. Cooley put those who were left in the back of her station wagon, which was so old some of the wood paneling had come loose on the driver's side.

"Don't tarry. Go straight home. I'm going to call your people to make sure you made it safely."

At the far end of the building, the drama shop students worked away, oblivious to the news that had put an end to the rehearsal. Mrs. Cooley drove down to the end of the parking lot and leaned out of her window to tell Mr. Oaklyn what was going on.

Words drowned out by distance, the drone of power tools, their conversation played out in pantomime. I could read the twists of Mr. Oaklyn's face, as Mrs. Cooley's lips moved quickly. It didn't take long to tell bad news.

Mr. Oaklyn waved his hands at his students, motioning for the sawing and hammering to cease. His students picked up their unfinished city and took it inside. The girl who was painting dragged her signs into the building—thick brown letters against a fiery orange sun.

"I need to keep my knife on me," Henry said.

"What good is a knife?" Booker said. "If they want your black ass, they'll get you."

Henry shook his head, and scratched wide marks through the cloudy sideburns formed by his sweat mixing with the powder in his hair meant to make him look old.

"Trying to scare us."

"It worked," Booker said.

On the way home, we passed the Afro-American Archive on the corner of King and Sansom. It used to be the colored library, and its architecture was almost identical to the gleaming white library building on Government, but its scale was about a quarter of the size. It had sat boarded up for ten years, but it had been reopened a few years before.

Twin flagpoles jutted out from the building's facade at a forty-five-degree angle. The one on the right of the door carried the American flag. Mobile was called the City of Six Flags—Great Britain, France, Spain, the Alabama Republic, the United States, the Confederacy. The six flags flew in front of government buildings downtown, but on that Saturday, in front of the old colored library, there was a seventh flag: a silver-lettered sentence on a black cloth banner. It had been in a glass case inside one of the exhibits, but that morning someone had moved it outside.

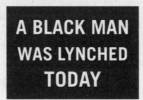

A BLACK MAN WAS LYNCHED TODAY

Lorraine leaned against the window, her Afro spread against the glass. She ran her fingers through the silky hair of the wig in her bag, with the folded crumpled script lodged into the side pocket. Her eye makeup mixed with the tears, and a dark line ran from her eye to the place where the dimples should have been.

The bay winds cut through the trees on either side of the archive, shaking the mimosa on one side and the live oak on the other. The gusts coming off the water can have their way with the sturdiest trees, snapping the various flags against their poles. That thick dusty banner stayed in its place, too heavy to follow the wind.

Late Saturday afternoon, Ricky Boone rode by and threw the *Mobile Press* onto the porch. When I went outside to pick up the evening paper, the street was quiet except for the spring locusts that had started their evening calling. The insects were the only life outside when night approached. As the local news broadcasts started that evening, the bug-light blue of television screens flashed through opened windows along the street. A chorus of news voices rang out in high fidelity, announcing the same story that stretched across the front page that I held in my fingertips. The worse the news, the thicker the letters.

LOCAL MAN FOUND DEAD ON HERNDON AVE.

We ate dinner in front of the television that night. The story had made the national news. Michael's picture floated over the newscasters' shoulders as they called his name in that solemn diction that bad news requires. They pronounced "Alabama" like it was some foreign place—not the state I was in, watching a story I already knew by heart.

From the local news, we had learned of the new developments, Michael's bloody wallet found in a Dumpster with money still in it, the charred remains of a cross in front of the courthouse. As Detective Wilcox stood in front of a podium that matched the wood-paneled walls of the briefing room, he continued to maintain that there was no evidence that the two events—the hanging and the cross burning—were related.

"One plus one used to make two," my father said. "The police must use the new math."

During a commercial break, I took our plates to the dishwasher. It was strange seeing the kitchen table empty at dinnertime. We only ate in the den when television carried news on something in the world that required our attention. During the King funeral, we watched a mule and wagon pull Reverend King's body down Auburn Avenue as a wall of grievers lined both sides of the street.

Behind our funeral home, the garage was once a livery where we at one time kept the mules that my grandfather drove. Each mule had been named after area towns. Saraland. Chickasaw. Loxley. Plateau. My great-grandfather would lead them through downtown streets when some were still paved with wooden bricks. My grandfather told me about the days when the streets were flooded from the spring rains, and the splintered bricks broke free of their tar and floated in the street. Sometimes the wooden blocks clicked against the wagon wheels as they sloshed through water that had nowhere to run.

Dr. King's procession looked like something out of a history book, and I suppose that was the point. I was four years old that April when he was killed. I can't remember exactly when I realized what it meant for someone to be dead, but I wasn't much older than that when I figured that people didn't get out of those boxes. They said in Sunday school that the death of a believer should be a time of rejoicing and homecoming, but I knew different. I had never seen anybody rejoice at a funeral, especially that April when Reverend King died. I remember my mother crying as we watched his funeral on the black-and-white Zenith floor model. News of Michael Donald's murder came to us in color, on the cable-ready set that sat on top of the old one. My mother watched the news, gripping the third cup of coffee she had poured since dinner.

"You aren't going to be able to sleep tonight," my father told her as he sat on the couch, his arm around her shoulder.

"I won't sleep anyhow," she said.

Once we brought Paul home from the crime scene that morning, I had helped him up the stairs and to his bed. He was too tired to talk. He just turned on the radio like he always did. Paul liked to drift off to the sound of music, but WBLX wasn't playing any songs. The deejay was still taking phone calls; someone was yelling conspiracy theories and speculation, his anger filling the time slotted for "Midday Melodies."

Paul lay down and switched on his turntable, which sat right beside his bed, but before he could move the needle, he was out. I had slipped off his sneakers by the time Mama came in. She was sitting on the edge of his bed when I left to bury Mr. Whitfield. She was there when I came back.

"I'm going back up to check on him," she told us leaving Daddy and me sitting there in the living room, listening to the same bad news over and over.

In the same living room the night before, everything had been different. The University of Alabama–Birmingham played Indiana in the NCAA tournament. The week before, UAB had beaten Kansas in the biggest upset of the tournament. Birmingham was four hours north of Mobile, but the Blazers might as well have been a local team, as much as folks were talking about that win. We made so much noise during the Kansas game my mother yelled for us to be quiet, not that it did any good. She finally gave in and watched with us.

On that Friday night, everybody was hoping UAB could do it again, but the Cinderella run came to an ugly end when they ran into Indiana and Isiah Thomas.

"That brother can play some ball, can't he?" my daddy said.

Paul just sucked his teeth. "I'm going to work," he said. The next time I saw him was that morning on Herndon.

On my way to bed, I opened Paul's door, lifting it at the place where it always creaked. It was quiet except for the click of the changing clock numbers, which by then read three minutes after two. Narrow lines of streetlight came through the half-opened blinds and fell on Paul's desk. That was where he kept the bracket sheets and the envelope of rumpled bills, fifty-eight dollars worth. He had organized a two-dollar pool for a few of the brothers from the rec center and a couple guys from his job. I leafed through the stack of papers and found mine. I always filled out two brackets. On one, I picked the obvious winners. On the other, I mixed in a few long shots and maybes.

Friday night I had sat in front of the television with my bracket sheets, watching the highlights and hoping that my guesses had come out right. Most didn't. Twenty-four hours later, I didn't care about how many jumpers James Worthy had hit. March Madness had seemed like the most important thing in the world, but by Saturday evening, it was just a footnote in a story that overshadowed everything else.

"According to family accounts, Michael Donald left his home shortly after the end of the UAB basketball game and went to a nearby convenient store to buy a pack of cigarettes. That was the last time anyone saw him alive . . ."

The little bit of streetlight that missed Paul's desk fell across his bed. I had thought he was asleep until he turned his head my way.

"You got North Carolina and Indiana still in it," I told him. "You might win the money."

"Maybe," he said.

"I picked UAB to win on one of mine, so that one's done."

"The Cinderella team never wins," he said.

"Yeah. Would have been nice, though."

He nodded.

When I put the papers back on his desk, I noticed everything else that he had left there—stacks of pictures I hadn't seen in years, the colorful cardboard frames that held Little League photos. I held one up to the patches of light and tried to make out the faces. Among the All-Stars stood Michael Donald, a tall lanky youngster in the middle of the second row.

Those pictures had been in the attic for years. Angles of dust had settled on each frame, an outline of the frame that had rested on top of it. I wiped them clean with my shirttail, leaving only the stubborn dust that gathered in the corners. We had put away those photographs so long ago, I had forgotten about them. Against my feet, I felt the open banker's box and the lid with Paul's name written in his grade-school cursive. That box was filled with wrinkled first-place ribbons, autographed ticket stubs, and cheap little trophies. The door to the attic was over Paul's bed, and this box was among the many that lined the shelves up there.

"It'll be all right," I said, but Paul wasn't listening. He had drifted back to the sound sleep that for a few hours would give him relief from the memory that, when he opened his eyes, would surely be there waiting for him.

Early Sunday Morning

On the first edition of the sunrise news, a familiar scene was broadcast live from Government Street. The recognizable black faces, a dozen at least, had assumed the position, standing before a narrow podium on a downtown street flanked by the Old South architecture, colors more cheerful than the situation warranted. The podium carried a steel crown of microphones with channel numbers clipped to their bases. Half of the numbers were from stations I had never heard of.

It had been just over twenty-four hours since the body had been found. The police had already had their say, and the sordid theories had spread like kudzu. *Body found in known drug area. Love triangle. Jealous boyfriend. Wrong place at the wrong time.* Familiar words for dead black boys portrayed as complicit in their own demise. Michael Donald's body had been hanged on a Mobile street, and the police were doing the same thing to his name. The gathered activists wore their Sunday best, no doubt headed from the press conference to the various houses of worship. The collective was centered on the television, and those who stood on the ends were distorted by the curve of the screen. Nancy Freed headed the local NAACP and taught history at Bishop State. She spoke first. Whenever I saw her, she carried a big black pocketbook filled with voter registration cards and Starlight peppermints, both of which she handed out whenever she could.

"Like many of you around this city, this country, I am a grandmother and a mother. There is a mother in Mobile this morning, Beulah Mae Donald, who has lost a child. Once again, we must break the ground to bury another child. And in so doing, we bury any future he could have had."

Mrs. Freed had held prayer vigils for the mothers of the murdered Atlanta children. She had invited some of the mothers to Mobile, collected love offerings. On that Sunday, she would say those same prayers for Mobile.

"We need prayers and answers. Answers from the mayor. From the police department." She turned toward city hall as if anyone was there to hear her. "Answers for the Donald family. For the people of Mobile. Answers."

As she stepped back into the orderly row of activists, Lyle Ferguson stepped to the microphone. His name, face, and voice were well known. State senator. Civil rights lawyer. He could have passed for Nat King Cole, a tall man with diction as sharp as his clothes.

"I would like nothing more than to bid Mobile a good Sunday morning, but the goodness has been taken from it.

In the void that remains, the police have left us with accusations, apathy, and the first wave in what will surely be a steady stream of lies."

Lyle Ferguson had gone to the seminary before law school, but he didn't talk like some of the marquee preachers I had seen in person. They sometimes seemed distant, unable to come down from the pulpit, stuck in the stories of their glory days. Mr. Ferguson delivered his remarks with the right mix of the formal and the familiar—as he might deliver greetings to friends he ran into on the street.

"Michael Donald is dead, Mobile. It is a time for prayer, a time for grieving, a time for memorial. Just as the Bible said, there is time for all things. The time has come for the police to be forthright. The time has come, Mobile, for the city to stop hiding behind innuendo as they shirk their responsibility to the victim and his family."

Whether he spoke to a handful of people or to a packed auditorium, he addressed his remarks to Mobile. I suppose he wanted his listeners to see the city as one united place, no matter what.

"We have come a long way over the years, Mobile, but today we have been forced to look back to the times we thought were over. At the body of another young man who will never return home to his family."

Mr. Ferguson wasn't like the fire-and-brimstone preachers who, emotion obscuring their words, end their messages with grunts as thick as gravy, as if the evil they lament has gathered in their throats. His diction never wavered, and his volume never went to extremes. Perhaps that coolness was one reason why Mobile activists never achieved the acclaim of their colleagues a couple hundred miles north.

Montgomery. Selma. Birmingham. Mobile had not exploded like the others.

"Just like Jacob, we have been climbing this ladder since this city began. We all follow the same narrow path, Mobile. We must pick up the fallen if we want to continue onward."

The chorus of civic leaders behind Mr. Ferguson stood silently. It had been a generation since 1968, and in the years since, some of them had moved out of their familiar streets into West Mobile neighborhoods that were once all white. Into the historic districts. Lawyers and doctors had bought some of the majestic homes they used to drive past as children.

"Michael Donald left his family to go to the neighborhood convenience store, but the police have told us that he was in the wrong place at the wrong time. Tell me. On God's green earth, in a land governed by the Constitution, by the Fourteenth Amendment, is there a wrong place? I ask you, is there ever a right time for a man to be hanged on a city street? I say to you this morning, it's always the wrong time."

To Mr. Ferguson's right stood Lorraine's father, Sonny Watters. He had a voice like Isaac Hayes, with a bald head to match. He had a gap in his mouth wide enough to fit another tooth in. His beard grew as wild and peppery as he was. He wiped the sweat away as he stepped to the podium. When he dropped his hands down hard on the podium, the tangle of microphones knocked together, sending a burst of sound through the television, a prelude to Sonny's thunder.

"They say this brother 'may have been' involved in a drug deal gone wrong. To borrow a line from our president, 'There they go again.' He waited for the amens to subside. "I don't know about you, but I can't think of a time when a drug deal has ever gone right." Amens again. "Drugs didn't have anything to do with this. We all know what this is. A lynching." The words *lynching* and *drugs* were heavier than the rest. After years of practice, and instinct perhaps, Sonny knew how to weight the words, play them against one another. "Lynched. The police won't say the word, but we all know good and well. Good and well."

When Mr. Watters was young, they called him Sonny Boy. People had said that he and some other boys had jumped the fence and pissed in the whites-only swimming pool. The perpetrators took a picture of themselves and sent it, with their faces cut out, to the mayor and to the newspaper.

MUNICIPAL POOL VANDALIZED

To Remain Closed Indefinitely Pending Investigation

Nobody could prove who did it, but Sonny's parents thought it best that he finish high school with relatives up North. Mr. Watters said all that time in Chicago was no better than Alabama—"Twice as cold, twice the people, and the white folks twice as evil." After law school he came back home and went into business with Lyle.

"The Donald family has retained Ferguson and Watters to pursue a wrongful death action against the guilty parties. People may ask what our role is in this investigation. See, Lyle and me, we're here to keep the Mobile Police Department honest."

Sonny and Lyle were the Odd Couple of Mobile civil rights. I'm sure that many of their opponents would rather negotiate with Lyle than deal with Sonny's antics. He looked as rough as he sometimes acted. The men and women around him wore Sunday clothes, but Mr. Watters, who had more than once called himself "a field hand for my people," stood at the podium in rumpled slacks and a white shirt, open-collared, with his sleeves rolled up.

"Unfortunately, honesty hasn't always been a part of the job description for the police force, especially when dealing with our people. Today I must appeal to their sense of integrity, because we need the Mobile Police Department. Before we can do our job, they've got to do theirs."

Before I started dating Lorraine, I had every reason to be intimidated by Mr. Watters. I had met him before, and he knew me because of my parents. He had been nice enough. But dating his daughter was something altogether different. The summer of my first date with Lorraine, I had to ask Sonny's permission. "I know it's crazy," she said. "But he thinks people still do that kind of thing. Just play along, it'll be painless." People only say "painless" right before it hurts. I thought about that when Mr. Watters invited me to lunch. We met across the street from the courthouse at a sandwich shop wedged between two bail bond offices.

"Young boys your age sometimes go out with a young lady and get a little too mannish. I'm not worried 'cause I know your people. You don't seem the type to act a fool. But I gave my Lorraine cab fare in case anything goes awry."

Awry. He said the word dry and gravelly, so I felt it along the back of my neck.

"Lunch is on me," he said. "I got a verdict yesterday. That fish sandwich was paid for courtesy of justice and equal opportunity."

I could see then why juries liked Sonny Watters. Why he was the first one people called when things went wrong. He was a little too loud and a little too country, but somehow it worked. Sometimes that was the only way to make people pay attention.

Ask yourself this question: If this had been a white child found dead in a black neighborhood, would they be knocking on every door?" *Yes, sir.* "Searching high and low?" *Yes, indeed.* "If this had been a white child, would they paint him as a sinner and not a saint?" *Lord, no.* The crowd agreed, and the silent chorus that had stood shoulder to shoulder then exulted, some raising their right hands, others shaking and nodding their solemn heads.

"Just like Lyle said, we walk the same narrow path. The brothers and sisters who fall along the way are left for us to carry. If there is no justice for Michael Donald today, there may be no justice for any of us tomorrow."

Sonny and Lyle were in their early fifties, younger than most of the others. On that morning, they had fallen into an old posture and all of a sudden looked like the younger versions I had seen in photographs, holding picket signs in front of Woolworth's and the Greyhound station. They hadn't changed much in that span of years, but others among them showed just how hard the years had been.

Standing behind Lyle was his father, Council Ferguson. He was of the generation that predated Dr. King, tracing his lineage back to the A. Philip Randolph days. He had helped to organize the porters that worked the trains from Mobile up to Detroit and Chicago. He had helped to break open the unions for the black workers at the mill, the stevedores, and the construction workers on the bay bridge.

We liberated France, and then we came home to liberate Alabama. I had been in the audience when Council Ferguson had said that, at some commemoration program—what was being commemorated, I don't recall. He was once a big man by any account, and when he stood at the pulpit, Mr. Ferguson was even bigger, his arms stretched wide as if he had sprouted there. In the time after those days, his body had bent under the weight of his hardest years. His latest stroke was another in a long list of setbacks. *Ask the Lord to look in on Brother Ferguson.* He was just over seventy years old, but could have passed for a man twenty years older. He should have been at home resting on that Sunday morning, but everyone expected to see him on such occasions. At the same time, everyone knew that a press conference was the last place he needed to be.

Oxygen tubes ran across a thin face covered with lines, wrinkles, and veins. He was one of the oldest among those gathered that morning. The last lynching in Mobile had happened when he was a child. Even for Council, such things seemed to be before his time. When he stepped up to the podium, he raised a right hand as his frail fingers quaked like leaves all around. He looked up, squinting, as if the poem he prepared to recite were written somewhere above him. His voice was much weaker than I had ever heard it before, but it didn't matter. Everything around him was so silent that his words were quiet but clear.

". . . *any man's death diminishes me, because I am involved in mankind; and therefore never send to know for whom the bell tolls; it tolls for thee.*"

Then the amens came.

"Today, during our hour of worship, I ask you to let the bell toll for Michael Donald."

Many of the black churches of Mobile were modest buildings. Others were storefront churches. They had no bells to toll. Organs and tambourines would have to suffice. When I stepped out of the door that morning to retrieve the Sunday paper, I listened for bells, but I heard nothing. If any bells were ringing, they were too far away to hear.

The television played the trumpet solo of *CBS Sunday Morning,* and from a room away Charles Kuralt talked in a heavy whisper. I usually enjoyed the leisure of those mornings, because Sunday was the one day that people were rarely buried. Most times, my father would have the paper in his lap, reading it out loud even if no one was listening. He was quiet that morning, and the newsprint pages went unturned as the morning edition rested on the far edge of the table, heavy and unread. My mother had made a place for Paul at the breakfast table.

"He can't stay in his room forever," she had said.

Her cake batter sat thickening beside the stove. Before she started breakfast, Mama had turned on the oven and started mixing a cake for the Donald family. It had always seemed like a strange custom, but the homes of mourning families were always filled with the food that people brought them, as if grief was a hunger that could be overcome a spoonful at a time. My mother spent many a weekend making food for people. I had never been much on sweets, probably because whenever I saw the light on in the oven, I wondered who had died.

Over our heads came the creaking of the hallway floorboards as Paul made his way down for breakfast. Charles Kuralt went through the day's headlines; we were among them. *"Yesterday, in Mobile, Alabama, the body of a—"* That was all I heard of it. Paul had reached the living room by then and switched off the television before he came through the kitchen door.

"Are you feeling any better?" my mother asked as she turned off the mixer, lifted the blades from the bowl.

"No, ma'am. Same as yesterday."

Paul wore a T-shirt and a pair of navy sweats with no drawstring. A bleach splatter ran down the leg.

"You should eat something," Daddy said.

Paul nodded his head and sat down. He stared into the bowl in front of him, looking into the yellow pool of melted butter on the skin of the unstirred grits. I passed him the plate of bacon and waited for him to say something, anything. But he didn't. Paul just took a few slices and passed the plate. My mother had her hand on the wooden serving spoon. She looked into the CorningWare as if waiting for her words to cool.

"I thought all of this was over."

I was born in 1963, but I remembered only bits and pieces of the segregated world. But the little bit that I could recall was vivid. My brother and I were with Mama in the

Kress store buying Halloween candy when we watched a clerk scrape the Whites Only off the wall over the drinking fountain. The brother who did it used a straight razor and every so often knocked it against the lip of the garbage can, discarding each of his finished letters before moving on to the next. By that time, moments like those were no longer landmarks, just something for Paul and me to step around as we reached for our Reese's Cups.

Mama sat at the end of the table with her hands clasped and her fingers moving as if kneading something invisible. She had been anxious all morning, straightening things that weren't even crooked. She offered that morning a grace shorter than the eloquent prayers she usually said.

"Thy will be done."

Mama placed four slices of toast on a plate and set them down on the table. She never ate when things were heavy on her mind. Instead, she drank a glass of juice and returned to her cake. The mixer blades had just started turning again when the phone rang, and my mother turned off the power as my father took the call.

"Deacon residence. Randall Deacon speaking . . . Yes, Mrs. Donald."

We didn't say anything to one another. It was like she had just walked into the room.

"We are all very sorry for your loss. . . . I spoke to him a few times when he visited the house with Paul. . . . A nice young man . . . Well, we all pray they're doing what they can. . . . Yes, ma'am. . . . Yes, I'll speak to them tomorrow and arrange everything. . . ."

As he looked over at Paul, he passed his fingers over the carved wood corners, the chipped place on the edge of the glass.

"He's shaken, but he'll pull through. . . . Yes, ma'am. Just a second."

My father put the receiver to his chest, and looked at Paul. He didn't move, just sat there staring down at the table.

"Paul, Mrs. Donald is asking for you."

Paul walked over and took the receiver. Between the silences, I listened to the words Paul offered: *I'm sorry. Thank you. Yes, ma'am.* Over and over.

I have always wondered about the kind of strength those first days required of the Donald family. It was hard enough to handle the details that dying forced—caskets, flowers, headstones. Then on top of that, add the extra weight of murder. I imagine they had to rush to tell faraway family before they heard it secondhand. Still, no real answers had come. Despite all of that, Mrs. Donald had taken a moment to comfort my brother.

"Yes, ma'am, thank you."

Daddy never left my brother's side. He held Paul's shoulders as he talked to Mrs. Donald and rested his forehead against the wall.

"I'll pray for you, too," he said, trying to hide the shaking in his voice. He handed the phone to my father and returned to the table.

"Yes, ma'am. . . . We'll take care of everything. . . . Yes, ma'am. . . . God bless you, too."

My father hung up the phone and sat down heavy in his chair.

"You okay?" he asked Paul.

He shook his head. "I need to be excused."

Paul disappeared up the stairs, and my mother went with him, leaving just my father and me at the table. Daddy took hold of the spoon in the blue-flowered dish and stirred under the skin that had formed on congealed grits. He turned on the clock radio on the counter, and the AM gospel came through just loud enough to hear. My father poured two cups of coffee for us and sat back down. He took a slice of dry toast and crunched it slowly.

"They want us to handle the arrangements."

My mouth got dry when he said out loud what I already knew. Before I started working full-time with my father, he reminded me of the people I might see on the table. Friends and family. No one dies before their time, he would say, as if there was a good time.

"The call comes when it's meant to, and it's not for us to question."

If this were to be my profession, he would tell me, I would have to be ready for them. I wasn't ready, and I was more and more sure that I never would be. But certain things were expected of me. Seven generations in the service.

"After school tomorrow, I'm going to need you to go to the morgue to claim the body."

Daddy finished the last of his coffee, emptied the pot into the chipped mug, and drank it black.

"Yes, sir." At times, it felt like "Yes, sir" was all I ever said to him.

"I'm going upstairs to check on your mom and your brother. As soon as they feel up to it, we'll go on to church. I think we all need it."

I nodded.

"How are you?" my father asked, as he rolled down his sleeves and took the cuff links from his pocket.

"Fine."

"You sure?"

"No, but you know—fine."

"I know the feeling." He stood up and walked toward the door to the living room. "Soak the pots and put the plates in the dishwasher. And keep your head up."

"Yes, sir."

He left me there with what was left of breakfast, grits that were as hard and cold as the toast beside the bowl. I cleared the table, ran the sink faucet as hot as it would go, and spooned what remained of our breakfast into the rush of scalding water.

On the way to church that morning, a radio sermon came through the speakers behind my head. As the preacher rattled on about heaven, Paul stared into my father's headrest mouthing the memorized scriptures—blessed are the persecuted, blessed are the meek—as if two voices made them twice as true. We passed a dozen churches between our house and Bethel. I'm sure all of those pastors prepared to do the same thing the preacher on the radio did, wrapping Michael Donald's body in the scriptures.

As we sat in the crowded sanctuary, the sweat rolled down Reverend Gallery's temples as he doled out the comfort verses like penicillin. "Let justice roll down like the waters"— as amens filled his pauses, I looked up at the still baptismal water in the pool behind the pulpit—"and righteousness like a mighty stream."

Paul and I had been baptized in that very pool on a Sunday morning ten years before. My brother had gone in first, and he was much more excited about the prospect than I was. As Reverend Gallery dipped Paul backward into the water, a chord rang from the brass pipes that flanked the baptismal. We were so close to the music that it sounded like a train with no desire to stop. I had always been the type to stay as far away from the front of the church as I could. I had only joined because my brother did, and I was tired of my parents asking when I would get saved. I really didn't even know what I was getting saved from.

When Reverend Gallery lifted Paul's head out of the water, he came up smiling. He patted me on my shoulder with his dripping hand as they ushered him past me on the narrow steps. With the reverend waiting in the pool, I took my turn in the water. I had believed that the experience would somehow change me. I had thought that something magical would happen while I was under that water, and I would come up new and improved. As Reverend Gallery held me underwater, my only thoughts were of the pain of his grip against my nose. I snuck a peek to see if the world looked different when you got saved. The only thing that was different was the way the music sounded when my ears were submerged. I kept my eyes open, and all I saw was the churn of the water and the spread of Reverend Gallery's fingers across my face. When I came to the surface, no transformation waited for me. I only felt the sting of the chlorine that had seeped into my nose and the waterlogged white robe that weighed me down as I climbed those steps to where my brother stood, still excited.

Most every Sunday of our youth, I sat right next to my brother, but when it came to religion we couldn't have been further apart. Paul had believed the same faith my parents did, and he often nodded along with Reverend Gallery when he preached some of the very words he spoke on that day after the lynching.

"We must have faith, beloved, but what is faith? Faith is the substance of things hoped for, and the evidence of things not seen."

I had watched grieving families use their faith to keep them from falling apart. It eased their minds to believe that there was a piece of their loved one still living, something beyond the body. I even told them what they wanted to hear, quoted some of the scriptures I'd heard so many times, I'd memorized them. I reasoned that it was part of my job, giving them whatever counsel they needed to get through, whether I believed it or not.

"We know not the day or the hour, but we do know, beloved, that there is a city called heaven."

I had made more trips to churches for funerals than I had for worship, and each time I listened to the words the ministers used for death. Transition. Home going. Passing. But I had drained the last of the blood from the bodies that lay beneath the flowers. By my lights, dead was dead. I sometimes watched the still baptismal waters and waited for any sign of a spirit that could do the impossible, raise the dead simply by calling their names.

I didn't have much reason to open a Bible, but I had heard what seemed like all of it through sermons and eulogies. Of all the words offered in churches, I was drawn to the unspoken words carved into the communion table beneath the pulpit: "This Do in Remembrance of Me." Before some funerals, I helped my father move the heavy table those words adorned so the casket could take its place.

Reverend Gallery closed his Bible and returned to his seat, and the choir sang. That was the only part that did me any good. It didn't require faith to feel the music. On Sunday mornings, sometimes I wished the singing would never stop.

Because once it was over, and all that was left were the scattered amens, there was nothing left for me to feel.

Paul had said, only half joking, on more than one occasion that I was going to hell in gasoline drawers. When Reverend Gallery started the benediction, Paul always gripped my hand a little too tight.

> *May the Lord watch between me and thee,*
> *while we are absent one from another.*

Each Sunday I bowed my head and said those words along with everyone else, like I was supposed to. Whenever the verse was spoken, I looked around the church and was reminded of how many people didn't make it from one Sunday to the next, their names moved from the sick and shut-in lists to the funeral notices I would type. It seemed like those prayers were just a way of buying time, the faithful begging God to spare them from one Sunday to the next. Those final minutes of the hour of worship were the only time each Sunday that I said Amen.

Monday

Murphy was the oldest public high school in Alabama, and Mr. Barrett had tended the grounds since before it was integrated. He kept the bright beige brick immaculate and the Spanish-tiled roof intact. He arrived before anyone else each morning to remove any trash that had collected on the front lawn and—when circumstances warranted—to change the letters on the sign in front of the school. For weeks, the sign had listed the final rites for our senior class.

SAMUEL S. MURPHY HIGH SCHOOL

SENIOR DAY	MAY 15
PROM	MAY 16
FINAL EXAMS	MAY 19–22
GRADUATION EXERCISES	MAY 23

By the time I got to school on Monday, Mr. Barrett had already climbed his ladder again to make new words.

IN MEMORIAM:
MICHAEL DONALD
MURPHY HIGH SCHOOL CLASS OF 1980
REST IN PEACE

"It's a terrible thang," Mr. Barrett said. He stood at the side entrance, tending to his next order of business, layering a fresh coat of paint onto the iron railings that ran alongside the stairs. "That Donald boy was good people. Never caused no trouble or nothing."

"Yes, sir. He was."

"Stringing folks up. Thought all that was water under the bridge. I guess it ain't."

In the summer and on weekends, Mr. Barrett did maintenance work around the funeral home. When I passed my certification exam, Mr. Barrett was the first person Daddy told because he wanted him to repaint the sign out front. I watched out the office window as "Deacon Memorial: Six Generations in the Service" was transformed to "Seven" with a few strokes of Mr. Barrett's brush.

"Who's taking the body?" Mr. Barrett asked, as he covered the last of the primer with the black paint.

"We are," I told him. "The service is Saturday."

"Your people do such good work," he said. "Always did. You know your father had my baby brother Cornelius when he died over at the shipyard." Mr. Barrett dipped his brush in the bucket, pressed out the excess along the rim. "When your people finished with him, you never would have known."

Before he touched the brush to the metal, I walked past him toward the door.

"Roy," he said. "And you. How are you doing?"

"I'm fine, Mr. Barrett."

"Well, I'm praying for you, too," he said. "And don't get that paint on you."

Michael's old locker was just down the hall. Through the static-filled intercom boxes along that same hallway, our principal, Mr. Foley, called Michael's name. "I know that many of you have heard by now . . ."

I sat in homeroom as Mr. Foley finished his message. Mrs. Randolph sat at a desk covered with neat stacks of graded papers, red corrections between the lines—numbers and letter grades circled in the right-hand corner. Her roll book was flipped open to the attendance page. Checks and x's filled the boxes beside the names of the twenty-four seniors in her homeroom. Forty-some-odd boxes were left blank, one for each of the remaining days of school.

Most mornings Mrs. Randolph took the roll while Mr. Foley rambled on, told the usual suspects to quiet down or get detention. But on that Monday, she just looked each one of us in the face and recorded our presence with her eyes. She stared at the empty desk of Jacob Weary, late more than he was on time. When he tipped into the room, Mrs. Randolph didn't say a word. She just nodded her head and sat with her hands clasped too tight to be comfortable.

In his educated drawl, each of Mr. Foley's words came out succinctly: *Counseling. Prayer. Memorial Service. Flowers.* He finished with a moment of silence, but the quiet only amplified the arbitrary noises—the feedback of the PA system, the diesel engine of the city bus running a few minutes behind. Each morning Mr. Foley led our school prayers and left a few minutes of quiet time for us to fill in the blanks. Each head in the room would be bowed talking to God. I had never had anything to say. I would just fake it, staring down at whatever wisdom had been carved in my desk.

The moment of silence ended when the bells began, sending us from one class to the next. History. Civics. Chemistry. In most of the classes, I don't remember what we were supposed to learn that day. Most of the lesson plans were set aside, because everyone was distracted by what had happened. The lynching had settled into everything like smoke. While others spoke about the murder, I said nothing. Michael's body waited at the morgue. With that on my mind, there wasn't room for anything else.

I had Mr. Billups for art during sixth period, and I spent the better part of the hour staring at a blank piece of newsprint, looking out the window. The art room faced the south parking lot and the gymnasium. Ruben and Slim had sixth-period athletics, and they were walking out of the field house toward the section where we all parked. When I got outside, Ruben and Slim stood next to the drivers'-ed car. For detention, Buster Green had to wash it. He was on his knees scrubbing dead mosquitoes off the grill.

"You stay in detention, Buster," I told him. "When you finish, come over here and wash mine."

"Wash what? Your ass or your car, motherfucker?"

"See, Roy. And this fool wonders why he stays in detention," Ruben said, pulling on his shirt's alligator like it was a scab. "If they paid you minimum wage for washing that raggedy-ass car, you could have bought it by now."

Buster pointed to his ass and blew Ruben a kiss before he turned his attention to the brake dust on the rims.

"Avery beat my high score on the Pac-Man up at

Willie's. Now he's talking shit." He tapped the quarters that filled the pocket of his corduroys. "I got to go set him straight. Y'all going over there this afternoon?"

"My mama wants me home before dark," Slim told him. "She's scared they might try to string up somebody else."

"My folks want me home, too," Ruben said, tapping his Erasermate on the hood of the car.

Slim held on to the football cleats draped around his shoulders. His gym bag was by his feet.

"Coach Rudolph canceled spring practice," Ruben said. "He wants people to get home before it's too late."

"You think they'll fuck with somebody in broad daylight?" I asked him.

"No telling," Slim said.

Buster poured a bucket of soapy water over the hood and rinsed it with the hose snaked around his feet.

"Mike was good people," Buster said as he squeezed the trigger, working loose the dirt caked on the fender. "It's a goddamn shame."

"You know it was some crackers."

"Who else."

"I know you heard what the police are talking about," I said.

"That old bullshit."

Everybody nodded as Buster shot the hose into the rims, and dirty water moved along the dips in the pavement.

"My daddy gave me his pistol," Slim said. "He keeps it under the seat."

"But Michael was walking," I said. "Gun won't do you any good under the seat."

"That's why I got it on me." Slim reached over and clutched his book bag.

Slim was a six-five, 270-pound offensive tackle. He had taped some of his recruiting letters inside his locker. Alabama, Tennessee, Ole Miss. People on the field didn't want any part of him, let alone anybody on the street. I'd known him since kindergarten, and the only things that I knew scared him were flying roaches and snakes. Other than that, he was a rock.

"Could have been any one of us," Slim said, rubbing that bag like it had a genie.

Just about everybody I knew had a gun in the house, including us. My father kept one of his shotguns in the hall closet.

"Be careful with that," Ruben told him.

"Careful's why I got it."

The south parking lot cleared out faster than usual. Most everyone was out of the building by then. Lorraine's French class was at the far end of the hall, and she would be coming out the door any minute.

"Since nobody's going to the arcade, y'all can come over to my house and play spades," Buster said.

"Might as well," Slim said. "But Roy, you can't be my partner after last time."

"I'm working tonight," I told them.

"Damn. Your old man can't give one day off?"

"We're doing his funeral."

I didn't mention Michael's name, but they knew who I was talking about. I didn't go into any detail about what I did with my friends. In all the years I had known Ruben and Slim, they both had been to the funeral home a handful of times. I made it a point to close the viewing room door if a body was out. The last time they came, a body lay in state and the viewing room door was wide open. From then on, they rang the bell and waited outside.

"More power to you."

Whenever friends asked me what we do, I would say, "We do what we can" and then leave it at that. I left out the particulars. We drain fluids, manipulate tissue. Nobody wants to hear that, let alone imagine what that means.

"I don't see how you do it." Some days neither did I.

Slim was squeezing into the front seat of Ruben's Nova when Lorraine walked out.

"Hey, Lorraine," Buster said, wrapping the water hose around his arm, "I asked your girl Naomi to the prom and she looked at me like I was crazy. She must think Billy Dee Williams is coming to ask her stankin' ass."

"If her ass stinks, why are you always sniffin' around?"

"Oooh, Buster," Ruben said. "Don't let her jank you like that."

"Tell her she better ask somebody," Buster said. "I'm Buster Green the panty fiend."

"Let me borrow that bucket so I can bring you some of her bathwater," she said. "You can use it to rinse your nasty mouth."

"Damn, Lorraine," Slim said as Ruben backed out of his parking space, "how you wanna jank on that man so hard?"

"You know I'm playing with you, Buster," Lorraine said. "Naomi might be too fast for you, anyway."

"That's why I want to go with her."

Buster coiled the water hose and carried the buckets and rags into the utility room. Mr. Barrett was locking the back doors, shaking them to make sure they were closed. Lorraine looked around at the deserted parking lot, empty except for us, and the three driver's-ed cars.

"Feeling any better?" she asked me.

"Yeah," I said. "I'm fine."

She knew I was lying. Lorraine crossed her finger over my heart and looked at me.

"Not really."

"Me, neither," she said.

Lorraine's hand still covered my heart.

"Slim's got a pistol in his bag."

"He's probably not the only one," she said. "Folks are talking crazy. Everybody's scared."

The fastest way from school to Lorraine's house took us down Springhill right past the Herndon intersection. The street was still littered with yellow and blue—police tape and the barricades. A few blocks before we got to Herndon, I put on my blinker to turn off Springhill. Lorraine put her hand on my shoulder.

"I want to go by there to pay my respects."

I had no intention of going back over there. At first I thought that if I didn't say anything, she'd let it go. Pay her respects from a distance.

"Do you mind?" she said, her fingers tense on my collarbone.

"There's nothing to see."

"Still. I need to see where it happened."

I turned off my turn signal and drove the last couple blocks toward the crime scene. Herndon Avenue was only a block long, and except for the people who lived there, it was nothing more than a shortcut between the heavily traveled streets that met at Five Points. But that week it became as much a destination as a back way. Some of the visitors added their flowers to the neat line of bouquets along the strip of grass between the sidewalk and the curb. An elderly man removed his hat, staring into the tangle of branches as if Michael's body was still there.

In the early 1980s, most of the residents of Five Points were still white. Seeing so many black visitors on the street must have been odd for the residents. Some of the houses were well kept. Others were covered in blistered paint, their yards lined with broke-down cars and chained dogs. Some of the neighbors watched the foot traffic from their porches, sitting on the threadbare love seats and wing chairs they'd moved outside. Others opened their windows to look at a crime scene the whole world had come to see.

The hanging tree was small, with wiry limbs and a clustered trunk. Perhaps someone had tried to cut it down years before, and the shoots had come back defiant. It had grown so close to the sidewalk that its roots buckled the concrete, disrupting the path of anyone who tried to walk beneath it.

I had expected to see something more happening there, a crime scene investigation like the ones I watched on *Quincy*. On television, the authorities combined science and legwork to figure out the truth. On Herndon Avenue, there was nothing of the kind. Michael's tree stood alone, surrounded only by the barricades, blue wooden slats with MOBILE POLICE DEPARTMENT stenciled in white letters on either side. The only police presence was a lone officer tapping his rhythm on the side of his patrol car, the music too low for anyone else to hear.

The tree stood on the edge of a vacant lot where the unattended grass had grown thick and uneven. The lot was flanked by two neat houses, their windows facing the hanging tree. I looked from house to house, window to window, peering into the mesh of the bug screens, the overlapping slats of the crank windows. If people looked out at us, they were impossible to see. As far as I had heard, no eyewitnesses had come forward, but somebody had seen something. Knew something. They had to.

Lorraine had taken the rosary from her purse, most of the beads hidden in her fist. She stared toward the tree as she mouthed a silent Hail Mary. She opened her door, and I began to open mine until she stopped me.

"You don't have to get out. I'll just be a second."

Lorraine didn't close her door after she got out. Three rusty trash cans were on the curb right beside the car, and even with the lids closed, the smell of the garbage carried. The trash collectors, diverted that Saturday, had not returned. A week's worth of garbage was left for the Tuesday-morning haul.

Lorraine stood still in front of the car, and the light from the blinking hazard bounced off her jeans. Her left hand was pressed flat on the hood of the car, and she prayed with her eyes open. Once she mouthed an amen, she came back to the car. She put her beads back in her purse and took out a tissue, wiped the pollen and dust from her hands.

"You okay?" I asked her.

"Not really," she said. "It just makes you wonder—about everything."

She ripped the tissue between her fingernails and dropped the pieces into my ashtray, along with the Juicy Fruit wrappers and the broken Stanza nameplate that had fallen off the bumper. I drove away, forgetting my hazards were on until I reached the end of the block. We turned the corner, and for the second time in three days, I watched the hanging tree disappear in the rearview.

"Student council is planning a memorial service on Friday," Lorraine said, touching my arm with a hand that still carried the warmth of the car hood. "People wanted me to ask you about where to send flowers. A lot of people have never been to a funeral."

"I wish I'd never been."

When we pulled into Lorraine's driveway, her little brother was in the front yard, dragging the lawn sprinkler from one side to the other. Mrs. Watters watched her son from the porch.

"She won't let him go anywhere by himself," Lorraine said.

Mrs. Watters said something to Corey, and when he ran to the side of the house, she walked right behind him, peering around the corner.

"Baseball tryouts were supposed to start this week, but they got canceled," she said. "And the basketball playoffs are this week. They haven't decided what they're going to do. People are still scared."

Corey wore jeans with grass-stained knees and a jersey for the O'Neil's Barber Supply Mustangs, the team he'd played for the year before. He had grown a lot in a year's time. The shirttail stopped just below his belt.

"People are saying this may be just like in Atlanta. They still haven't caught who killed those boys."

Mrs. Watters reached down and uncurled a kink in the hose. A few seconds later wide circles of water reached all the way to the driveway, a foot or two from the car.

"Come inside for a while."

"I can't. We have to pick him up from the morgue this afternoon."

"Oh."

Lorraine dug her fingernail into the broken spine of her calculus book.

"I can't imagine," she told me.

"I can. In an hour or so I won't have to," I said. "I just wish—"

I didn't finish my thought. There was no point to it. We'd had that conversation so many times already.

"I know," she said. "At some point you need to talk to your father."

She made it all sound easy. But the reality was that certain things were expected of me. I had watched some other funeral homes fall apart because the families walked away from the business. When my father and I drove past those buildings, crumbled or sold away, he told me the cautionary tales. Sinful, he called it. I never offered a response. My father had a reputation for warmth and kindness, but that was with clients. In the end, he was a businessman, and for us business and family were one and the same. He'd let Paul walk away because he knew he had me—or at least, that was what he assumed. Lorraine didn't understand, and I couldn't make her.

"Did you find your prom dress yet?"

"Yeah, I found one at this store called change the subject," she said, pinching my arm. "My aunt found one for me in Birmingham. That way I won't walk into the Civic Center and see some other girl with my dress on her ass."

"I'm sure your ass will look better in it."

"I know."

"Except Naomi's ass. Maybe Theresa."

"Keep playing," she said. "You ordered your tux, right?"

"Powder blue, with ruffles."

"Please."

Corey held his hands out over the sprinkler, and the spray of water ricocheted off his palms, darkening the green cotton jersey. Lorraine leaned back into the window and looked at me with her nose turned up.

"You were joking about a blue tux. You had to be."

"My daddy would kill me if I left the house in a powder-blue tux."

"As he should."

Lorraine joined her brother and mother on the porch, and I rolled the window down to speak to them.

"You and Paul coming to my game Wednesday?" Corey asked. "We playing for the championship."

"*We're* playing," his mother said.

"We'll be there," I told him. "Hey, Mrs. Watters."

"Hello, Roy," she said. "Call us so we'll know you made it home safely."

Claiborne Street was quiet, except for the hiss of water that came through the sprinkler. The trees on Claiborne carried the yellow ribbons for the dead children in Atlanta, twenty black boys killed over two years. The shredded and stained ribbons for the first of the victims had succumbed to the elements, only to be replaced by the fresh ribbons for the latest bodies to be found. Over on Herndon Avenue, the remnants of yellow police tape lay about the street, broken ends attached to the trees. A different color yellow, but a reminder just the same.

After I dropped off Lorraine and returned home, I was surprised by the gurgles of the iron. Paul was ironing his work clothes.

"I thought Mr. Davie gave you the week off?"

"He told me I could have it if I want it." He rested the

iron, and the steam poured out in a long wheeze. "I don't want it."

"You might need to take a couple of days. Until—"

"Until everything gets back to normal?" He shook his head.

He creased the legs of his trousers and draped them over the edge of the clothes basket. He grabbed a shirt and laid it across the ironing board.

"It's all people were talking about over at South Alabama today," he said.

"Same over at Murphy," I said.

Paul poured another cupful of water in the iron, and it hissed and steamed as he smoothed away the wrinkles around the Gulf Land Paper logo. He hung up the work shirt with the other two. He always ironed a week's worth at the same time. On the other end of the clothes rod that ran the length of the room hung the white shirts my father and I wore, identical but for the monograms.

It would have been so much easier for me if my brother had just worked in the business like I did. But the bodies had never scared me like they did Paul. When our father first allowed us into the prep room, he showed us the body of a man who had died of natural causes. By all appearances, he was just sleeping. Daddy never wanted us to see his work as something to be feared, so he started off by letting us see the parts we could handle. The ugliness of it we ended up finding on our own.

When Paul and I were too young to stay at home alone, we would spend time in the summer messing around behind the funeral home in the big yard. My father let us do whatever we wanted as long as we didn't get too loud. We had nailed a milk crate to the gingko tree, and if it was nice out we'd play basketball until I got tired of losing. When it rained or got too hot, we stayed in our father's study and played Uno, or hooked our Pong game up to the TV. Daddy's one steadfast rule was to stay out of the preparation room. "It's no place for you boys to be playing."

One rainy summer morning, when our father was distracted by his work in his office, I sneaked into the vault to see what was inside. Paul wanted no part of it.

"You gonna get whipped if he sees you in there."

"Long as you don't tell."

"I ain't no tattletale."

The metal door wasn't as heavy as it looked. It was the kind of door that would have creaked in movies, but it opened without much sound. I moved a few feet inside the vault, but Paul stood just outside. He wanted me to come out so we could turn around and leave, but he knew I'd call him chicken if he left before I did. Paul was six inches taller, twenty pounds heavier, and twice as fast as I was. In most things that seemed important in your youth—sports, the attention of girls—he had me beat. I enjoyed for once seeing him afraid.

"Scary ass."

He shook his head but said nothing. The overhead light had clicked on when the door opened, and the regulator came alive. Cold air poured from the ceiling vent down on us and the three gurneys that filled the space. The one closest to us was empty. The far gurney held the body of an elderly woman who'd died in her sleep the night before. She was barely five feet tall, so tiny that she barely disturbed the sheet that covered her body. The middle gurney was the body I wanted to see.

A man named Dexter Kyle had died in an explosion on

a gas rig just south of Bayou La Batre. I'd heard my father and grandfather discussing it that morning, whether or not they could open the casket.

"Quit acting like a chicken," I told Paul.

"You a damn chicken. I'll kick your stank ass, wait till we get outside."

"Well, we ain't outside now."

Paul let go of the steel door, and it took its time swinging shut. As he stood in the middle of the doorjamb, the door closed on his back and nudged him those last few inches inside.

"I dare you to lift the cover," I said.

"You lift it."

"All right, we both lift it. First one to let go is a sissy. Dollar bet."

Paul never backed down—from a fight, from a game—even if he knew he couldn't win. When he grabbed his edge of the canvas, I grabbed mine.

"One. Two. Three."

We pulled back the canvas only to find a second covering, this one a thick sheet of plastic, but the contours of the body beneath the sheet were distorted beyond what was natural. I had only wanted to see what had happened to Dexter Kyle, but when I saw the greasy blood spots that stained the covering, I wasn't curious anymore.

"If you're scared, we can go back outside," I told him.

When Paul grabbed his edge of the second sheet, I had no choice but to do the same. His hand shook more than mine did. When the regulator went silent, there was nothing left but the sound of our own shallow breathing.

"One."

I looked through the window, hoping to see Daddy ready to rip the door open and start yelling, but there was nothing there but the shelves.

"Two."

A whipping would have been better than what was under the sheet, but a bet was a bet. Paul stared me down with a tight grip on his corner of plastic.

"Three."

The cold of the vault dulled the odor, but the stench of gas and fishy waters lingered with the smell of Dexter Kyle's burns. The regulator, as if it had been holding its breath, kicked on once more.

His body had been torn to pieces. The right side of his skull had collapsed inward, and the white of his remaining eye had hemorrhaged to deep crimson. The debris that struck him had been searing hot, because the edges of skin around his wounds were burned to a crisp. The charred flesh of his right hand left exposed the slim bones at the end of the smashed forearm. His severed left arm lay wrapped in plastic. Though the skin was jagged around the wound, the arm didn't have a scratch.

I don't remember letting go of that plastic, but my side of the gurney was again covered while Paul kept holding on. He stood frozen with the edge of plastic wrinkled in his fist, his face twisted like he'd stared at the sun.

"Paul. Let go."

He didn't look away until I pushed the door, and he was awakened by the rush of outside air that forced the regulator to restore the chill. We slammed the vault shut behind us and ran out the back door and across the street to the park. I'd never seen Paul run as fast as he did when he jumped the three-foot park fence before I'd even cleared the sidewalk.

The rain had stopped, and the smell of ozone was as thick as the humidity. Paul sat on the bottom rung of the monkey bars with his head between his legs and threw up. He went to the drinking fountain and rinsed his mouth and his hands. When he returned, water matted his hair, and his Oilers T-shirt was soaked. Scraped paint covered his right shoulder where he must have brushed against the building when he went flying around the corner.

"I told you I ain't no damn chicken."

Paul had always run faster than I had. Most times after our races, I struggled to catch my breath while my brother talked mess and held his hand out for what I owed him. But that time he kept his hands in his pockets. I ripped open the Velcro wallet seal and took out a crisp dollar from my allowance. Paul shook his head.

"I don't want it."

"Take it."

"I don't have to take shit."

I grabbed his hand and slapped the dollar into his palm. He looked at the paper for a moment, then he crumpled it into his pocket. Paul came and sat in the swing next to me. He didn't say anything about the body, and neither did I. We just sat there in our swings and stared across the street at the house that bore our name.

I saw Dexter Kyle's body in the chapel on the day of his wake. He lay in his casket as whole as the day he was born. His face wore the appearance of peace, mouth and eyes closed, and his arms lay neatly folded across his chest.

"This is how everyone will remember him." This is what my father said after the difficult restorations. In the years since, I've seen bodies troubled as bad as Dexter Kyle's, but that day it became real. Until he found Michael, Dexter Kyle was the last body Paul had seen. In the family photo that adorns the church fans, my brother was there with us standing on the front steps. That's about as close as he got. He didn't come back into the preparation room again.

The children who played in the park would sometimes run across the street and stare into our windows, dare each other to ring the doorbell. They always said the house was haunted. Sitting on the swings, accompanied by my brother and the memory of Dexter Kyle, I saw the building the way those children did. The way Paul did. It was a house full of bodies.

The starch on Paul's cuffs sizzled when he pressed the iron down.

"I saw him last night while I was sleeping. It's not as bad when I'm awake."

He picked from the shirt collar a piece of lint and flicked it from his fingertips. It caught the light from the bay window as it fell to the linoleum near the bucket that held a pair of soaking coveralls. One of the others was in the custody of the Mobile Police Department.

"Do me a favor, Roy. Keep telling me everything will be all right. Maybe I'll start believing."

"I will."

"You better hurry, Daddy's waiting. I know he probably wants to get started on him. He was—" Paul measured his words. He wrapped the cord around the base of the iron, and set it on top of the washing machine. He folded the ironing board and set it in the corner. He turned toward the window and lowered his head. "His face. You all might have to close the casket."

As uncomfortable as funerals can be, sometimes people need to see the faces to say their good-byes. Closed caskets only remind the mourner of the damage that couldn't be undone.

"We'll do everything we can."

His breaths were as heavy as the exhales of the iron.

"They messed him up something terrible." He turned his head toward me. "Mike was never dirty. He was always clean as a whistle, you know?"

"Yeah, I know."

"I know you'll clean him up right."

When the phone rang, I knew who it was before I answered.

"Yes, sir. I'm just now changing clothes. I'm on my way."

Paul looked out the window. Mr. Lockhart and his son were in their driveway, playing basketball. Billy was four years old. He threw the ball as high as he could, and it would make it halfway up to the goal before it came back down. It didn't seem to matter that it wasn't even close.

"This time last week, we were running folks off the court," Paul said, his clothes folded over his arm. He turned his back to me. Didn't want me to see his eyes tearing up.

"Clean him up good," he told me.

"I'll do everything I can."

"You always do."

Our funeral home was on the corner of Carlisle Street and MLK. Many things about King Avenue had changed over the years, primarily the name. Lots of folks still called it Jefferson Davis Avenue, some out of habit and others out of spite. At some point, everyone settled on calling it the Avenue and left it at that.

The Avenue had been an amazing place once, the street where you could get a little of everything. When the storefronts still had stores, my mother bought my first Easter suit at Besteda Brothers tailor shop. All of our birthday cakes came from Craig's Bakery Shop until they closed. Before the west-side malls and shops, the Avenue sidewalks were thick with people spending money on Saturday afternoons. By the late 1970s, some businesses had simply gone to the west side, and others were gone for good. The funeral homes never left. Azalea. Johnson-Allen. Christian Benevolent. They, like us, remained in the part of Mobile known to many black folks as 'cross town. They came to these same streets when it was time to bury their dead.

I parked by the garage and walked around to the front. My father stood on the steps, leaning against the mailbox and smoking a cigarette. He had quit on orders of his doctor two years before, but on certain days I'd catch him having one, taking long drags that brought out his frown lines.

He looked me up and down before he pressed his fingers to his collarbones, sign language telling me to straighten my tie. I moved it to one side and then the other. He nodded. My father had always been a clean dresser: sharp creases, dimpled ties, high-shined oxfords. He kept the extras simple: pocket watch, wire-rimmed glasses, and a cigarette lighter engraved with his initials, RJD.

"My last one, I promise," he said.

He looked up and down the street as if he expected company. Down the block, a hearse pulled into Christian Benevolent. Yellow funeral parking cones lined the street at Lovett's. Lucille Winbush was setting some out in front of Azalea. With everything that had happened with Michael Donald, it was easy to forget that other people were dying, too.

My father pulled hard one last time on the Marlboro before he dropped it on the concrete and stamped it out, placed the butt in the palm of his hand. He had already pulled the van around, so I got in the passenger's seat and waited for him to get in.

"I got a call just before you got here," he said. "There's an intake that I need to be here for."

I looked at the driver's seat, empty except for the keys he'd left there.

"Ready?" he asked me.

I tightened my jaw and swallowed. Lied.

"Yes, sir."

The medical examiner's plan had been very specific. My father explained to me what they had worked out over the phone. Bertrand, one of my father's drivers, would drive a hearse to the main entrance of the morgue and wait. A few minutes later, I was supposed to drive the cargo van to a side entrance where Dr. Warner would turn over Michael's remains. We would meet at 4:15. Dr. Warner didn't want us to wait too long outside because the photographers and news cameras were waiting, and the coroner hoped to avoid another spectacle.

When I drove past the front entrance, four photographers were already there waiting. A Channel 9 station wagon idled near the covered entryway on the side of the main building. A newswoman mouthed her practice words as she stood beside an empty tripod. They all were looking at Bertrand leaning against the 1981 Cadillac Crown Sovereign, the newest in our fleet, polishing out smudges with a shammy. He played his part perfectly, even looking at his watch and then to the door. The photographers must have had the picture framed in their heads, a body bag rolled out of the morgue and loaded into the shiny black hearse. They never looked my way as I drove around back. It was just then 4:45. If Dr. Warner had kept to the schedule, at that moment he was rolling Michael's body down the long corridor through the unfinished new wing, away from the waiting cameras, his plan to preserve some semblance of privacy for the family, even if it seemed too late.

Just beyond the Dumpsters, I got out of the van to move aside the orange cones that blocked the parking lot entrance. The blacktop still had its brand-new luster, and the lines hadn't been painted yet. The new wing of the hospital was scheduled to open early that summer. From the street, the top of the new building was hidden behind the scaffolding, and surrounded by stacks of brick that would complete the last corner of the facade.

The yellow pollen that covered the shipping dock had mixed with the reddish dust of bricks. After only a few steps, it was all over my shoes. I polished them religiously. But ultimately it seemed pointless. Walking through the cemetery grass, stepping through the red clay around fresh-made graves, the shine was fleeting.

A Danger sign had gotten wet and wrinkled by the spring rains. The paper had broken away from the tape that held it to the double doors. Through the windows just above the sign, Dr. Warner came into view one hundred feet down the corridor. He walked at the front right side of the gurney, and an assistant pushed from behind.

We're supposed to open the bag and make sure we have the right body, but that time I didn't have to. The look on Dr. Warner's face was proof enough. Besides, I only wanted to open that bag once. I rolled the gurney to the bumper and locked the wheels. The metal was still cold to the touch, and the spring humidity had made a thin fog along the steel. Dr. Warner gently gathered the bag around Michael's ankles and pushed from behind, and his assistant lifted from underneath. As I lifted from the front, I felt the weight of Michael's shoulders and head against the slick plastic that was as cold as the metal below it.

I thought about Bertrand sitting out front. The hearse he'd driven was plush. Whenever the pallbearers slid the casket onto the chrome rollers, it rested against the soft interior. The cargo van was just an empty space with nothing to soften the bare walls. It was unembellished, just like the bodies it was meant to carry.

"Roy, I need you to sign for him," Dr. Warner said.

While I signed the triplicate forms, the coroner stared down at the body bag as if he could see through the plastic. He handed me a copy of the death certificate, which smelled of the blue-black ink that had smeared in places. Another envelope held the autopsy report. The coroner always provided the morticians with their findings to help us do our work. The particulars of death—wounds, swelling, lacerations—dictate the restoration. I glanced down at the paper, Michael's filled-in blanks. Cause of death: Asphyxiation. Mechanism of Death: Plastic rope. Time of death: Approx. 12:00 A.M. Height. 6'0". Weight: 150 lbs. Age: 19.

He glanced toward the parking lot entrance through horn-rimmed glasses that dated him. No news vans. No cameras. His plan had worked, but all things considered, that wasn't much solace. I had known Dr. Warner for years. He fished the same waters my grandfather did, and when we transferred bodies, there was often small talk about rods and reels, artificial lures and such. On that day, there wasn't much for Dr. Warner to say, just a sad proclamation before he disappeared down the corridor.

"I've never seen anything like it," he said. "A sin and a shame."

When I drove around the corner, Bertrand was still standing beside the hearse with his arms crossed, shammy in one hand and the other cradling his chin. He had driven for my father since well before I was born. Just about every Saturday morning, he drove one of our family cars, and in the afternoon he would go to mass at St. Augustine's. He didn't make eye contact when I passed him. He just dipped his head and made a quiet cross, thumb against the salt and pepper of his beard. The photographers looked toward the automatic doors for the body I carried. I wondered how long they would stand there, waiting in vain.

When I took the mortician certification classes at Bishop State College, everyone there was older than I was. I wondered who these people were and what possessed them to want to do what I had been born into. The man who sat next to me was a retired army sergeant. In the baseball cap that rested on his knee, he had made sharp creases like the ones he had worn in the service.

"What year are you in school?" he had asked me.

"Freshman."

"At Bishop?"

"No, sir. High school."

He stared like he was looking for the rest of me. I suppose that when they looked at the fifteen-year-old among them, they wondered what possessed me to be there as well. When the instructor called the roll the first day—*young Mr. Deacon*—everyone recognized my last name and turned all the way around to look at me. At that moment, I wished I had taken the empty seat in the front of the room instead of the one in the back.

In the prep room, there was nowhere for me to hide. When Michael's body bag was placed on the table, the room was quiet but for the ventilation hum, which was so familiar that it could be mistaken for silence. My father stepped back and waited for me to make the assessment. The preparation room quickly became familiar. The porcelain table. The steel light fixtures. The sinks, the tanks, the hoses. The ventilator. The scalpels and the sutures. The sound of the drainage rising above the hum of the lights. The sound of the scrubbing once our work was done. But being familiar didn't mean being comfortable. Being certified to be there didn't mean I was ready.

"Just take one good look to see what needs to be done." One good look. When I first started, those words had made sense.

I expected the worst when my father took hold of the plastic. After he opened the bag, I could still hear the zipper. The tracks might as well have run on forever. I didn't look at first. I kept my eyes on the five-by-seven of Michael that was pinned to the light above the table. It was a senior picture, taken in his cap and gown. Daddy removed it from the clothespin and held it close to Michael's body.

His face was so swollen that he looked like a stranger. The right side of Michael's face bore the waffled imprint of a jackboot cast in red clay. The medical examiner's theory was that the assailant placed his boot on Michael's face to hold him still, then pulled the rope tight. He was killed while he was still on the ground. The treeing was just for show.

I touched his face. "His jaw. It's broken right here. And here."

Dr. Warner concluded that Michael had taken over a hundred blows. A vague scent of pinesap rose from his body, but no pine trees grew on Herndon. He had abrasions from being dragged through the woods. A stubble of pine needles clung to the mud on his cheeks.

"I guess killing him wasn't enough," my father said, moving the light close to the wound. "Lord." Michael's neck size was fourteen and three-quarters inches. The noose had been tightened to twelve. On top of all that, Michael's throat had been sliced three times.

When my legs got shaky, I leaned against the counter. My elbow rattled a tray of crushers, sending the smallest one to the floor.

"You need to go outside and get some air?" Daddy asked, his eyes never leaving the table.

"No, sir. I'm fine."

Michael had lost much of his blood from the neck wounds, and the remaining fluid had pooled in his legs as he hung for all those hours.

"Edema in both legs," I told my father.

Michael's spine doglegged just below his hairline, where the bones had snapped. My father placed his hands on either side of Michael's head and gently rocked it from one side to the other. The movement of Michael's head at the slightest touch coupled with the rope burn and the scars made restoration seem hopeless. I wasn't prepared to put him back together. To make him look like the person I had

seen all those times at school, the rec center, and all manner of places. At graduation the spring before, Michael had
crossed the stage just after Paul did. And just like that, he was
on our table.

"May I be excused?"

He nodded. The vacuum seemed to suck all the color
out of the room, leaving only the steel gray, the white of the
porcelain, the cream of the tile, Michael's ashen skin. When
I moved the overhead light aside, the metal hood was hot to
the touch. I left my hand there for a moment, feeling the only
warm thing in the room.

"Son, if you'd like to go home, I'll understand."

He didn't mean it. He wanted me there as much as I
wanted to be gone.

"I'll be back soon."

"Take your time," he said. "We'll be here for a while."

The hall window was halfway open, as was the window
at the top of the stairs. A crossbreeze ran through the house
unencumbered. The ginkgo out back already had full-grown
leaves. Every autumn, the air carried the odor of the tree's
fruit as it rotted on the ground among the yellow leaves. On
that spring evening, the fruit was still months away, and the
air was cool and empty. But the relief the breeze gave was
enough to let me forget, for a few minutes at least, where I
was and what I was doing.

Black-and-white photographs lined the wall. The an-
tique frames contain the oldest of our family pictures, faces
from each of the seven generations that the sign out front
decried. A pewter frame carried a grainy brown photo with
hand-painted color. The couple in the center picture were
Paulo and Grace Deacon.

I was in the eighth grade when *Roots* was published.

My history teacher that year gave us an assignment: trace our families as far back as we could go. For some students the names went back a few generations before they became harder to find. For me the answers were easy to locate. I didn't even need to ask. All I had to do was just look at the mortuary wall.

Grace was born on Captain Timothy Meaher's plantation, but Paulo was among the many smuggled into Mobile well into the 1850s, arranged like cornrows along the bottom of the boats. He was a boy when he was captured, and Paulo was the name the Portuguese gave him in Dahomey. Captain Meaher was fond of Mina slaves, because they made their livelihood on the water and were skilled at building boats. He brought them to America to work in his shipyards. As far as we could tell, Paulo was brought over sometime in the early 1840s. He became a carpenter, building the captain's slave ships.

Many who crossed the water never made it to shore. At night when the smugglers entered the bay, they had to watch out for the navy ships that patrolled it. The dead and dying on their boats were dumped into the waters. Some were weighted with chains and sank to the bottoms, but others washed ashore.

Many of the bodies were burned by patrollers or left for the animals. If the slaves got the bodies first, they did what they could to bury them. The carpenters built coffins with whatever wood they could find or steal. Paulo became one of the deacons at the slave church built on Old Hill, and he later became caretaker of the cemetery.

There were no names to place on their markers, so the rows of anonymous dead share a single stone, an uneven piece of rock with "Jubilee" cut across the face. The few people who gathered at their funerals heard the same words.

> *Ye shall return to thine own possession,*
> *Ye shall return unto thine own family.*
> *It shall be jubilee unto you.*

After emancipation, Paulo and Grace Deacon continued to fill the rows at Old Hill, and the colored cemeteries of Mobile County. That is how it started, these seven generations in the service. When I left my father and the body of Michael Donald, I didn't need to be reminded of what I had been born into. Anytime I thought of letting the chain of generations end with me, I ended up in front of that wall, met by staring faces that followed me around the room. I sat down on the long wooden bench and closed my eyes. When I opened them, there on the bench beneath the photographs was my grandfather.

"I didn't mean to startle you."

He leaned forward in the chair and wiped a few specks of dust from his shoes. His starched cuffs carried the familiar monogram, TPD. Thaddeus Paul Deacon. "You were resting. I didn't want to disturb you."

"I just needed some air."

"Take as much time as you need."

"I don't think there's enough," I told him.

The lines of his face were well settled. The only smooth place left was on the top of his head. The last bit of hair that covered his temples was cut low and neat. The wrinkles on his forehead gave him the look of endless contemplation. I hadn't heard him walk down the hallway. Mr. Barrett had replaced the hardwood floors five years before. They never creaked after that. Everyone walked across them as quiet as ghosts.

"Daddy didn't tell me you were coming."

"He doesn't know I'm here," he said as he stood and walked to the window.

In some of the pictures behind me, my grandfather was a boy. He didn't talk much about the lynchings in his lifetime, but he had told my father about one that happened in 1909. Gloria Upchurch. Everybody knew that Colonel John did what he pleased to the women who worked on his farm. The day Gloria went missing, they found Colonel John half dead in his smokehouse. When a mob went after Gloria, her friends and relations waited and hoped she had escaped. The waiting and hoping ended the next morning, when someone came by the funeral home to bring news nobody wanted. Gloria had been hanged from a pecan tree in Tillman's Corner.

My grandfather, his father, and a few others took a mule and wagon out to go get her remains. Even in the dense acres, a lynched body was not hard to find. They found a mass of wagon tracks that chewed up the ground of a small clearing. A trail of garbage told them they were close. Empty Coca-Cola bottles and chicken bones covered the ground where the crowd had watched. Gloria's naked body had been hoisted fifty feet off the ground so that the circle of watchers could see her unobstructed.

Once the body was brought down, the wagon returned to Mobile, where the Upchurch family had gathered. Paulo Deacon was at least eighty years old by then. He waited with Gloria's people on the funeral-home gallery, standing on the same steps where he took his last picture, a former slave beside the grandfather who sat across from me in our vestibule.

"When's the family coming?"

"Tomorrow afternoon."

"I went to high school with his uncle," he said. "Good people."

Granddaddy checked his watch, wound it, and returned it to his vest pocket. He had been retired for ten years. Most days he fished or took his morning walks along the beach in Daphne. He only wore his three-piece suits to church, to funerals, and to go freshen up the flowers on my grandmother's grave.

"I understand the young man was a friend to you and Paul."

"Yes, sir. He went to Murphy."

"I stopped by the house to see your brother, but he was already gone. I wanted to see how both of you are doing."

"I'm okay."

"If you see your brother before I do, tell him that I want to sit down with him."

"Yes, sir."

He walked over and straightened a photograph that wasn't even crooked.

"I hoped that we had left all this behind." He walked over and closed the window. "You get to a certain age and think such things are behind you for good. But here we are."

He placed his arms behind his back, and his fingers trembled until one hand caught the other. "How far along are you?"

"The assessment."

"Will he have an open casket?" he asked.

"It'll take some work."

"They always do," he said, rubbing his temples. "Did I tell you that I went to grade school with his uncle?"

"Yes, sir. You mentioned it."

"Good people." He motioned toward the door to the prep room.

I could see my car from the window, and I thought about leaving. My father and grandfather had managed without me all those years before, and they could have gotten by without me then. I had been waiting for the right time to tell them that I wasn't built for it, but my grandfather stood in front of me, his hand on the doorknob. The faces on the wall stared. I stood and walked toward the door he held open.

My father didn't seem surprised to see him. We all stood there in starched shirts and good slacks, sleeves rolled up ready to do what was required. With fresh gloves from the box on the counter, we returned to the table.

"I talked to your brother at lunchtime," my father told me, moving the light from one side of Michael's head to the other. "Did you talk to him today?"

"I talked to him for a while before I came."

"How was he holding up?"

"With Paul it's always hard to tell. He was on his way to work."

"The boy shouldn't be going back to work so soon," my grandfather said.

"Maybe it'll help things get back to normal," I said.

My grandfather had his hands on Michael's temples, making the same moves and turns my father had minutes before.

"Maybe this is our normal," he said.

It took forty minutes to drain the blood from Michael's body. Once the embalming was complete, my father and grandfather worked on his face, addressing the bruises and the swelling. They cleaned the caked mud from his cheeks, and rinsed the grit from his hair. While they worked on his face, I washed his hands and cleared his fingernails of the blood, gravel, and mud. My father came and watched over my shoulder as I cleared the scrapes and cuts on his knuckles.

"He put up a fight."

Melanin helps to obscure some bruises, making them difficult to distinguish from the dark skin they've stained. Under the strong light, all of the bruises that covered him head to toe were plain to see. The defensive wounds that covered Michael's palms appeared bold against the pale skin.

Seeing Michael's hands and face, I thought of my schoolyard brawls. After the fights I'd won, I remembered how the rush of victory dulled the pain of taken blows. Then I thought of the fights I had lost, when I felt the pain of knuckles against my face, and the hot rush of blood coming to the surface. Those fights seemed important at the time, but we were all just kids. There was nothing at stake besides pride or shame.

"Too bad he didn't take one of them with him."

My grandfather had been stifled by the shaking in his hands and a memory that sometimes failed him. We worried that he wouldn't be able to live alone much longer, but as he worked around Michael's head, stitching the ruptured skin and reshaping his face, his hands were steady and his memory was sound.

He remembered things we had never known. How to dress rope-burned skin. How to wire a neck, broken and distended, to make the bones straight again. Arrange the

high, starched collar and necktie so they hid the marks that
makeup could not conceal. I watched him as he worked, cradling Michael's head in his hands. He held it like he held
mine in the waters along the bay, on the summer afternoon
he tried to teach me to float. I floated for a while, but when I
opened my eyes and realized his hands were gone, and what I
felt along my neck and back was just a memory of his fingers,
I sank like a rock.

Tuesday Afternoon

The afternoon temperature had crept up past 75, and people around my neighborhood took advantage, found escape in their outdoor distractions. When I got home to change my clothes, Mr. Lockhart from next door was outside firing up his new gas grill. His tools covered the pavement at his feet.

"Lava rocks," he told me as he dropped the shiny grate into its grooves. "Then you pour the mesquite wood on top to get that smoke taste."

He explained it like it was science.

"You too good for charcoal?" I asked him.

"At least now I can smoke meat like your daddy—shit, maybe even better."

"I'll tell him you said that."

"Go ahead. Run, tell it all you want."

A wide grin spread across his face, but then he saw

something over his shoulder that made his face go tight. His eyes stayed on the car that had pulled up in front of the house. "You got company."

Unmarked police cars only seem to draw more attention to themselves. Heavy metal with too many antennaes, dull black rims with a little cap of chrome. Detective Wilcox walked up the sidewalk and opened the gate. He looked like he had dropped ten pounds since Saturday. He was pale, even more so than before. The only color in his face came from his eyes.

"Hello—Roy, right?"

"Yes."

He stood at the gate and surveyed everything. The porch. The garage. The hedges.

"Nice place," he said. "I must be in the wrong business."

Mr. Lockhart said something under his breath. I couldn't make out the words, but I could imagine.

"Is your brother home?"

"No."

"How's he doing?"

"He's fine."

"You expecting him soon?"

"He has late classes, and after that I'm not sure if he's coming straight home. You can leave a message for him."

He ran his hand across his face. The afternoon whiskers had started to come in. And the pleasant face, a little bit of a smile, seemed painful to hold. His face showed the hint of the frown lines that were years away from being permanent.

"Well, I just had a few more questions about Michael. Some of his activities."

Mr. Lockhart stood over his grill, staring dead into Detective Wilcox's face and making no effort to disguise his eavesdropping.

"From the looks of things, we think that he was just in the wrong place at the wrong time."

"Now you're saying he wasn't into drugs?"

"No, we're just saying he was the victim of unfortunate circumstances. Any idea who might have had it out for him?"

"We went through this already," I said. "Nobody had it out for him."

"You can't be certain."

"Then why ask me?"

I measured my voice when I answered his questions. I didn't want to sound disrespectful, but he'd only asked one question, and it had already grown tiresome.

"Well, truth told, I think I might have come across the wrong way the other day. I know the department has had some tension in its interaction with the black community, but I'm happy to say things are changing for the better."

His words were too measured. He talked like he was still at the podium, standing behind the city shield.

"The department has no desire to impugn anybody's character."

Nobody stood in front of your house talking about impugning anything. That wasn't a front-porch word.

Mr. Lockhart said something under his breath as he poured the layer of lava rocks into his brand-new grill. Detective Wilcox kept his hands in his pockets, rustling what sounded like a dollar's worth of change.

"It's a mess. That's the one thing I know for sure," he said in a changed voice, like he was pulling me aside. "The rest we're just trying to figure out, same as everybody else."

Wilcox leaned against the chain-link fence. Behind his head, I saw Mr. Lockhart, his face warped by the invisible wall of heat that rose from the grill. He wasn't blinking. He stood there, arms crossed, staring into the back of Detective Wilcox's head.

"I need to get ready for work," I told him. "Is there something in particular you need to ask?"

He walked onto the porch and put his hand on the back of one of the rattan chairs.

"May I?"

Detective Wilcox sat down heavy, as if he carried more than his two hundred or so pounds. The seatback creaked as he shifted his weight.

"Look, you and your brother come from a nice home, nice family, things are a little different for you than they are for somebody who lives over in the Orange Grove projects like your friend."

"You think they asked where he lived before they took him?"

"There's plenty about your friend that you might not have known about. He could have had words with somebody," he said. "Maybe they wanted to get back at him."

His words of wisdom sounded untested, like he was trying them on for size before he could believe them himself. When he leaned forward, I could see the wooden butt of his pistol poking through the vents of his sport coat.

"You want to know what I think?"

He didn't give me time to say no.

"There are a lot of drugs changing hands around Herndon. Maybe Donald was in the area—for whatever reason—and he walked into a bad scene."

Mr. Lockhart held his stare on Wilcox, with a box of matches still in his hand.

"There hasn't been a lynching in Mobile in sixty years. I checked. Why'd anybody do something like that now?"

"You tell me."

Wilcox stood from his seat and straightened the creases of his pants.

"Tell your brother I stopped by," he said. "I'd like to ask some follow-up questions."

As he walked down the steps, Wilcox saw Mr. Lockhart staring. The detective nodded his head.

"Good afternoon, sir."

"Y'all catch them crackers that killed that boy?" Mr. Lockhart said, his voice as loud and country as I had ever heard it.

Detective Wilcox kept walking, but the blood rushed to his head and darkened the skin around the neatly cropped line of his neck as he got in his unmarked car and drove away. Relations with the police had not always been smooth. Sometimes things were quiet for a while, then something happened that reminded us. A few weeks before the murder, Chief Davidson had referred to a suspect as a nigger during a press briefing. His defenders said the chief had not used a racial slur, had said "nigra," which was a "commonly used colloquial reference for Afro-Americans." The tension went deeper than a careless word. A few years before, members of the street crimes unit had threatened a suspect with a noose while trying to get a confession. It didn't happen in the police station, but on a city street.

Sergeant Kincaid was one of the first few black officers to get promoted, but we could still count the senior officers on one hand. Seemed like the young cops who busted heads in the 1950s and '60s had been promoted, and they were still pretty much running things. The young Wilcoxes of the world might have meant well, but in a lot of ways they were just as bad. At least with the old ones you knew where you stood.

"So that's the man they got in charge," Mr. Lockhart said. "You think he's up to it?"

"I hope so."

"You and me both," he said. "If not . . ." He never finished his thought. Mr. Lockhart shook his head, still holding the same unlit match as the police car disappeared down our peaceful street.

Michael's family was scheduled to arrive at five thirty to view the restoration. We had placed his body in the lift and lowered him into the casket. Bertrand had gone to the Donald home earlier that day to pick up clothes from his family. The wooden hanger that had carried them was now on the counter. I sliced down the back of the suit and shirt with a sewing knife so that we could wrap the clothes around him. Once we arranged his shirt and suit, all that remained was the tie, dark red with blue stripes, that I had draped around my neck. I had struggled three times trying to make the knot with the dimple just so. Makeup, sutures, and synthetic skin concealed the rope burns and his slashed throat. Michael's reconstructed neck lay exposed between the open ends of his collar. I made the knot in Michael's necktie for the fourth time, and the dimple was worse than the ones before. Tying my own tie was so easy that I never thought twice about it. It was hard to tie someone else's.

The Donald family would arrive soon, and I had been trifling with the necktie for half an hour. It had to be right. I only had one chance to cut the loop. I had just started over when my father called me through the intercom.

"You need to bring the casket to the viewing room."

"Yes, sir. I'll be up in a second."

I released the intercom button and turned back around, and there was Paul standing in the doorway. He wore a faded South Alabama T-shirt and jeans that had frayed at the bottom. He looked around the room he hadn't visited in ten years.

"Still looks the same back here," he said.

Paul looked at the tie draped around my neck and grabbed both ends. Once he finished the second loop, he guided the end with his finger so that the dimple was just right.

"Thanks," I told him. "I don't know what's wrong with me today."

"Same thing's wrong with everybody."

I sliced through the loop and centered the tie in place. The skin above the collar was firm, and all signs of the trauma had been covered. Paul stood across from me and looked down at Michael's face.

"He started his masonry classes this quarter," Paul said. "Wanted me to talk to Daddy about making a new sign out front. Just kept forgetting. Telling him I'd get around to it."

He dropped his head and closed his eyes.

"At first when I saw him out there, it looked like he was alive. Like somebody just standing on the street. Then I saw that rope, his blood."

Paul picked up the wooden hanger that lay on the counter with the makeup cases. He looked toward the vault, which held two bodies, the latest in the hundreds that had been there since his last time through the door.

"With everything you did to him, it still won't matter. I can't help but to see him in that tree."

"Maybe," I said. "After while, it'll—"

My father was calling me through the intercom.

"I need to let you get back to work," Paul said.

"No. Wait for me. I'll be right back."

"Don't tell them I'm down here. They keep asking me if I'm okay, and I'm tired of lying."

"Okay. But just wait a minute. I'll be back."

I rolled the casket down the hall. The old floor had grooves from years of wheels that followed that same path, but on the new wood, the load shifted side to side. When I reached the viewing room, my father was pulling a few crumpled leaves from the flower arrangements. Just as we centered the casket and opened the lid, my mother called out to us from the next room.

"They caught them," she said, her nervous hands moving quickly as she jerked the rabbit ears on the little TV in the office, trying in vain to get the picture clear. The SPECIAL REPORT banner jumped across the screen of the worn-out set. She finally smacked the console, and the picture came in as sharp as the words.

"Mobile police arrested three men this afternoon in connection with the weekend murder of Michael Donald . . ."

They looked like I imagined they would. Three long-haired white men, who looked no older than I was, were marched through the back door of the police station in handcuffs. Thomas Holman, twenty-two. Theodore Holman, twenty-six. Herbert Moody, twenty-three.

"Unidentified police sources say two eyewitnesses place the suspects on Herndon Avenue on the evening in question . . ."

As my parents watched, I ran back down the hallway to tell Paul. The arrests should have been a small comfort. At the very least, the killers couldn't lynch anybody else. But by the time I got to the prep room, Paul was already gone. I walked out the door and looked through the window, at the homemade basketball rack that we had never taken down. Just as I opened the window to call for him, the door chimes rang through the hall. Soon after the chimes rang, my father's voice came through the wall, calling my name again.

"Yes, sir. I'm on my way."

I had gone to Lorraine's house after school as many times as I had gone to my own, but on that evening, walking to the door with my mother and Paul, it felt oddly official. Sonny and Lyle had a cramped downtown office, but Mr. Watters did much of his business from home. Sometimes when I brought Lorraine home at the curfew that her parents had set—11:00 P.M, not a minute later—the light would still be on. If I came by at seven in the morning to give Lorraine a ride to school, he was already up working on somebody's case, catching somebody else doing wrong. "Nailing one more motherfucker to the wall," as he liked to say.

"Sonny just wants to ask you a few questions," my mother said to Paul on the way over. "The police are talking about that young man something terrible. Lyle's going to make a statement tomorrow. He wants to talk to some of Michael's friends first."

Mr. Watters had asked for a copy of the autopsy report,

and my father asked me to bring it to him. The families get copies if they want them, but it wasn't the kind of thing that Mr. Watters wanted to ask the Donald family about so soon. It wasn't anything a family wanted to leaf through. The location of every wound. How much blood was lost. Mr. Watters and Mr. Ferguson had made a living exposing ugly details. I had in my hands twenty pages' worth.

Lorraine answered the door. Her father must not have told her we were coming, because she looked surprised. My mother was the first to the door, and she acted like she hadn't seen Lorraine in years.

"Hey, sweetheart," my mother said. "I'm looking forward to that play."

"I'm on my way to rehearsal in a few minutes," she said. "I'm sad this'll be my last one."

"The last one in high school, but then you'll have college and Broadway and Hollywood."

Mama's voice jumped an octave, and she talked to Lorraine in her daughter-I-never-had voice.

"Everybody's in the study," Lorraine told us.

Paul and Mama walked in and left the door slightly open. Through the crack in the door, I heard Mr. Watters greeting my mother and then Paul. I stayed outside for a minute with Lorraine. She sat on the stairs, looking toward the door that was opened just enough to hear the hum of conversation. Sometimes when I brought her home, she would sit in her father's office and talk to him while he worked. Lorraine said that she had wanted to be a lawyer when she was little. I'd asked her what changed her mind. Told me she had come to her senses.

"This is how it always starts," she said. "First phone calls. Then these meetings. The press conferences."

"You talk like it's a bad thing," I told her.

"It can be."

She turned her back against the wall and pressed her feet along the railing. I sat down just beneath her and leaned against her. When she put her hand on my neck, the bracelet her mother gave her jangled, filled with the charms she'd collected, the ones I'd given her.

"My favorite part is when crazy-ass white folks start calling the house talking about nigger this and nigger that."

She pressed her feet against the railing that was loose enough to twist, rattle in its dry socket.

"Sometimes they send letters. You'd be surprised at how many people don't know that *nigger* has two g's. *Niger* is a country."

"It's a river, too."

She leaned over and rested her chin on my head. I could smell the cocoa butter on her skin, the Sulfur-8 Hair Food she rubbed in her scalp. Her bag sat by the door, stuffed with all her things. I asked her once why she needed so much.

"You just never know," she told me.

Lorraine's house had been the frequent site of such gatherings. I had been there several times when Sonny had a room full of people. Lorraine said that most of them came by unannounced at all kinds of hours.

"I'm glad they're doing all this," she said. "But the fact they still have to do it—"

She didn't finish her thought, just ended it with head-shakes and a sigh.

"I gotta go," she said. "Rehearsal."

She kissed me on the cheek before she disappeared through the door and got behind the wheel of her mother's car. A little while later, a minute at the most, the blue

Cougar passed the window as Lorraine flew down the street toward Dunbar.

You all know my youngest, Roy," my mother said when I walked into the study. They all nodded hello, offered the usual welcomes. *Looking more and more like your daddy every day.* I took the last empty chair brought in from the dining room, and sat next to the leather couch where Mama and Council sat. Paul sat in a chair like mine by the window.

They were all in there. Sonny Watters. Sergeant Kincaid. Nancy Freed. Council Ferguson and Lyle. Mr. Ferguson's secretary, Carole Sanford, sat at the small conference table in the corner. Mr. Watters was in his leather chair. Lyle sat at his desk.

The only time I saw all of them together anymore was during Black History Month. One program or another. They'd talk about "the struggle," then we'd sing "We Shall Overcome" and have refreshments. The same kind of history lesson played out on Sonny's walls. His framed mug shots. Pictures with the famous. Proclamations. I had seen everyone in that room at a podium somewhere, telling their war stories. It was odd to hear tales of something that had just happened, was still happening. Sergeant Kincaid continued with the story he must have started before I entered.

"As far as I know, they have two witnesses. One is a drug offender. He rolled over on these other three so he'd get a suspended sentence."

"He's reliable?" Lyle asked.

"Hardly. He's a junkie," Kincaid said, shrugging his shoulders. "The other witness is a fifteen-year-old girl that was going with one of the boys."

"A grown man courting a child," Mrs. Freed said. "They should have put him under the jail for that a long time ago."

"So, three junkies picked up a black boy, killed him, and hung his body in a tree across town? In Five Points?"

"That's what the brain trust says. And so it is."

"It smells funny."

"Smells like some bullshit," Sonny said.

"The Anderson trial ends in a mistrial," Nancy said. "Then a couple of days later, the cops find a burned cross and a body hanging from a tree."

Josephus Anderson was a black man on trial for killing a white police officer in Birmingham. The trial had been moved to Mobile, the logic being that we supposedly had less racial tension than Birmingham. It must have seemed like a good idea at the time.

"And the wallet," Sergeant Kincaid said, his hands talking as loud as his voice. "They found that in a Dumpster over by Bishop State."

He unfolded his arms, rubbed his hands against his trousers.

"Still had money in it. Watch was still in his pocket, too. What kind of junkies would kill a man and leave all that on him?"

"And those boys they arrested live way out in the county," Sergeant Kincaid said. "So why in the hell would they come into town to hang a body on a street they didn't live on?"

"Doesn't wash," Lyle said. "Are they considering any other motives?"

"Still floating the white-girl theory. If he wasn't so bruised up, they'd just say he killed himself and be done with it."

"What other suspects did they have?"

"Not a one," he said. "Can't find what you're not looking for."

Sergeant Kincaid couldn't sit still. The story he needed to tell had him nervous, so anxious that he needed to shift his weight back and forth, one leg planted on the rug and the other on the hardwood, clicking as he moved his feet. He finally just had to stand up.

"I had to cut him down," he said. "A couple of the police were out there taking pictures. You should have heard the shit they were talking on the radios. Didn't make a difference I was listening."

Kincaid sat back in his chair and sat rubbing his hands, working his empty fists like he still held those hedgers he used to cut the rope. Mr. Watters poured him a glass of water from the little pitcher on the end table. As Sonny handed over the glass, he looked my way, then down at the roll of paper I had twisted and crushed nervously in my hands. I handed it to him before he asked. He reached over to the desk and took his reading glasses. He kept them in the tray with the pipes he collected. Sonny folded over each page, peering down through the razor-thin reading glasses designed for a nose much narrower than his.

"They took their time with him, didn't they?"

He spoke to no one in particular, his eyes still fixed on the words. The room was church quiet for a moment as Sonny flipped through the pages. He moved his fingers in circles along the contours of the armrest, retracing the faded grooves he'd worn in the leather.

"I heard something else this afternoon," Kincaid said. "Guess who owns property up and down Herndon Avenue? Bennie Jack Hays."

Lyle and Sonny looked at one another. They recognized the name.

"He's Ku Klux," Nancy said.

"He's still at it," Sergeant Kincaid said. "Some of the schoolchildren went around putting yellow ribbons on the trees for the kids in Atlanta. Hays and some of his people ripped 'em down."

"That's a damn shame."

"He got citing for littering, that's it. The department didn't want it getting out when it happened," Kincaid told us. "Didn't want to be embarrassed. Just like they didn't want this out."

"You know Tina Lambert?" Nancy said. "She works the switchboard at City Hall. Been getting calls from all over. *Nightline. 60 Minutes.* All kinds of places."

"That's the last thing they want," Lyle said. "The city will never admit there's Klan still in Mobile. They're breaking ground on a convention center downtown. The mayor wants cruise ships in the docks in a few years. Something like this is bad for business."

Lyle sat down on the armrest of the love seat, and at that moment he looked as tired as his father did.

"Go federal, then."

"U.S. attorney just got appointed. He won't step on the D.A. anyway. There's no future in prosecuting Klan murders."

Lyle rolled his head back for a minute and rubbed his hand across his mouth.

"We just have to show that Hays was involved," he said. "It'll take us a little time and some digging, but we'll find something. Once we have everything in order, then we go to the police."

"I'll see what I can find," Sergeant Kincaid said. "It's hard, though. Sometimes it gets quiet when I walk in a room."

"Get what you can," Sonny said. "In the meantime we need to speak out about the drug business. If we let it go, it might as well be true. That's why we need the young people from the rec center."

Paul had been silent this whole time, staring out the window into the empty space where Lorraine's car had been.

"I want to make a statement tomorrow at the gymnasium," Sonny said. "Talk about his character, tell them what Michael's friends say about the allegations. His family gave me some names, numbers. I wanted you and some of the other boys to bring a few words."

Paul sat, and finally turned his head back around.

"The Converse he had on were brand new. Leather ones. He'd been saving up from his mailroom job at the newspaper," Paul said, looking around the room until his eyes stopped at me. No one said anything.

"You might want to tell them that in your statement," Paul said. "That their drug dealer was saving a few dollars a week for a new pair of sneakers."

"I think y'all can say it better," Lyle said.

"Okay." Paul rubbed his temples, dropped his head before his eyes got too watery.

"Tomorrow at four. Give us time to make the six o'clock news. How's that with everybody?"

They all agreed. Once the tasks were assigned—phone calls, car pools—everyone prepared to go.

"Before we leave—" Council Ferguson grabbed his son's hand on one side and my mother's on the other, ready to pray. Everyone joined hands and waited for him to start. He asked God to grant peace for Michael Donald. For his family. "Touch them, Lord." For us all. Then he did something that I couldn't understand. He prayed for the killers. He prayed for Bennie Jack Hays. "Look into their hearts, oh Lord." I opened my eyes just then. Council held up his right hand; his fingers, weak and bone thin, trembled. "Grant us strength, oh Lord, along this journey for what is just."

He had grown winded. Before he could finish, he took a long pause to catch his breath.

"We know that, Lord, you work in mysterious ways, your wonders to behold. Thy will be done, in your son Jesus' name. And all the people said . . ."

They all said "Amen," robust and all together. Maybe the strength of their final word made the prayer a little stronger, improved the odds of its granting. I mouthed the words along with them. My absence of faith didn't mean I didn't have any hope.

Once the prayers and good-byes were finished, Mr. Watters walked everybody out and stood in the front yard as the assembled folks walked to their cars.

"Mr. Watters," Paul said. "It would be nice if I could do something more than that."

"Showing up tomorrow will be a lot of help."

"Not just that," he said. "On the case."

Sonny looked him up and down, like he used to do me while I waited for Lorraine to get dressed.

"You might be a little young," he said. "What can you do?"

"Anything you all want me to," he said. "I'm pre-law."

He was lying. He didn't have a major yet.

"Well, I'll be pre-law when I declare my major."

"How are your grades?"

"A's." My mother cut her eyes at him. "For the most part."

"That's fine," he said. "You'll be mostly running for fish sandwiches and soda water. Then after that we'll see."

"Anything you want me to do."

"Stop by this time tomorrow, and we can get a schedule together."

My mother hadn't weighed in when we were outside, but she said her piece when we got in the car.

"Two jobs and school, Paul?"

"Just one job. I can't work at the paper mill forever," he said. "You said so yourself."

I suppose she was happy about the prospect, and I knew my father would be. When we were in private, he had said Paul needed a proper job. My brother contended that he didn't mind working like regular folks, but Daddy had always said that being regular was the same as being common. And he didn't intend to raise common children. My mother had been a bit more patient, but that's just how she was.

"Sonny and Lyle will expect a lot," Mama said.

She had always encouraged us in pragmatic tones, not too much praise and just enough criticism. No matter what we were doing—Easter speeches, spelling tests, Little League games—she would ask us how we thought we did before she shared her thoughts. She wanted us to put our own weight on things, learn to be even keel, especially when the world wasn't.

"You sure you want to get involved in something like this?" Mama asked him.

"I'm in it already," he said. "But at least I can say I did a little bit."

She nodded, never taking her eyes off the road.

"Sometimes that's all we can do."

Wednesday

The King Avenue Rec Center was one of those old gymnasiums, red bricks and wood. The broken lights on the scoreboard made it hard to tell the eights from the sixes. The side walls faced east and west, and the long windows just below the rafters caught the sun coming and going. On that afternoon, the gym was full of light and people. That morning at school, Mr. Foley had announced the press conference in his homeroom remarks, and a Murphy contingent—students, teachers, staff, even Mr. Foley himself—had turned out. The stands were filled, as were the folding chairs that lined the floor from the top of one key to the other. More people sat on the second story, along the track that circled the gym.

The podium that was used for award ceremonies and banquets had been rolled out on the floor, straddling the foul line. Sonny and Lyle stood behind it, and the risers that flanked them were filled with those who had come to speak on Michael's behalf. Earl, Tunk, and Pony from the basketball team stood there next to Paul. Michael's pastor was there, and church members from Revelation Baptist who had known him his whole life, and some of his coworkers from the newspaper. Family and friends delivered kind words on the brief life of Michael Donald. *Christian youth. Good student. Teammate. Hard worker. Loved his family.*

The voices of the speakers quivered, and even the uplifting words were heavy. It was hard to hear stories about a dead teenager. Those memories would be the last ones any of the friends and families would be able to make. I was always anxious to get the eulogies out of my head. Words that somber lingered too long and didn't leave much room for anything else.

A girl went to the microphone and sang "Going Up Yonder." No organ or drums or tambourines—just her voice and the ones that answered. She was a small girl, a hundred pounds if that. She had a voice that should have come from someone much older. As beautiful as her song was, it was a strange sound for a place meant for play, free from the cares and thoughts of living and dying.

On other days, the squeaks of sneakers on the court mixed with the sound of runners' feet beating the boards of the overhead track as they made their miles. The ones up there leaned against the railing, or sat on the edge of the wooden planks that made the track, their legs dangling over the edge.

The doors and windows were left open to vent the heat, and the echoes could be heard along the Avenue. People must have heard that singing as well, because they had gathered at the exits, looking in.

From where they stood, the stage could not be seen, but they only had to look to the rafters to understand. Among the old championship banners and the American flag, faded from too much light, hung a hand-painted banner. It was made from the long paper rolls cheerleaders used to drape the walls in spirit. On this sign, the cheerful colors were missing. Those letters made from a darker blue said it all: "Michael Donald was a friend of ours."

Thursday

A familiar El Camino with Michigan plates was parked near the back window when I got over to the funeral home. On the couch in the office, my cousin Maurice slept with his shoes off and his mouth wide open. When I smacked the side of his head, he sat up with the print of the velvet covering his face.

"That shit was unnecessary, cuz," he said. "You could have just said you were happy to see me or something."

"When did you get in?"

"Late last night," he said, still yawning. "Don't ever fall for a woman who can't drive a stick. I have to drive the whole goddamn way. Jeanine's over at Granddaddy's, probably still sleeping."

"He letting y'all sleep in the same room?"

"That's grown-folk business."

The couch had wrinkled his clothes. He straightened up his tie and wiped the sleep from the corners of his eyes.

"My daddy didn't waste any time putting you to work."

"Damn straight. Had me working like a slave all day," he said. "Wants me to help you out tonight, too."

He squinted at the clock, grabbed his glasses. It was going on four fifteen.

"What took you so long? I thought they let special ed out early."

"It's good to see you, too."

Maurice's father, my uncle Greg, had a dental practice in Detroit, but he was still in the funeral-home business. He had invested in a few mortuaries all over Michigan, and Maurice helped to manage the money they brought in. Uncle Greg said putting money into funeral homes was safer than Fort Knox. He and my father had started to invest in some around the Gulf. Maurice had come down to oversee two funeral homes they'd bought, one across the Mississippi line in Pascagoula and one up in Clarke County. One was on the verge of bankruptcy, and the other had been closed since the first of the year. Maurice planned to stay through the summer to get things turned around, and then he and Jeanine were going back to Michigan to get married.

"We need to get over to the morgue so we don't cut it too close," he said.

Maurice passed me the work order that lay on the desk. It was for a woman named Brenda Calderon. In town visiting from Chicago, she had died in a car accident in Satsuma on Wednesday morning. Dr. Warner had completed his autopsy that afternoon. The Calderon family hired the Pratt-London Funeral Home in Chicago to direct the funeral arrangements, and they'd contracted with us to embalm Mrs. Calderon's body and ship her remains north. Her niece Angela, who she was down here visiting, was going to meet us at the train station. She would take her aunt's casket home on the ten o'clock train. From time to time, we shipped the remains of people who had died far from home, and we received the bodies of those who wanted to be buried down home. Many were sent by way of the trains. The Crescent from the East Coast. The Sunset Limited over from Los Angeles. The City of New Orleans down from Chicago.

On the way to morgue, Maurice hit the preset tabs looking for a station. Earl the Squirrel played the five o'clock Happy Hour. "Sippin' music," he liked to call it.

"Squirrelly Earl's killing me, cuz. Can I get some Shalamar? Some Ray Parker Jr.? Only so much of this down-home blues I can take."

As much as he talked about us "country-ass, down-south Negroes," his drawl was heavier than mine was.

"Jeanine was looking for a radio station on the way down, and between Huntsville and Birmingham we couldn't get a damn thing but country music and static," he said.

"She's a long-ass way from Detroit."

"Her and me both."

For every song Squirrel played, he talked twice as long. *"The Happy Hour is being brought to you by Suzy Q's Beauty Supply, Mobile's choice for TCB hair care products. Suzie Q's. The Q stands for Quality."*

Maurice turned the dial, shooting over the static and pausing at the clear patches of sound. He passed over the bass line of "Another One Bites the Dust," turned back until the signal got clear.

"You know these some white boys, right? From England? Ain't that some shit."

Once the song ended, Maurice started searching again, but nothing good was on. He had to settle for Squirrel and a Marvin Sease double play.

"I'm like Jeanine about this grown-folk music," he said, shaking his head. "She grew up in the city like I did, and she doesn't have people down here. She didn't know a damn thing about the South. Asking all kind of crazy questions about tractors and cotton and shit.

"I'm trying to tell her that things aren't so bad, and she started believing it until we heard about that boy they strung up."

We passed the Mobile Infirmary, where both Maurice and I were born ten years apart. A teenager in painting clothes stood in the slender front yard. He held a ladder against the building and stared up at another man who cleaned the columns, running a wire brush over the dust that had gathered on the leaves carved around the capitals.

"What do I say to my lady when she hears about somebody getting lynched in the city I was born in?" Maurice said.

"At least they caught them," I said.

Maurice just shook his head.

"Those kind of crackers are just like roaches—for every one you catch, there's a dozen somewhere hiding."

Just before the light turned green, the painter climbed down from his ladder. He took a rag from his pocket and wiped a few splatters from the blades of the cabbage palm near the gate.

"Could have been you or Paul in that tree. Could have been me."

The afternoon traffic was thick. That week brought the warmest weather of the year, and most people couldn't wait to enjoy it. The cars ignored the yellow lights, and the drivers seemed eager to get home, salvage a little bit of daylight.

"You're mighty quiet," Maurice said, knuckling me in the shoulder.

"I'm just trying to figure how many times I've been to the morgue this month," I told him. "I just get tired of seeing bodies, and this week's been some shit."

"You can't take it to heart," he said. "Like this woman tonight. We do our work and get her where she's going. That's all there is to it."

Maurice was never fazed by what we saw every day. When he got drafted for Vietnam, he spent his time working at the mortuary at Dover Air Force Base, preparing the bodies shipped back from the war. He said that being a mortician kept him out of the jungle. He appreciated the family business as much as Uncle Greg did. He believed what his father always said, "God takes care of the souls, and we get the rest." Maurice ran his hand over the razor bumps that lined his neck. While Squirrel spun his records and talked his noise, Maurice pulled on his cigarette one last time before he flicked it out the window.

"Damn you, Squirrel."

He switched off the radio, leaving us in silence as we turned into the parking lot toward the morgue.

Dr. Warner's secretary sat at her typewriter, flanked by two wire baskets, one carrying a scattered pile of *Reader's Digest,* the other holding a stack of blank death certificates. Gertrude Price's fingers never touched the keys. The ends of her nails fell lightly on the keys, whisper quiet as she filled the empty boxes with the particulars.

Trudy wore one of the three argyle sweaters she kept folded on the top shelf of her bookcase. The office she shared with Dr. Warner was separated from the morgue by a door that was always open, at least when I was there. The chill didn't bother me anymore. Their tables and vaults were just larger versions of our own. Our prep room is just the flip side of the morgue, filled with the same arrangement of porcelain and steel.

"Sorry to make you wait, Roy," Trudy said. "This goddamn ribbon." She looked at me, then up to the corrugated tiles that made up the ceiling. "Forgive me, Lord."

"Take your time."

Across the room, Dr. Warner sat behind his desk beneath a *Doonesbury* calendar that counted the passed days of March, a thick marker line drawn across their boxes. He was retiring soon, and maybe he wanted the last year or so to pass much faster than the rest. The calendar hung from the beige brick wall, surrounded by school-day portraits of snaggletoothed grandchildren and family photos taken at the Dauphin Island house he was always talking about.

The wall clock had been removed from its nail, and Dr. Warner turned the knob squinting out the window at the sign in front of the Gulf Coast Trust. He double-checked the time against his wristwatch.

"It was spring-forward time last Sunday, Roy," Dr. Warner told me. "I set every clock except for this one. Got all mine at home set except for one on that videocassette recorder my daughter gave me for Christmas. Just flashes twelve o'clock all the damn time. You got one?"

"No, not yet."

"More trouble than they're worth."

He turned the clock over and wiped a gauze pad across the face in circles, clearing away the dust that had gathered since the fall. Once that was done, he climbed up on his chair and moved the clock along the wall, trying to catch the nail.

"You have no business on that chair like that," Trudy said, tabbing her way from one box to the next.

"If I fall, the good news is, the emergency room is right downstairs."

"Wouldn't need an autopsy," Trudy said. "I'd tell Martha and your children you died of stupidity."

Dr. Warner scraped the clock against the wall until the notch met the nail. Before he climbed down, he straightened his diplomas.

"You by yourself, Roy?" he said, easing his feet back into the scuffed penny loafers.

"No, my cousin Maurice is downstairs."

"I was glad to hear his father bought that Adams place over in Clarke County. From what I gather, their work hasn't been what it used to be."

The sagging bookcase beside Dr. Warner's desk shelved the composition books he used to scribble autopsy notes. They were the same kind we wrote our schoolwork in, ink blotches on both covers. Trudy had one open on her desk, with the cover pinned down by a *Garfield* coffee mug—she moistened her thumb against her tongue before turning each page, looking for notes required to fill Brenda Calderon's last boxes. I assumed that her body was the one on the gurney just inside the doorway that led to the other room.

"What did you find?"

"Heart attack. She was dead before the car ran off the road. Didn't feel a thing."

Brenda Calderon had borrowed her niece's car to visit some friends in Citronelle, but never made it.

"We know not the day, nor the hour," Dr. Warner said.

Trudy turned the carriage dial and pulled the paper out of the rollers. She got up and made a Xerox copy, handed me the paper while it was still warm.

"Sorry to make you wait, Roy," Trudy said on her way out the door. "And it's such a nice day out. You probably have somewhere to be just like I do."

"Don't break anything tonight you might need tomorrow," Dr. Warner told her. He took his plaid sport jacket from the coatrack, leaving the lab coat in its place.

Dr. Warner had worn that same plaid jacket when he taught the forensics section of my certification class. That was the first time I'd seen him outside the morgue. We had always exchanged greetings when I came with my father, but his class was the first time I got to understand what he did.

My classmates and I watched Dr. Warner perform his autopsies. I had never seen what was done to the bodies, only the marks that remained when we took possession. The replaced skull bones, the Y incision on the chest. At the end of it, the coroner closed those bodies with thick sutures, a sickle-shaped needle. By the time his work was complete, Dr. Warner could sometimes learn more about a victim's life than a name could ever tell. The training was needed because many of my classmates lived out in the country, municipalities that didn't have coroners of their own. The morticians were called to crime scenes by the local police, asked to transport the bodies to the state lab, or sometimes required to draw the first conclusions from the remains.

"Sometimes the body is the only eyewitness," Dr. Warner had told us. "The forensics might be the only thing we can trust."

Dr. Warner grabbed the rails of Brenda Calderon's gurney and pushed it toward the door. He smoothed down his lapels and straightened the shirt collar that was shiny in places where the iron had burned the starch.

"When's the funeral?"

"Monday in Chicago."

He leaned against the bookcase, resting his head against the crooked line of notebook spines on the shelf behind him. "I meant the Donald funeral."

For as long as I'd known Dr. Warner, he'd never once asked about a funeral. It just seemed to me like the last place a pathologist would be.

"Saturday. Revelation Baptist Church. Eleven o'clock."

"My wife and I want to pay our respects."

Dr. Warner sat down in his chair. The patches of wood beneath his fingers were a shade lighter where he'd worn the stain away.

"You knew him?"

"He went to Murphy," I said. "Graduated in the same class as my brother."

Dr. Warner looked toward the autopsy room, kept his eyes trained on the empty table. "It boggles the mind."

"You heard what the police said about him? The drug talk."

"The police say a lot of things," he said. "His blood said different. Clean as a whistle. No drugs. No liquor."

"Now they're saying he was in the wrong place at the wrong time," I said.

Dr. Warner rubbed his wrists and looked at his palms like he could read the lines.

"You don't kill a man like that unless you have it in your

heart," he said, taking his tam from the bottom desk drawer, twisting the hat in his fingers. "I've autopsied over two thousand bodies. This was the worst I've ever seen."

Dr. Warner took a Sharpie from the broken coffee cup that held his pencils. He stood in front of the calendar, near the line of old photos dated by their details, fishtailed cars, stacked hairdos, clothes that had long since gone out of fashion. Some objects in his pictures were unchanging; green shutters on the white cottage, the distant lighthouse, and a line of trees that grew beyond the focus.

He drew a line across March 27 with the same marker he had probably used to write "Spring Forward" in the margins. In the haste of all that had happened that week, moving ahead had been all but forgotten. He crossed through the reminder.

"Never made much sense to me. Fall comes, we turn around and go right back."

We said our good-byes. As he held the door for me, I rolled Brenda Calderon's body to the elevator, well ahead of schedule to meet her evening train.

After we laid Mrs. Calderon on the table, Maurice brought a stack of eight-tracks from the utility room shelf. My father played gospel music while we worked—Mighty Clouds of Joy, Jackson Southernaires. When he wasn't there, I played what Daddy called Monday-to-Saturday music to pass the time. Despite his aversion to grown-folks music, Maurice liked to find something he thought the departed might like. He thought they might be looking down on us while we were looking down on them. Might as well make them comfortable.

"Bobby Blue Bland or Little Milton, which one you think she liked?"

"Bobby."

"Everybody likes Bobby," he said. "Especially folks in Chicago. What part?"

"South Side. Her niece said she taught junior high school for thirty years," I told him. "Five children. Four girls and a boy. Six grandkids."

"A shame," Maurice said, looking up at the clock behind him. "I guess we better get going if we want to get her on that train."

Before Maurice pushed play, he looked back at Mrs. Calderon and offered her a prayer.

"May the Lord bless you and keep you; may the Lord make his face to shine upon you, and be gracious unto you. May the Lord lift up His countenance upon you, and give you peace."

Shortly after the amen, the horns from *Two Steps from the Blues* came through the speakers. Once we finished the restoration, I rolled in the silver casket. Maurice looked at her face and made the sign of the cross. Before we loaded her in, I took the paperwork on the counter. Among the papers, an Amtrak cargo slip for her journey.

"When she took that train down here from Chicago, I guess she never figured she'd be going home like this," Maurice said. "I suppose we all have to get home some kind of way."

With the hearse curtains closed, Maurice and I made our way to the GM&O Station. When people saw the drapes pulled, they stared a bit longer, wondering who was inside. Folks sometimes look to see if any cars are trailing us, their headlights running no matter the time of day. When we reached the station, I checked to see if the train was on time. Maurice put a quarter in the soda machine and bought a Nehi, and we sat on the wooden benches and waited.

"Going to school in New Orleans will do you some good. Some fine-ass ladies over that way, too. Shit, if I was a single man—" He looked over and leaned against the bench. "What about you and ol' girl?"

"She'll be in D.C., so we decided to, you know, play it by ear."

"You remember that girl I brought home for Mardi Gras that one year? Yeah, we said we would play it by ear. She's married to a ballplayer now."

A heavyset man with thick gray hair waxed the marble floor. His yellow Wet Floor sign had fallen over, and a half-empty bottle of blue solution sat on the mahogany shoeshine station. As he moved the buffer in slow circles, the orange cord snaked across the floor.

"Sometimes things don't work out. A few years from now, it won't even matter. She'll just be that girl you dated back in high school. That's how it goes."

The train station was nearly empty, and the low rumble of the buffer was joined by the sound of Maurice whistling the same song he'd whistled while we were working earlier. I had envied the way he could look at our work like it was just another job. Maurice drained the last of his soda and twisted the tab around his finger, bending the sliver of tin until it separated from the ring.

Out on the platform, a redcap stood near the casket. I thought about all the places I would rather be than waiting to put a dead woman on a train. Before they would switch trains for Chicago, the Sunset Limited would take Brenda and her niece over to New Orleans. I remembered all the times I had been there for weekend trips, staying a couple of days at a time. In a few months, I would be there for good. I didn't have to spend my evenings doing the work I had never chosen.

"After school I want to do something else."

Maurice dropped the soda tab into the empty can and stared at me. This was when he was supposed to say, "I understand. Take your time and figure things out." But he didn't. It was scary how much he looked like my father.

"What did Uncle Randy say about all this?"

"I haven't told him."

"You're burying somebody you knew Saturday," he said. "That's always hard. But after a while you'll see that there's worse ways to make a living."

"My mind's already made."

"Someday you'll be grateful your people had something to pass down," Maurice said. "Every time I unloaded a body up at Dover, all I could say was, 'Thank God it's not me.' I prayed for every single one, but then I moved on to the next. It's just business."

I wished I hadn't opened my mouth. I suppose I was testing the waters, seeing how my revelation would fly, but I guess I knew it wouldn't fly at all. Maybe it might be a better idea to wait until I was gone to say something to my father, but there were expectations. Coming home on a weekend every now and then. Make sure people see my face, he had said. Get them ready for what he assumed was inevitable, when my face was the only one there.

"You should hear some of what your daddy says about you, cuz," he told me. "Talking about how good you are at running things. The place in Clarke County we bought, the one over in Pascagoula, who do you think they want to run all that?"

He pointed at me just as the arrival board shuffled its names and times. The Alabama Star was boarding for Montgomery on track two, and the Sunset Limited we waited for was half an hour away.

"Why can't you run it?" I asked him.

"I'm going back to Michigan to run things up there. All this down here is going to be your side of the world. What else do you want to do?"

"Anything but this."

"Let me pull your coat," he said. "All those funeral homes my daddy put money in around Michigan used to be owned by black folk whose kids wanted to do something else. Now who's making the money? Us. And the ones we didn't buy got snatched up by white folks."

I didn't have anything to say in response. I might as well have been talking to the pictures on the mortuary wall.

"Why do you think Randy has you handling jobs alone? He knows you can handle it. Watch. When that lady's niece gets here, you'll say everything you need to say—do everything your daddy would do if he was here."

The last boarding call for the Alabama Star came over the loudspeaker and echoed through the station. The hum of the buffer went silent, and the custodian came around the corner and pulled the plug from the wall, then closed the brass cap that covered the outlet.

"Some things just get in your blood," he said, slapping me hard on the shoulder. "Some folks were born bowlegged. We were born morticians."

The board shuffled once more, and the Montgomery-bound train left the station, heading north on tracks that ran along the river.

"It'll pass, Roy. This ain't the most regular job in the world, but you'll settle in."

Maurice looked at me for a moment, but all I could do was shake my head.

"You sure you're sure?"

"Yeah."

Maurice leaned back against the bench and shook the empty soda can, rattling the broken tab inside before he tossed it in the trash bin across from us.

"My daddy thinks I'm coming back to help out some weekends," I said. "Before I go to school, I'll have to tell him I won't."

"Good luck with that." Maurice shrugged his shoulders. "He might lose his damn mind."

"Yeah, I know."

Fifteen minutes later, a young woman came through the automatic doors with a thin suit bag and a large suitcase. Maurice held the small Deacon Memorial placard with Angela Calderon neatly printed, but we didn't need it because the thick cheeks and smooth, gentle face were familiar. The niece looked so much like her aunt that it gave me a chill.

"Miss Calderon, I'm Roy Deacon. We spoke on the phone. Once again, we're sorry for your loss."

"Yes, I remember your voice."

She looked at me like she knew me. She had a resilient face. It was all there, the signs of sleeplessness and tears, but she held it all together. At least at first. Angela looked around the train station, and her vibrant features grew heavy. The blue handkerchief in her hand was moist, and her damp lashes drew attention to her heavy eyes. Her aunt had died almost instantly. Sometimes people say quick deaths are painless, but there's always pain for somebody.

"I picked her up right here on Monday," she said, staring at the heavy door to track two. "She had a ticket home on tomorrow's train."

She looked down at the suitcase.

"That was hers," she said.

As I took her aunt's bag and escorted Angela to the platform, I said all the things Maurice predicted. I invoked the God I didn't much believe in, and said things I had heard my father and mother and grandfather say. Made sure someone would meet her on time in Chicago.

I suppose everything that Maurice said was meant to make me change my mind, but like I had told him, my mind was already made. Maybe my brother was right in not wanting to spend his life filling cemeteries. At the very least, he had faith that death was not the end of things. Maybe if I felt the same way, things would have been different. The church people were always saying, "Let go and let God." Maybe then I wouldn't have to dread the ring of the phone, bringing those calls that announced someone's end.

As Angela climbed the steps of the train, Maurice stood near the redcaps at the far end of the platform, watched them as they eased the casket onto the last freight car. When Angela got to the top of the steps, she thanked me and called me Mr. Deacon, which still sounded strange to me. Maurice came and stood next to me on the platform just as the Sunset Limited started to move down the line.

"God bless both of them," he said. "Lord knows that's a long ride. Even when you want to go."

Friday Night

Most every day, the streets around us were lined with the yellow Funeral Parking signs so common on those blocks. Michael Donald's wake was scheduled for seven thirty. The time change had given us an extra hour of light, and the days lingered a little longer. By six thirty, what was left of the sunlight was fading. Young people streamed into the doorway, well-groomed teenagers wearing Sunday clothes and solemn faces. They kept coming. As the hour grew closer, the little yellow signs that lined the grass were obscured by dusk light and the cars that lined the avenue.

Paul's brakes squealed as he came to a slow stop in front of the mortuary. He looked around, embarrassed for having broken the quiet that had settled over the street. He had picked up Pony, Earl, and Tunk. Earl and Pony rode up front, and Tunk rode in the back. They all wore the darkest suits they owned.

When Tunk made his awkward steps down from the payload, he stumbled and kicked over one of the yellow signs, sending the metal legs scraping across the sidewalk. He caught his balance and looked around to see if anybody had seen him. Any other time, the rest of them would have janked him for days. I could count the times I had seen Tunk out of sneakers. The shoes he'd just stumbled over must have belonged to someone else, his father, one of his brothers. The toes were turned up from years of another man's steps.

Paul was the last one out of the truck. He stared out of his window, looking at our building like it had never been there before. Earl, Pony, and Tunk waited for him on the sidewalk. They shared the same nervous moves, hands in their pockets, tugging at their ties, fidgeting away the nerves. They weren't in a hurry to get inside. None of them had seen Michael's body in that casket except for Paul, and he was still in the car, staring down into his lap.

Pony went over and leaned against the truck. The rolls of skin on the back of his neck went taut as he lowered his head. He must have been praying. After a while, they nodded together. Paul's inside door handle was broken, so he had to reach outside to open his door. They had been champions in the men's twenty-one-and-under basketball league at the rec center. Paul had a picture of them on his bedroom mirror. Seeing them standing together on the sidewalk only made it more obvious who was missing. The four who remained gathered themselves as best they could, and together they took anxious steps.

Earl was the first one to the door. He didn't say anything

at first, just lifted his chin. I nodded back. Pony was right behind him. He leaned over to me and whispered, "What should
I say, you know, to his people?"

His eyes quickly left me and surveyed the foyer that he'd
never entered, instead opting to wait on the porch those few
times he'd come with Paul.

"Just say what's on your mind."

Pony tensed up and breathed in.

"What's on my mind ain't got nothing to do with talking."

He closed his eyes long enough for the gathered tears to
stay in place, at least for a few minutes more.

"I feel like whippin' somebody's ass. Got our boy laid
out like this."

He stared into the petals of my boutonniere before his
eyes lifted, looking past me into the chapel. The lid of the
opened casket could be seen at the front of the room. He
looked straight up toward the slow whirl of the ceiling fan.

"Don't make no goddamn sense."

Tunk kept his head down as he passed me, and the three
of them made their way to the front of the chapel. I turned
away, facing the opened front doorway, though there was
no one coming. It's hard to know how anybody will take it. I
didn't want to see them break down, like so many of the others who were sitting in those rows. Rocking. Sobbing. It was
a hard walk for anybody who had to make it.

Paul hesitated. As I stood just outside the viewing room
doorway, he came out and stood beside me. He leaned against
the opened door and ran his fingers along the wood, piano
strokes along the frame.

"Help me understand it," he said.

"Wish I could."

Paul pulled out his handkerchief and rubbed it over his

face. His eyes were too red for any more tears. All he could do was close them and lean his head against the wall as air eased down from the ceiling fan, the only thing in that place that gave any relief.

A wide porch wrapped all the way around the mortuary, and it was often a gathering place for mourners looking for a reprieve. By ten o'clock, the lights were off inside, and my parents had left for the night. Everyone who had come to pay their respects had gone home except for Paul and the boys. Earl sat on the side steps that led to the garage. Pony was on top of the wood railing with his back against one of the posts. His legs were outstretched, his empty shoes arranged on the porch. Paul leaned against the windowsill with his arms crossed. Tunk had left twenty minutes before, going to the corner store for some wine.

A police car rolled by at an easy pace.

"Sumbitches," Pony said.

Deaths were hard enough for people to handle, but murders made the grieving that much slower. It was hard to pay respects to the murdered without dwelling on the crime. I suppose the police thought the arrests might ease the tension. Chief Davidson had announced the arrests like he was announcing bingo winners, as if we should all enjoy our piece of the shared fortune.

"These three suspects are known drug users, with past criminal records. We hope that these arrests show the people of Mobile that we are working hard to suppress drug trafficking in this city, and to stem the resultant criminal activity. Citizens of Mobile should be able to sleep well tonight knowing that these murderers have been taken off the streets, and that the Mobile Police

Department continues to protect and serve all the citizens of the Port City."

As ass-backwards as the police chief was, he knew what he was doing. The tactic was working. The national news broadcasts that had jumped on the story over the weekend weren't following as closely. Nothing I had heard about the story in the preceding day or two had mentioned the word *lynching*. As long as the police called it a drug murder, not many people were willing to say otherwise—at least, not publicly.

The police car disappeared behind the tall bushes that separated the backyard from the street. The shrubbery ran the length of the garages, each of the six bays filled with hearses and funeral cars, chrome grills gleaming ready for the next morning. The vehicles were more ready than any of us on the porch would ever be.

Thirty minutes after he left, Tunk came into the yard, looking over each shoulder again and again. I saw the tell-tale outline of what he tried to conceal in the inside pocket of his jacket. By the shape of the bottle, it was a pint of Thunderbird.

"I'm usually a Mad Dog man, but all they had was the big bottles," he said as the paper bag rustled against the polyester of his suit. "I wanted to be discreet."

The thin metal of the bottle cap snapped with a turn of Tunk's wrist. He waved the bottle under his nose, like the Bird was so much finer than it actually was. He tipped the bottle until the wine was just at the lip.

"For the brother who ain't here."

Tunk dipped his hand a little more, pouring a long stream of wine into the briars.

"For the brother who ain't here," said the chorus.

After two pulls on the wine bottle, Tunk passed it to

Earl, who passed it to Pony. Once Paul took it from Pony, he passed it to me. Thunderbird tasted cheap, like Communion wine, but I didn't mind. I needed it. Standing there, across the lawn from the waiting funeral cars, I took my swallows and kept the bottle circling around the porch.

Around eleven thirty, we were halfway through the third bottle. With each pass, the bottle got lighter and the words got bolder. Tunk decided we should go down to the jail. No one speculated on what we would do once we got there, but fuck it, we were going. It had been a night of mourning and seventy-five-cent wine, so a trip to the jailhouse made as much sense as anything else.

I got in the front seat of the truck with Paul and Earl. Tunk and Pony rode in the back. Pony sat on two of the cinder blocks that my brother kept to brace anything he had to carry. Tunk lay flat on his back with his hands under his head. He didn't pay any mind to the rust and dirt.

There was no reason to be downtown after dark, even on a Friday night. The stores were closed with dimmed window lights shining down on the displays. Even the green lights were gone for the night, replaced by the flashing reds and yellows. The city jail was down on Royal Street, a few feet away from the interstate. When I-10 cut right through the black neighborhood called Down the Bay, this thin sliver of neighborhood was separated from the rest. The main thoroughfares—Canal, Palmetto, Charleston—had been reduced to side streets and dead ends. The little piece of Texas Street on the river side of the highway was renamed Short Texas Street, because it was only three blocks long. Sometimes when we drove under the concrete legs of the highway, my parents gave me a phantom tour, telling me what used to exist on those streets. Who used to live there. What businesses used to thrive. A few houses were scattered between the vacant lots, and the ones that weren't empty were so raggedy they should have been. Nobody wants to live near the highway. The only people who ended up on that side—poor or criminals in that jail—didn't have much choice.

In those few blocks between the highway and the river, the city changed. The smell of the river, fish and diesel, was strong no matter which way the wind carried. The waterfront cranes, with lights along their arms and spines, brightened it all, but beacons only made the worn places easier to see. The houses and the grass disappeared, replaced by old fences, rusted and curled, railroad tracks lined with empty tankers, and stacks of shipping containers, paint oxidized from years of water and sun.

On the sidewalk across the street was as close as I had ever been to the jail. The main building was shaped like an octagon, as if four walls weren't enough. It was made of concrete, thick and brown like the ruins of the forts scattered along the bay. I had looked down on the jail from the interstate, watching the small figures chase basketballs around the concrete yard. They were surrounded by five-story walls on three sides, razor wire on the other.

Underneath the bus shelter on the corner, there were two news boxes, one for the *Mobile Press* and the other for the *Register.* The *Register* box was empty, the last of the morning papers gone from the door rack. A copy of the *Press* remained, and the three faces on the front page stared out, stringy-haired and wild-eyed. Thomas Holman, twenty-two. Theodore Holman, twenty-six. Herbert Moody, twenty-three. Killers and junkies.

"Give me some change," said Tunk, his speech thick

and syrupy like the wine he'd drunk on the way over. "Give me some change, goddamn."

Paul reached into the Crown Royal sack under the seat and held a case-quarter between his fingers. When Tunk dropped the coin in the slot, it rattled against the others at the bottom of the box. He took the last two papers and tossed them into the corner of the bus shelter. He'd taken off his tie and stuffed it in his back pocket. A small edge of maroon paisley hung from beneath his shirttail as he stood with his back to us, unfastening his pants. With the quiet along that street, we could all hear the splatter of piss on the newsprint.

"Motherfuckers," he said, looking over at the jail.

I stared up at the thin slats of glass that passed for windows, looking to see if Tunk's invocation had brought them within sight. No one was there. If anyone stared back, I couldn't see them. We were a sad little mob. Drunk, angry boys in rumpled dress clothes. Fact was, they were safer than we were.

"Hell, they might not even be in here," Earl said. "For all we know."

Earl didn't even get out of the truck. He leaned his head against the passenger-side window, staring up at the top of the jail, the Slinky coils of razor wire that wrapped the whole way around.

"As long as they're somewhere," Pony said.

"They need to be in Atmore," Earl said. "In that chair."

"White folks don't get the chair. They get life."

"I hope they get fucked in the ass in Atmore," Tunk said. "See how they like that."

Tunk was standing in the middle of the street, teetering. If a car had come around the corner, he'd have been hit for sure. I got him out of the street and helped him up on the tailgate.

"I need me a cigarette," he said. The more he drank, the heavier and slower his voice became. "Give me a cigarette." He repeated himself just above a whisper.

I blew into a crushed pack I had in my coat pocket and gave him my last one. I put my lighter in his hand.

"If I could," he said, flicking the lighter, "I'd burn that motherfucker down."

My butane was almost gone. The weak little flame barely cleared the steel. Hardly enough to burn tobacco, let alone anything else. Tunk craned his neck, looking at the lights along the top of the jail that shone down into the empty yard. The basketball rims that rose from each corner had been stripped of their nets. Everything was brick and steel. Nothing to burn.

"Fuck it."

By that time, it was twelve o'clock. Seven days before, Michael had left home around 11:00 P.M. and vanished. The medical examiner had estimated that his time of death was round about midnight. A week to the day.

"I'm tired, man," Pony said. "I need to get home."

He jumped in the back with Tunk, and I climbed inside next to Earl. The only one still outside was Paul. He stood where Tunk's paisley tie had fallen from his back pocket. Paul picked it up and shook off the dirt before he folded it twice and walked back to the truck.

We sat in that strip of Mobile between the highway and the river. On top of the pylons in front of us, Interstate 10 went from Jacksonville to Los Angeles. A few miles away it ran into I-65, and that stretched damn near to Canada. The water could take you just about anyplace else. A line of merchant ships sat along the river, their countries printed in big letters along their sides. Earl stared out at the docks, where the ships grew taller the closer we got.

"I signed up yesterday," Earl said. "In a couple of weeks I'll be gone."

Earl used to talk about joining the merchant marine, but I thought it was just because he hated school. Paul used to mess with him about it, said he got ready to enlist every time grades came out. The merchant marine was something people threatened their kids with when they got out of line. They used to call Earl crazy, but all of a sudden packing up and leaving didn't seem so strange.

"For a minute I was scared, but then I said fuck it. My boy got snatched up walking down the street. Plenty of shit to be scared of right here."

I sat on the front seat between my brother and Earl, who had his arm dangling out the window, his fingers outstretched into the little bit of breeze that still blew as we turned onto Government Street, passed the little storefront with "Ferguson and Watters" stenciled on the window.

"When do you start up with Sonny Watters?" Earl asked him.

"He told me to stop by Monday morning, before I go to class."

"What you think you'll be doing?"

"Everything he tells me to."

Earl nodded.

The gauntlet of streetlights blinked red and yellow all the way up Government Street. Farther ahead, the light poles were obscured by the thick masses of foliage, and the signals were just flashes blinking among the leaves.

"You'll have to write me a letter and let me know how you make out. Got no idea where I'll be," Earl said, looking toward the place where the river meets the bay. "Wherever it is, I'll be a long way from this shit."

Saturday wasn't even an hour old, but the funeral might as well have started already. I looked through the back window and saw the back of Pony's head pressed against the glass. Tunk sat against the fender. When we got caught at the first of the red lights, I heard his wheezing above the idling engine. Tunk had his suit jacket pulled over his face to hide it, but he did the kind of crying that was impossible to hide. It only got stronger as we made our way home.

I was the first one dressed on the morning of the funeral. When I got downstairs, Paul sat at the breakfast table, pouring milk into a cereal bowl. He always poured the milk first, then stirred in two spoonfuls of sugar before he poured the Rice Krispies. He wore the Murphy homecoming T-shirt from two years before. The silver clasp of his herringbone chain had worked its way around to the front. He rolled the thin metal in his fingers, flicking it open and closed.

"Are you riding to the church with Mama?"

"I'm not sure I'm going," he said, staring into his bowl. His eyes were heavy, and he rubbed along his collarbone as he stirred a slow whirlpool in his milk. "I don't know if I want to watch when you put him in the ground."

"You might be sorry if you don't come," I told him.

"I'm sorry already. Sorry he's dead," he said. "Sorry we have to bury him in the first place."

I couldn't begin to say how many funerals I had already been to, but I could count on one hand the funerals Paul had seen. We had not lost many kin during our lifetimes. Our father's mother had died when we were babies. There had been other deaths, old and distant relatives we barely knew. The loss of friends can sometimes be harder. Losing a bond you made, instead of one you came into the world with. The liquor we'd all drank the night before hadn't helped. I could still feel it kicking me in my gut and in my head, and Paul probably did, too. Maybe he needed to hear a eulogy to help him cope. The true believers need to hear the preacher speak of ascension and eternity like it was the most natural thing in the world.

"Maybe it'll help for you to come."

"Maybe it won't," he said. "Maybe the last thing I need is to see him one more time. I've been praying about it, but I just don't know."

He dredged the sludge of sugar from his bowl and let it fall back to the bottom. He'd barely eaten it. The snap-crackle-popping had long since stopped as the soggy Rice Krispies floated in the bowl.

"How's your head feel?" he asked me.

"Like shit."

"Mine, too. But the liquor had no part in that," he said, getting up from the table. "It'd be easy if it was just a hangover."

Paul dropped his bowl into the sink and went upstairs. Through the walls, I heard the hot water rushing up the pipes as he started his shower. I tried to think of something I could go upstairs and say to make him change his mind. It helped people sometimes to sit in a room full of folks who felt the same way. Being alone with it was like being outnumbered.

It was sure to be one of the biggest funerals the city had seen. Before I even got there, there would probably be people on the church steps already waiting as we brought in the casket. There was still so much disbelief. About what had happened. Why it happened here. But the disbelief would be gone soon. When the hearse pulled up and the casket came out, things got real in a hurry. I suppose I could understand why Paul didn't want to go. But me, I had no choice. I was what my father liked to call duty-bound. It was my job to deliver Michael's body to the church on time. I picked up my keys and closed the door. I had a schedule to keep.

As I drove Michael's body to the Revelation sanctuary, I thought about the last time I'd seen him alive. Fat Tuesday. Mardi Gras had come and gone three weeks before Michael's murder, and Mobile had been a different place then. From the Friday before until sundown on Fat Tuesday, the city shuts down so everyone can party. No work, no school. Carnival was my favorite time of year for one simple reason: funerals almost never happen during Mardi Gras. That's partly out of tradition, and partly logistics. Funeral processions can't move through the streets that have been closed for parades that start every morning and keep rolling until well after dark. The only processions that pass through the barricaded streets are those meant for revelers. Dozens of parades roll down Government Street and circle Bienville Square before returning uptown. Each parade is sponsored by one of the

Carnival Krews: the Order of Pharaohs, the Mystics of Time, the Krew of Columbus. Their members are mostly white. Like most other cities along the Gulf Coast, Mobile still has its black parades. The biggest is the Mammoth Parade that rolls every Fat Tuesday afternoon.

I had never seen as many black folks at one place at one time as I'd seen on the corner of Broad and Government at three thirty on Mardi Gras day. The Mammoth Parade took a different route than the others, snaking through the black neighborhoods that circled downtown, passing the frat houses and the social clubs and going over by Bishop State. It stretched for miles, with masked horsemen wearing the purple, green, and gold Carnival colors, Mardi Gras Indians, black cowboys, and marching bands from all over. The Mammoth Parade always had a couple dozen floats, each sponsored by a local club.

Once we each turned sixteen, Paul and I joined a club called the Porters, started by some of the old men who had worked on the trains. If we paid thirty-five dollars, washed cars, and came to the meetings once a month, we could ride the float come Mardi Gras. We had to buy our own throwes, and the drinking policy was BYOB. Everyone on our steam engine float had ten or fifteen bags—hard candy, bubblegum, beads, doubloons—and as many boxes of MoonPies.

The golden rule of riding a float was that you never showed your face. Violators got fined or kicked off. Under the dark narrow masks, it was hard to see once the sun went down. The branches of the thick trees that lined either side of Government Street made a canopy that brought dusk too early. As the parade made the final turn onto Broad, beneath the trees and my mask, it was hard to see who was who. I aimed at the voices that yelled my name, throwing blindly when the day was at its darkest, in those minutes after the sun has gone and just before the streetlights kicked on.

All of our friends were waiting toward the end of the route we had started three hours before. It felt like everybody I knew in the world was on those sidewalks. People would claim the same places year after year. Slim and Ruben were always in the supermarket parking lot. My folks waited in their folding chairs in front of the Elks Lodge. The Watters always cooked out on the ball field behind Dunbar. On Mardi Gras I realized how many people I knew as I saw their faces among the thousands waiting to catch the good throwes we saved until the end.

I always threw beads a few strands at a time, making sure I didn't run out. My brother had no such worries. He ripped open his last bags and threw them all at once, handfuls of beads and MoonPies and anything else. The gold and silver beads caught the glint of the streetlight as they flew high, some landing in the trees while the rest disappeared into the crowd of hands. Pony's voice was always the loudest, and when he started hollering, Paul aimed his throwes toward his collected friends. Earl and Tunk caught what they could in upside-down umbrellas, and Michael stood next to them, arms out to catch what came his way. Paul threw as much as he could for as long as he could, until the float moved out of reach. Then we rounded the corner onto the Avenue, and that was the last time I saw Michael Donald alive.

The papers said that hundreds of thousands packed the streets during the Mardi Gras season, but early on that funeral morning, along those same city streets, there were few souls in sight. The only evidence of revelry were the odd strands of silver beads left among the branches, too high for the cleaning crews to reach. On that warm and vacant morning, as we made our way to Revelation, there was nobody there but us.

The sanctuary of the church tried in vain to hold all of Michael's mourners, as the hundreds who gathered poured onto the front steps and covered both sides of the street. A curtain of flowers flanked the casket, more orchids and lilies than I'd ever seen in one place. The flowers had been delivered from all over the country. Churches. Schools. Organizations. Before Maurice and Bertrand drove the family cars that morning, they shuttled flowers from the funeral home in the back of the van. A small bouquet decorated the table that I stood beside in the back of the church. Around the arrangement, even stacks of funeral programs carried raised letters.

IN MEMORIAM
MICHAEL A. DONALD
1961–1981

The pulpit overflowed with the reverend doctors of the world, known and unknown. Most of them I had never seen in person until that day. Joseph Lowery. Jesse Jackson. Ralph Abernathy. Andrew Young. All of their voices were familiar, called upon to use an old vocabulary that they might have thought was no longer needed. Lynching was one of our old demons. I'm sure it seemed like a safe assumption.

One of them mentioned Emmett Till. My parents had told me about him. When he was murdered, his mother didn't let the morticians repair his face. She wanted the world to see the skull of a head swollen to twice its size. Maybe she'd gotten it right. No restoration. No makeup. Maybe the world needed to see how ugly it really was underneath.

When the service was complete, my father closed the casket and tightened the seal. I stood in the vestibule as the pallbearers carried the casket down the aisle. On the wall behind them, in stained glass, Jesus stumbled on the road to Calvary. Next to him stood Simon of Cyrene, the man who helped him carry his load. As Simon reached down over Jesus, his mouth was near the ear of Christ. Whenever I was in Revelation, whenever I was burying one of their own, I looked at that wall and wondered about the Cyrenean. I wondered what he said.

The pallbearers reached the door and met the sunlight of the March afternoon. The man at the front right looked down as he walked over the threshold. He looked back to the others and whispered. The others nodded and lowered their heads as they crossed over. They looked down as they left the church, careful of the spot he warned them of—where the carpet had curled away from the tacks—careful not to stumble.

I opened the payload door on the hearse, and the pallbearers slid the casket onto the metal rollers. My parents, Bertrand, and Maurice escorted the family to their cars. The ones lined up behind us had turned their lights on, ready to get in line. Three police cars waited on the street along with a couple on horseback. Two police officers sat on their motorcycles, ready to lead the procession through the red lights and intersections. It had always amazed me how quickly we moved, as if it mattered how fast you reached the cemetery, as if burial was an appointment that couldn't wait.

When I opened the door, Paul sat in the passenger seat with his hands in his lap, his shoulders heavy. I can't say that

I was glad to see him, because I knew it would be a tough road either way. The guilt of not coming could be as bad as the unease of being there, making that ride from the church to the cemetery. Seeing the end of it.

I had been down those streets too many times. Pleasant Valley. Duval. St. Stephens Road. There were all manner of ways a procession could go, and I knew them all. Every church. Every cemetery. The combinations. Macedonia to Little Bethel. Saint Peters to Sacred Heart. New Canaan to Azalea Gardens. For Michael, we left Revelation and made our way to Whispering Pines.

Out of my window, it was another weekend for the rest of the world. People lived their lives on Saturdays, free from work and school. Children played in front yards, and people did their shopping in the strip malls along our route. A woman from the fish market on Duval stood on a short ladder and changed the sign, setting the prices for mullet, white trout, and whatever else had come off the boats. When she saw us coming, she stopped placing her letters, joined the procession with her eyes. Some knew who we were, where we were headed. Two old men removed their hats as we passed down St. Stephens Road. The route from Revelation to Whispering Pines usually took twenty minutes. With a police escort, it took ten.

Before we could get there, we had to stop at the railroad tracks. The bells that warned of the approaching train drowned out the lights and sirens that had cleared our path. The motorcycle cops had both feet on the ground as fourteen railcars snaked through the city toward the docks. It carried no caboose, just engines at both ends. Soon after the last engine rolled past, the lights and chimes stopped, and we made our way the last few miles toward the red clay of Whispering Pines Road.

The cemetery was just what the name said. An open field in the middle of the Mobile County pinelands, far enough from the main road that there was nothing to hear. The clearing was dotted with flat grave markers, some shiny but most dull from the pollen and the years. Michael's marker was yet to be made. His grave was marked by a green awning, a fresh mound of earth, and the people who gathered around. In the center of the south lawn, silver rods suspended the casket above the hole. After the familiar words, *ashes*, then *dust*, we lowered Michael Donald's body into the ground.

The gravediggers were discreet. They stood at a respectful distance, waiting for the mourners to leave. After the amens and the parting words, they shoveled clay of all colors into the grave. I was always among the last to leave, making sure that the grave was filled. As the men completed their task, I watched the vehicles disappear through the gate and wondered how many cars I'd led there during my many visits.

Paul stood by me the whole time. The road dust had colored his pants legs red, and gathered in the seams of his wingtips. Blades of just-cut grass tangled in his shoestrings.

"So this is it," he said. "This is where we'll all end up."

Paul waved his foot over a dandelion, sending the seeds flying across the open field as the diggers finished their work. It would take a while for the grass to return, but it would in time. It always did. The sky above Whispering Pines was open, and it drew the eyes of people as they left. Some of them looked up, mouthing words, prayers I'm sure. I believe my brother was praying, too. His head was neither up nor down, he just looked straight ahead at that grave and worked his hands, closing his fists and spreading his fingers.

"I hope you're wrong," Paul said. "This can't be it. I pray to God it's not."

"Sometimes I hope I'm wrong, too."

As we walked toward the hearse, I read the headstones of the cluster of graves. Many bore names and dates, while others carried messages of remembrance: *Father. Wife. Sister. Friend.* Over at Old Hill I thought about the Jubilee marker. The slaves believed their dying day was the first day of freedom. I hoped they were right. As my brother walked back down the cemetery road toward the hearse, I tried to warm up to the notion that beyond this world, something wonderful waited. I wished I could believe that was true.

PART TWO

Part Two

Good Friday

That afternoon I drove to Atmore for the wake of Dr. Abigail Jameson. She had been one of the first black doctors in Escambia County. Dr. Jameson was among the generation of notable black firsts, and by 1981 many of them were passing on. Lots of people, well beyond the circles of friends and families, wanted to pay their respects. The service was bigger than most people's funerals. The trip was an hour each way, and I didn't get back to Mobile until after nine.

When I got in the house, Paul was sitting at the kitchen table, eating dinner. He still had on his work clothes, the shirt and tie he had to wear when he was in Sonny and Lyle's office downtown. It was usual for somebody to be a little rumpled at the end of the day, but he was an absolute mess. A wide smear of black ink started just below Paul's collar and went clear across his shirt to just under the pocket. A thin strip of unstained cotton ran across the middle of the shirt, where his tie must have gotten splattered instead. He'd already taken it off, so I'm sure it was ruined just like the shirt was. As Paul sat there eating, he didn't seem to mind. Then I saw why. Reading the monogram on the pocket, I realized the shirt was mine.

"I had a little problem with the Xerox machine at Lyle's office."

"A little problem," I said.

"I was out of clean ones," he said. "My bad."

Paul had been working for Lyle and Sonny for three weeks. Most of his classes were in the morning, so Paul came home in the afternoons to put on a shirt and tie and then went to work. It was a change those first few evenings, seeing him coming through the door late in the evening dressed like that. Outside of church, Paul was never one for dressing. We had gone to Catholic school through eighth grade, and on most days after school, Paul's shirttail was out before we got to the parking lot.

Back then, he always had something on his clothes. When we were real little, it was finger paint, grass stains, chocolate milk—a little blood from whatever scrapes he got from fighting or jumping off the monkey bars. Ruining clothes was nothing new for him, but up to that point he'd only destroyed his own. My $3.35 an hour didn't go that far at the mall.

"Come see me on payday," I told him.

My father got home from Atmore about a half hour after I did. He had started sorting through the mail when he saw the stain. Paul explained before Daddy had time to ask.

"Xerox machine," he said, his mouth full of rice.

"He got in a fight with it," I said.

"I guess I know who won."

"Guess whose shirt it is?" I said.

"Tattlin' ass," Paul said under his breath.

"These things happen," Daddy told us. "You can't expect to go through life without getting a little dirt on yourself."

I thought my father was losing his mind. He was usually a stickler about such things. He could spot a scuff on my shoes from across the room, and if he did, I'd hear about it.

"I'll take it to the cleaners," Paul said. "They might be able to fix it."

"That's not coming out," my father said, just as casual. "You'll have to buy a new one."

He looked at me when he said it, like I was the one covered in ink.

"New shirts cost money," I said. "On what you're paying me—"

I suppose I felt like instigating that night. But I couldn't begin to count the times I'd asked him for a raise politely and directly with no luck. Maybe if I made him feel guilty, I might get somewhere. My father didn't answer right off. Maybe he didn't hear me, which would just save him the trouble of saying no. He put some coffee in the percolator and filled the pot with water.

"Maybe you're right," he said. He stuck a fork in the pot of red beans and rice and ate from there, something he only did when my mother wasn't around to tell him how nasty it was. "You probably deserve a little extra."

Paul looked at me and closed his mouth just before the rice fell out. He was as shocked as I was. Our cheap-ass daddy offering to give somebody a raise.

"Five dollars an hour."

I suppose I had my brother to thank for the benevolence.

When Daddy found out Sonny and Lyle had given Paul a job, he was happy to hear the news. Of course, he had a sermon ready for any occasion. Through tragedy sometimes the Lord shows us our purpose, opens windows—something to that effect. He was worse than a preacher sometimes. Preachers would sermonize once a week, but I had to hear my father every day. He'd already checked on the in-state tuition for the University of Alabama School of Law. He'd talked about Tulane, too.

"How about that," he'd said. "Your senior year at Xavier would be his first year of law school. Maybe I could buy a little place for y'all, and you could rent the extra rooms out."

Since he was so keen on investing in our futures, I guess an extra dollar or two an hour wasn't much of a sacrifice.

"Sunday after church y'all can take my credit card out to the mall and get a few shirts and ties. You probably could use a couple of suits, too."

That was when I knew he'd gone stone crazy. Once I started working, I had to buy my own clothes. The only things he gave us were under the tree on Christmas, mainly drawers and socks. Tube socks for Paul, dress socks for me. Getting that credit card from him had always been out of the question.

"You need a few new shirts anyway," he told me. "Yours have been a little dingy. That bleach turns them yellow after a while."

Paul looked at the collar of the shirt he was wearing, stared down at the sleeves.

"He's right," he told me. "It is a little dingy."

He had the nerve to make jokes.

"I need to go change anyway," Paul said. "Lyle gave me some boxes to drop off at Sonny's house."

"What kind of boxes?" Daddy said.

"Stop being nosy," I said.

Paul's work had monopolized the dinner conversation for those few weeks. It was a relief for me, because I didn't have to continue whatever conversation my father and I had at work. I could just listen to somebody else for a change.

"I carry boxes back and forth when Sonny works from his house. Lyle wanted me to drop off some probate stuff. Tax. Lien records."

We had all been brought up to speed on the life and times of Bennie Jack Hays and the remnants of Klan still left in Mobile. With his history—vandalism, assault, arson—it was hard to believe that he was still a free man, but he was. He was in his sixties, and had inherited some property from some relatives who died a few years before. Ever since, he had started supporting himself as a landlord, renting out a few houses and run-down apartments on Herndon Avenue.

"Of all the streets in Mobile," Paul said. "They say it can't be a coincidence."

"These boxes you shuttle around. Where are Sonny and Lyle getting all that?" Daddy asked.

"Sonny said he knows every maid and janitor that works in the courthouse," he said. "Says sometimes they find things that he might be interested in."

"Find things. Sonny might mess around and find himself in jail. Again," Daddy said. "Whatever works, I guess. It takes somebody who knows how to hustle."

Once the percolator finished bubbling, he unplugged it and poured himself a cup. He fixed himself a bowl of beans and rice before he sat down.

"It was Sonny who pissed in that pool," he said, smiling.

"Yeah, we know."

Before Paul went upstairs, he took off my shirt and threw it in the corner of the washroom.

"Yep," Daddy said. "That shirt is ruined." As if there was any question.

He kept stirring around in his coffee, but the little bit of sugar had long since dissolved. His mind was somewhere else.

"It's good that your brother has a decent job," he said. "It'll be good for you, too."

How that was, I couldn't imagine.

"You know how much me and Greg paid lawyers to close on those two places we just bought? Tax codes, estate law, contracts. Imagine being able to keep that money in the family. That'll be nice for you and your brother, working together."

He finally finished his stirring. Before he placed the spoon on the saucer, he knocked it against the side of the cup. A gesture that served no purpose, something I never quite understood.

"Sonny and Lyle will be old one day, just like I will. People will be coming to young folks like you and Paul."

He had a deep-set smile that let the wrinkles of his face settle around it. It was the kind he usually saved for graduation days, award ceremonies.

"I think I might turn in early," he said. "A long ride over to Atmore tomorrow. I figure we get to the church around eight thirty, we'll be in good shape."

I nodded, but he wasn't looking at me. He was already headed upstairs.

I walked outside with Paul before he drove over to Sonny's. He had my shirt in his hand, ready to throw it in the garbage on the edge of the driveway. The weather seemed to have finally broken. In the weeks before, the days were warm, but the nights had been freezing—a swing that seemed to be too severe. The days and nights were almost even. It was the kind of weather that was warm enough to tease us, make us hope it was finally there to stay.

"What are you and Lorraine doing tonight?"

"There's a party at the Skate Haven tonight," I told him. "You should come. Doesn't make sense working on Friday night."

"I don't mind," he said. "Kind of worn out from the week. It's not too bad. At least if I'm tired, it helps me sleep," he said. "Otherwise—"

We stood at the end of the driveway and watched the boys across the street. Ricky Boone had already thrown the last of his papers. When he got to his yard, he threw aside the canvas bag along with his bike. The other boys from the street had already started playing basketball in his driveway.

"I went back to the gym for the first time yesterday. I halfway expected to see Mike."

The boys played with a ball that didn't have enough air, and a goal that didn't have a net. But they didn't seem to mind. It was Friday night of a weekend that felt as good as summer.

"I played for a while, but nobody showed but me and Tunk," he said. "Pony's asked for more hours at the grocery store. And Earl's going to New Orleans in a couple weeks to take his test. Said he's studying hard."

"I can't imagine Earl studying for anything."

"Neither could I," he said. "Motivated, I guess."

One of the things about living in a small place was that you could grow up when you wanted to. Hang out with the same friends. Go to the same places for years. No need to change habits. But then, maybe something happens, and everything changes all at once.

"It's kind of hard, you know," he told me. "They still have that banner up in the gym."

The boys across the street played on a goal Paul had helped Ricky's father put in the ground five years earlier.

"I went over to Mr. Davie's house and gave him my notice. He told me I can come back to the mill part-time this summer, but I think it's time for me to do something else."

Paul tugged at the cotton on the edge of the ink stain. It was dry enough to be powdery, but even after the loose bits came off, the rest of it stayed deep in the fabric.

"It's in there good, I guess," he said. "You know what the worst part of it is? The tie I had on was yours, too."

"Which one?"

"Your favorite." He just shrugged his shoulders.

"It's just a tie," I told him.

Paul threw my shirt away before he got into his truck. Sometimes he'd run across the street and play twenty-one with Ricky and his friends. But that night he just honked his horn as he made his way over to Sonny's house with the boxes. I had seen Sonny in his office, fishing through dusty boxes, through papers that looked as old as he was. He had said that there was an answer to everything somewhere. Maybe that was true, at least this time.

The day before I had gone to Whispering Pines to file the papers for a new plot. Towering above Michael's grave marker was a trophy. I looked at the date. March 6, 1981.

King Recreation Center
Young Men's Basketball
Under 21 Champions

Those trophies were always set on the end of the scorer's table so the players could see what awaited the winners. I was late to the game, and got there just in time to see Pony and Mike take it off the table, lift it up. It would be the last one they won together.

I didn't know who left it at the cemetery. The caretaker would let it stay for a while, but soon he would put it with the rest. The flowers they throw away or burn on the trash pile with the clippings. The rest they keep in the shed behind the caretaker's house. Rows of shelves line those walls with spaces that correspond to each numbered plot. A cemetery in numbers, filled with all manner of things people have left behind.

Opening Night

The Dunbar production of *A Raisin in the Sun* opened on the last week in April. It was just after Easter, and some people couldn't resist the urge to show off their new clothes one more time. The audience was a sea of gleaming polyester, which didn't mix well with the hot weather. Twenty feet above, a dozen fans spun in futility against the heat. The men who sat in the audience had responded in kind, draping their suit jackets across the backs of the auditorium chairs.

I didn't like sitting in the rows of cramped seats, so I went up to the lighting booth to keep Marcus company. The view was better from up there. As I watched the people fill the seats below, Marcus studied the pages of the script taped to the wall.

"I'm trying not to fuck up tonight," he said, running his

finger along the crooked dimple in his tie. "That's my number one priority."

"You'll be fine."

"This is how Billy Dee Williams started," he said, tapping the side of the spotlight. "Light man."

"Where'd you hear that?"

"Mrs. Cooley told me. At first I told her I didn't want to work the lights, but then she said, 'That's how my man Billy Dee started out.' My man Billy Dee, like he cooks her eggs every morning."

"Maybe he did," I told him. "Maybe she had his nose open."

"I couldn't blame him. If Mrs. Cooley was twenty years younger. I'd drink her bathwater with her ass still in it." He looked around. "Don't tell anybody I said that."

A lime green phone sat on the table next to the light board, and each of the clear square buttons below the num bers was labeled. STAGE RIGHT. STAGE LEFT. DRAMATURGE. SHOP. OFFICE. The stage-right button started blinking as a low buzz came from the base.

"Speak of the devil," Marcus said. "Her ears must be burning."

He picked up the phone, said "Yes, ma'am" five or six times, and hung up the phone.

"Called to tell me ten minutes till showtime," he said. "Like I can't read that big-ass clock right in front of my damn face."

The clock on the wall matched every other clock I had seen in a Mobile public school. A red hand ticked away the seconds. For hours and minutes, thick black hands that barely moved, especially for students who counted down the minutes as hard as Marcus did. When the clock crept its way to 7:55, Marcus spread his fingers along the light switches. As he blinked the lights three times, the heavy hum of blended conversations dipped all at once.

"I like it when they do that," he said, smiling. He leaned back in his seat, a poot of air squeezed out of the torn vinyl.

"Mrs. Cooley's doing *Macbeth* for the summer workshop," he said. "And *The Dutchman* this fall. She asked me to audition. Might be my ticket out this booth. Somebody can shine this light on my ass for a change."

Mrs. Cooley's husband, Cleo, made his way down front to his usual seat, holding his usual bundle of flowers. Many of the people in the roped-off rows had bouquets as well. Corey and Mrs. Watters sat in the third row with parrot roses for Lorraine. Her mother had draped her scarf over the seat along the aisle for Sonny. From time to time, she looked at her watch. Corey turned all the way around, looking at the door.

Marcus kept his eyes on the clock and his hands on the light board, ready to move once eight o'clock came. Tardiness would have repercussions. Mrs. Cooley didn't subscribe to the notion of colored people's time, as so stated in the memo that Lorraine had taped to the inside of her three-ring binder.

Dear Students:

Time, like gold, frankincense, and myrrh, is a gift from God on high. To waste it is blasphemy against your God-given talent. Be on time, no, be early. If you are late for rehearsal or a show, then you might as well keep your asses at home.

With love,
Mrs. Eartha Cooley

An orange laminated copy of that same memo had been taped to the wall below the clock, inches away from Marcus's head. He had apparently taken the note to heart. At straight-up eight o'clock, he brought the lights down and nodded his head, a silent ovation to his first good turn.

The curtain came up to reveal the set I had only seen in unfinished bits and pieces that had lined the outside wall. I had seen enough plays at Dunbar to recognize the re-cycled lamps, tables, and chairs, stripped and repainted as the scripts required. The raggedy couch in the middle of the stage had been covered in worn-out plastic.

A few minutes into the play, Lorraine took the stage in a flannel nightgown and bare feet. Her mother looked back at the center doors once more to see if Sonny would make it this time. As Lorraine delivered her first line, Mrs. Watters put the scarf in her lap. After she gave up the last empty seat, her eyes never left the stage.

In the few rehearsals I had watched, the actors' voices projected past the empty seats and ricocheted off the walls. The same empty seats were filled with the friends and family willing to pay two dollars a ticket. Instead of the return of their own words, what came back was the reaction of the audience. Silence, laughter, and the sounds people made when something rang true.

During intermission, I went outside to smoke a cigarette. I patted every pocket twice before I remembered my lighter was sitting on the dashboard. When I opened my car door, the smell of the flowers on the passenger seat overpowered my pine-tree air freshener. I had bought the bouquet from Emma Long's shop over on Thurman Street. Sometimes her delivery trucks came to our street two or three times a day, bringing to all the funeral homes the arrangements people feel obliged to send. We did so much business with her that she offered me anything I wanted at no charge. Something felt wrong about taking surplus funeral flowers. I chose a sixty-dollar arrangement of roses and orchids, and I insisted on paying.

"All right," she had told me, shaking her head, the bracelets on her arm clanking together as she stretched her hand out to take my folded twenty-dollar bills. "If you're set on spending it, I'll take it."

There on the back steps of the auditorium was Beneatha Younger herself. Lorraine had done her first scenes in her bare feet and had not seen fit to put on any shoes before she stepped outside. She stood in the splatters of paint the set builders had left, a mass of fresh purple and green. Layers had collected over the years, the bright new splotches on top of others that had been there so long the colors had turned as gray as the concrete.

Lorraine looked toward the street, into the parking lot. She was looking for Sonny's Continental, but she knew as well as I did that it was probably still parked in their driveway.

"If he was coming, I guess he'd be here by now."

"You were great," I told her.

She took the pack of cigarettes from my shirt pocket.

"I appreciate your attempt at changing the subject."

Lorraine's voice was much smaller than it had been onstage.

"You worry about things you can't change," I told her.

"I'm being childish," she said, somewhere between a question and a confession.

"No. You just want your father to see your last play."

"Very last."

Her eyes followed the car that turned into the parking lot, a Riviera with a radio as loud as the engine. No parking spaces were left, and the driver exited as quickly as he entered. Once the car was out of earshot, the only noise to be heard came from the stage door, cracked open just enough for the commotion to seep out. Mrs. Cooley's voice rose above it all, shouting her mix of encouragement and threats.

"There'll be other plays," Lorraine said, running her toe through a straight line of sawdust. "That was always true until now."

"He's got tomorrow and Sunday."

"He's going to Montgomery tomorrow. Won't be back until sometime Sunday."

She walked back to the door and pulled it shut, sealing in the voices. The only noises that reached us came from the folks at the other end of the auditorium, their odd bits of conversation traveling the length of the brick wall.

"Maybe," she said, smiling. Lorraine was hard to read sometimes, hard to tell at first if she was being sarcastic or being for real. "He's been sleeping in his study, you know. He said this case is the big one." She smiled again. "Until the next time somebody dies, or gets beaten, or fired." She just sighed, and the smoke she held in disappeared into the little bit of breeze that blew our way.

"Your mother's here," I reminded her. "Your brother, too."

She smiled. "They always are."

She held her wig up on her fist and turned it to face her, separating the hairs like she was looking into a mirror.

"I thought about something this afternoon. Maybe I should go to L.A. instead of New York after college," she said. "Then he can turn on the television and see me all the time. Won't have to leave the house."

She had her future all worked out in her head, never any bit of apprehension in her words. I envied her. Another car turned into the parking lot, but she didn't even look that way. Just then the floodlights that lined the wall blinked three times, and the folks down the wall filed back inside the auditorium. The muffled ruckus on the other side of the stage door grew louder as the door opened, and Freda Lumas stuck her head out.

"Lorraine—oh, hey, Roy—Lorraine, ten minutes."

She dropped her cigarette in the can with the others, burying the fire end in the shallow sand.

"This is it, Roy Deacon," she said. "After this they close the curtain on the Lorraine Watters era."

She was feeling grandiose, one of her third-person moods.

"Stop talking crazy."

"Don't fuck up my moment," she told me with a kiss on the cheek. She smelled like strawberry Afro Sheen and cigarette smoke. "I'm just trying to make it last."

She was halfway playing, but she was right. She walked up the steps into the back door of the stage and stood there for a moment like she was Diana Ross or somebody.

"See you on the other side."

Mrs. Cooley didn't mind me hanging around backstage for the tail end of the plays. That way I could always give Lorraine her flowers and avoid the crush of well-wishers that collected near the stage. As long as I stayed out of the way, everybody just floated around me, pretending like I wasn't there. A few feet inside the stage door, a wooden staircase led to a split-level storage room. About halfway up, there was a hidden corner. I could look between the side curtains and see most of the stage. With the painted-on details and the lights, it looked real from where I sat. Almost real, but not quite.

From backstage I could also see the other side of make-believe, see things as they really were. On the flip side of the panels with details painted on, skeletons of two-by-fours and chicken wire held everything together. It was all made from rough boards of pressed pine, donated scraps of Sheetrock, and two-by-fours with half-moon dimples around the nail holes where the shop class hammers had missed their marks. A thin layer of dust frosted the curtains. On the floor, faint markings drawn on the hardwood told the students where to stand. The actors had gone through those same paces for so long that they never looked down. They moved around like they believed they were some other place, like they weren't standing on that same stage made of warped boards. They all stood there onstage and said their lines, almost flawless, until it was all over.

After the play, Lorraine and I got to her house before her mother and Corey did. On the calendar on their refrigerator, April 24 had been circled and starred, with OPENING NIGHT underlined beneath it. Lorraine took what looked like the same felt-tipped marker and drew two faces. One had a smile and the other a frown. Beneath two ladybug magnets, a bright orange flyer announced the cast party that Mrs. Cooley was throwing at her house that evening. Written in the margins was a note from Lorraine's mother: "Rain, PLEASE don't forget Eartha's cake."

Right beside the bowls of leftover Easter candy, there was a cake covered in white icing with "Mrs. Cooley" written in green. The letters adorned the front of a marquee drawn with purple icing.

"When did she make that?"

"Please. She didn't make a damn thing. Probably got it from Winn-Dixie."

Lorraine opened the refrigerator door and took out a bottle of apple juice. She went to close the door but stopped halfway. She leaned and stuck her head in.

"Well, look here."

There behind the pickled beets was another cake, half the size of the other, with a marquee that said "Lorraine."

"Shit. Now I have to act all surprised," she said, moving the bowl of beets and opening the cake box. She scooped off a finger full of icing from the back of the cake, where nobody would notice. "She hates it when I ruin her surprises." She stared at it, turning her head sideways. The icing had cooled in thick white waves, and the letters had been drawn in blue and outlined in gold.

"It is sweet, though," she said.

"What kind is it?"

"As long as it's not German chocolate."

The only noise in the house was the hunt-and-peck rhythm of a typewriter down the hall. From the kitchen it was a straight shoot to the foyer. The only light was the bit that shined through the lead-glass door from the front porch and the light that bled out of Mr. Watters's study. Most evenings when I was over there, Sonny was at his desk, which was covered with a hill of open books and raggedy legal pads. On that night, Sonny sat on the floor with his back against the shelves that lined the far wall. His bifocals were caught in the squinting creases between his brow and his nose.

Stacks of paper surrounded him, weighted down with medallions Sonny had collected over the years, keys to the city from little places all over. Union Town. Enterprise. There was even a town called Equality, Alabama. Just as many keys were still in the thick wooden bowl on the end table. An ashtray sat between Sonny's feet, and smoke curled off the end of his cigar.

The offbeat typing came from Mr. Watters's desk, where Paul sat hunched over the typewriter that was older than he was, the carriage inching along as his fingers found the keys. Behind him was a blackboard, the kind with legs and hinges so Sonny could flip it over and write on both sides. The years of chalk had stained it so bad it never got clean, always ashy from the dust that gathered along the borders. Much of the handwriting on the board was Paul's. The chalkboard was lined with neat rows of bullet points, and lines connected to circles—some filled with words and others filled with question marks.

The pecking stopped once Paul looked up to see us. Mr. Watters kept his head down, oblivious, starring at the mass of notes all around him.

"Youngblood, put this on the board," Sonny said just before he looked up to see us at the doorway.

"You should have claimed Paul on your taxes," Lorraine announced as she sat on the corner of the desk.

"How was your show, baby?"

She cut her eyes, but he was looking down again. "Wonderful."

"You know I wanted to be there," he said, his voice trailing off as he fingered through the handful of pages, dealt each into the proper stack. "I had my jacket and my tie on"—he pointed over to the sport coat and tie that had fallen off the arm of the chair—"and my keys in my hand, and then Lyle called. Ain't that right, Paul?"

"I was sitting right here. He was halfway out the door. Said bye to me and everything."

Sonny pointed at Paul. "See."

"What do you expect him to say? He's on the payroll."

Sonny parted the sea of papers, clearing a space for Lorraine on the floor. She kicked off her shoes and sat down next to him.

"So it was Uncle Lyle's fault," she said. "He had good news, I'm sure."

"Sort of."

"The D.A. called Lyle at home. He wants to sit down and talk tomorrow morning."

"Why now, all of a sudden?"

"Everybody knew that drug story was bullshit. They probably can't indict until they call this what it is. That brother got lynched."

Sonny knocked the ash off what was left of his cigar and stuck it back in his mouth. The smoke whipped into the wake of the ceiling fan, which spun fast enough to raise the edges of the papers on the floor.

"They haven't indicted a soul, and it's been four weeks."

"Four weeks and five days," Paul said. His typing stopped for a moment as he stretched his fingers, and then the tapping started again.

"What are you going to tell them?"

"What they probably already know. A Klansman with a felony record owns property across the street from where a body was hanged." Mr. Watters made his case with his hands, each point enumerated with a tug on his heavy fingers. "And a burnt cross? On the same night?"

On the board behind Paul there was a list of names—Bennie Jack Hays, Henry Hays, and what seemed to be a who's who of South Alabama Klan. In parentheses next to the names were their titles: Exalted Cyclops. Imperial Wizard. Grand Titan. Names of their Klaverns. Koon Hunters Club. Alabama Rescue Squad. Written at the top of the board in red marker—"Josephus Anderson: Mistrial."

"If the police know we're on to it, then maybe they'll start to do right. Round up Hays's ass and all his people on that street," Sonny said, pointing in the direction of Herndon, like it was just outside his walls.

"Those three in jail might have done the killing, but Bennie Jack Hays was caught up in it. Probably some of those young boys living over there, too. If the police lean on one or two, somebody'll talk. We pay good tax money for that chair in Atmore. Time to strap one of them in it."

"You sound optimistic," Lorraine said.

"I got no choice, baby."

Sonny had his arm around Lorraine. When he looked over at her, he must have noticed that she still had her stage clothes on.

"Lyle and I got a meeting tomorrow up in Montgomery. The folks at the Law Center. And I'm speaking at a church Sunday morning, but I'll rush back so I can be in the front row."

Sonny hugged his daughter, then handed her a stack of papers and nodded toward Paul. No two pages were the same size. Each had been snatched from the pad with no regard for the perforations. Lorraine did what she could to line up the jagged edges before sending them along. She handed the pages to me, and I handed them to Paul, a bucket brigade of Sonny's scribbled-down theories for my brother to type up line by line.

"We need to go so we won't be late," Lorraine said.

"Take your brother with you," Sonny told me. "Works too much for a young man."

"That's all right," Paul said. "You'll be up all night trying to finish."

"Bullshit," Sonny said. "You need to be young and spry like I was at your age. Better ask somebody about Sonny Watters. The party didn't start till I walked in the room."

"You sure?"

"My wife's gonna be here to scold me in a few minutes, and I'd rather not have you see me get chastised."

Mr. Watters collected the last few notes and tapped them against the floor until the rumpled stack was as even as it could be. Lorraine was there beside him, gathering the last of the medallions that littered the floor and returning them to the wooden bowl.

"I'm sorry for missing you tonight," he said, just above a whisper. "When you get famous, I can go over to the Royal Theatre and see all your pictures—tell everybody, That's my baby girl."

As Paul gathered his things, Lorraine squeezed my hand. The Royal Theatre had been closed for three years. She kissed her father on the forehead, and the three of us left.

Sonny sat down at the desk and took over where Paul had left off. That was the last thing I heard as we walked down the hall, the ring of the typewriter as the letters reached the margins. Then came the click of the carriage as he pushed it back, started all over again.

* * *

When we got to the party, almost everybody was there already. The cake was supposed to be a surprise for Mrs. Cooley, so Lorraine waited in the car until it was clear. Eartha stood in her yard, setting dishes out on the long tables. When she went back in the house, Lorraine ran across the yard with the cake.

The Cooleys lived in Maysville. Across the street was an old house, dried-up empty, windows shaded with pollen and grime. The Cooleys' house was painted yellow and green, the bright kind of colors that fit right in underneath the cabbage palms. Her shutters were a color of green a little bit darker than the fresh cut grass where General Sherman, her bulldog, lay watching the people who filed through the gate. With each entry, the Beware of Dog sign rattled against the bent wire that held it in place.

The garage stood at the end of a simple driveway, twin strips of concrete with a patch of grass in between. A 1966 Impala sat in the garage with the hood up. The gutted parts had been arranged on the floor all around it. It had been like that for years. Cleophus Cooley had cornered Marcus and Booker for what would probably be one of those long conversations about that car. If he'd spent as much time working on it as he did talking, he would have finished years before.

There was not much front yard to speak of, but the side of the house was a quarter-acre wide. As green as that grass was, it was that much brighter because of the glow coming from the row of cabbage palms that ran just inside the chain-link fence. Strands of lights had been wrapped around the trunks, draped from tree to tree. The Cooleys left them up all year for their many parties. The bulbs were huge and clear. From a distance the wires were invisible, and the bright twirls of filament floated from tree to tree.

Paul and I waited for a while, sitting in the car with the windows down. "Machine Gun" played on the radio, and I had a thing about cutting off the car in the middle of a song I liked. It was like walking out of a good movie. When the song went off, I shut off the radio and reached for the door.

"You ready?" I asked him.

He wasn't listening. His mind must have been across town somewhere. He'd leaned his seat back, and sat with his hands behind his head.

"Ten years from now," he said, "where do you think you'll be?"

"The hell if I know."

"Something Sonny told me this afternoon. Said it might be ten years before they get a verdict."

Paul shifted in his seat again, and the vinyl moaned beneath his weight.

"I'll be damn near thirty," he said, turning his head to look at me. "Thirty."

I didn't say anything. Looking ten years into the future was beyond me.

"Ten years is just a long time to wait for something to happen," he said. "But at least you know it's coming, I suppose."

I thought about where we were ten years before. Kids. That was the time my brother had earned most of the mementos that had littered his floor in those days after Michael was murdered. In the weeks since, Paul had put away those boxes, returning the childhood trophies to the attic, between the rafters and the insulation.

There was a new clutter on his floor. Paul was still a

freshman at South Alabama. He hadn't declared a major yet, but he had already bought most of the pre-law books a semester ahead of time. They sat on his dresser along with the ones he borrowed from Sonny's shelves.

"Ten years from now, I'll have been out of law school four years."

He said as much without a hint of maybe. Paul had started talking about his future the same way Lorraine did, with a kind of certainty that I had never been able to find.

"However much time it takes, it'll be good to be there," he said. "In the courtroom with Lyle and Sonny when it comes down."

It was a comforting notion, the idea that there was some guaranteed good—however far away it might have been—but I didn't have that kind of patience to wait for something that was a world away.

Cleo Cooley was bringing a couple of old speakers out of the garage and lifting them onto a card table with his component system. On the table, he had set a ripped Winn-Dixie bag with eight-tracks spilling out. Cleo connected a tangle of extension cords to the line that fed the lights. The bulbs blinked, then after a crackle there was music, turned up as high as it could go. The Cooleys always invited their neighbors to the parties, so there was nobody to call the police when things got too loud. A few neighbors with covered dishes came through the gate, making just enough noise for Sherman to lift his head.

Paul leaned against the passenger door with his fingers grasping the side-view mirror that showed the small image of Myra James and her little crew, Rhonda Darnoll and Candace Jenkins, walking toward us. They were in all the musicals and had a little singing group called the Mobilites. They made the rounds during Black History Month singing an over-the-top rendition of "Lift Every Voice and Sing." Rhonda and Candace sang backup and beat tambourines.

Myra stopped and looked into the car—staring hard, like she was the police or somebody. She had always been mean as hell to me, probably because she and Lorraine had some static. With Paul, it was a whole different bag.

"I know that ain't Paul Deacon over there," she said, talking loud as usual.

"You know it is. How you been?"

"Same old same," she said. "Y'all got something to drink in there?"

"No," he said. "We might get some later."

Rhonda and Candace strained their necks to look inside the car and saw it was just me, and they both had a look of disappointment that they made no effort to hide. That was all right because they could kiss my ass.

"You see us standing here, Roy, and you can't open your mouth to speak?" Myra said.

"I just saw y'all up at Dunbar."

She looked at me like she wanted to cut me. She probably had a razor in her purse. Rhonda and Candace looked impatient, as if their lives would be incomplete if they missed the chicken salad, the lime sherbet and ginger ale punch, and the lemon ring cookies.

"Myra, bring your ass on before we miss the cake."

"Greedy asses," Myra said. "Y'all coming inside?"

"Yeah," Paul told her, his voice a little deeper, more deliberate. "We'll be there in a minute."

She just popped her gum, smiled, and left the gate open when she went into Mrs. Cooley's yard.

"She used to be kind of bony," Paul said, turning his head sideways out of the window. "Filled out nice."

"Fine as she is crazy. That's a bad combination."

"Where's old what's-his-name?"

"She quit him a few weeks ago."

Paul pulled a comb out of his back pocket and ran it through his hair, patted it down.

"I haven't seen Myra since Christmas."

"You haven't seen anybody," I told him. "You work too much."

He nodded. "It'll be worth it when it's over with," he said.

He opened the door and got out.

"You ready?"

"Yeah."

The cabbage palms threw their light down on the yellow wood of the house. Myra stood with her ass pressed into the diamonds of chain-link fence, pretending not to see Paul coming in. Lorraine looked over and motioned me to come over. She stood there holding the cake with the marquee candles burning, waiting for Mrs. Cooley to come out the side door. General Sherman lay sleeping just inside the fence. When I locked the gate, the Beware of Dog sign clanged against the ringlets that held it in place. Sherman opened his eyes, but didn't seem to mind us. Paul rubbed his stomach as we walked past him toward the first party we'd been to in what seemed like forever.

The Sunday-afternoon matinee of *A Raisin in the Sun* was the last show. I was sitting in the third row of the balcony when Sonny tipped in halfway through the third act and took the empty seat along the center aisle. I hadn't seen him since that Thursday night. Before Mr. Watters left for Montgomery, Paul asked him about his meeting with the D.A. "We'll see." That was his answer. It didn't sound promising. Sonny wasn't the type to keep good news a secret.

The lights on the side of the balcony seats shone against the tattered leather satchel Sonny carried. Sunlight bled around the edges of the drapes that covered the balcony windows. The daylight worked against the scene that had been set on the stage—the spotlight was just a little weaker, the colored lights not as bright.

Lorraine was onstage, but Sonny was barely paying attention. He looked toward the far side window, rubbing the leather of a bag too worn out to hold everything Sonny needed to carry. He grabbed a handful of notes from the outside pocket. As the play went through its paces, Sonny looked up for a moment, then looked back down at the work he held. After a while, his head remained down. At first, I couldn't tell if he was reading or sleeping. As Lorraine stood center stage projecting her last few lines, Sonny's head rolled to one side. His back rose with each breath as he slept in silence.

Sticking out of Sonny's bag was the Sunday paper, kinked and wrinkled, refolded so that it was thicker than it was supposed to be. He'd probably done the same thing most folks who'd followed that case did. We were overdue for a boldface headline, spelling out the indictment. In those days after the lynching, there was other big news. The space shuttle *Columbia* was making its way around the world. At school, we crowded around a television in the lunchroom the day President Reagan was shot. As big as those stories were, they seem to make our story seem a little bit smaller, the answers a little further away.

A note on the Donald case had finally appeared in that previous Friday's paper, but it wasn't the news anyone hoped for. The judge had reduced the bail for the three suspects from $250,000 to $150,000. Those men were only a $15,000 bond from walking out of jail. One of the most violent murders the city had ever seen, and all they needed was somebody's mama to put up her house and they'd be as free as the rest of us.

While there was no news on Michael's murder in the newspaper through April, there was big news from the police department. They had unveiled a brand-new fleet of police cars, state-of-the-art Chevrolet Caprices with supercharged engines and bucket seats. In the picture, below the fold on the front page, an officer stood with his foot on the step in the new uniforms they had adopted months before. Lynching or no, the Mobile Police Department, well dressed and turbo charged, had proudly stepped into the modern age of law enforcement. As far as the police were concerned, the Donald murder was off the books.

I had often heard people say that no news was good news, but as I sat in the matinee audience and watched Sonny, I wasn't so sure. He was dog-tired, dead to the world, and the fistful of yellow pages, his notes and theories, slipped from his grip and fell down the narrow steps of the mezzanine.

May

One of my father's high school friends, a man named Roscoe Grayne, came to the funeral home with his wife. He was in a wheelchair, and he wore an apple cap pulled low on his head. When his wife went in the office with my parents, Mr. Grayne waited outside.

"Which one are you?"

"Roy," I told him.

He extended his hand and made the firmest shake he could muster, but his body had lost too much. He had the grip of a man twice his age, and his hands were just as wrinkled. He and his wife had come home from Los Angeles for Christmas, and Mr. Grayne got sick the morning he was set to leave. They thought it was flu, but the doctors found cancer all over. He was too sick to go back home.

"You the oldest?"

"No, sir. That's my brother, Paul."

"He work here, too?"

"No, sir. Just me."

"Smart man," he said. "Not a bad business to be in. Your daddy always had some money in his pocket and some sharp shoes on his feet. He was the second cleanest brother at Dunbar High School, but he couldn't touch me."

I had seen the picture of my father and his friends wearing their tight suits and fried hair. They looked like they were posing for an album cover, and Roscoe Grayne stood in the middle like a lead singer. There in our hallway he was dressed as sharp as he was in the picture, but he no longer filled out the clothes that had once fit him to a tee. The door to the display room was wide open, and Mr. Grayne stared down the row of empty caskets. We kept half a dozen models on sight. The other styles filled the pages of the brochures on the near table.

"My wife didn't want me to come. At first she tried to hide where she was going, but I heard her on the phone with your people," he said. "I said fuck it, at least I get a chance to see old Randy one more time."

He worked up a smile, but his face showed his sickness. The face, robust in pictures, had been worn thin.

"When we'd go to parties, we'd stop by here and get your daddy," he said. "I wouldn't get out of the car. I'd just hit the horn. Your granddaddy hated that shit, but I'd be damned if I was coming up in here."

He looked into the showroom where the row of floor models waited.

"I guess you better show me a couple."

Some people like to help plan the details of their funeral. Maybe it's just a way to show that they've made their peace with it, and they're ready to go. There was something unnerving about watching someone pick his own casket, and the certainty of seeing him in it a few weeks later. When he made his request, I hesitated. I hoped he wasn't serious.

"Come on, Deacon," he said. "Get the hump out your back."

I rolled him into the showroom and stopped next to the first row. Mr. Grayne ran his hand along the Bronze Deluxe.

"My first Thunderbird was this color," he said. "You a Thunderbird man?"

"No, sir. I drive a Datsun."

"That's a pitiful way to get around," he said. "Save your money, and one day you can ride around in something nice."

Mr. Grayne took a handkerchief from his pocket and wiped the toe of his brown gators, then ran his fingers down the sharp crease of his trousers.

"Most folks don't ever ride in a Caddy until they get pushed into the ones y'all keep out back," he said. "That's a damn shame."

He shrugged his shoulders, then looked down the line at the next model.

"What do you call this one?" he said.

"That's the Corinthian."

He knocked on the shell. He rolled down the aisle a little farther. He came to a casket made of cedar with a charcoal finish.

"And this one?"

"That's the Sojourner."

"Hell of a name for a box," he said. "Specially one that won't be going but six feet."

He looked into the lining, from the toe to the head pillow. As he squeezed the satin, his head sank heavy against his sunken shoulders. He tried to cover his grimace with a smile.

"I miss California," he said. "We got a little garden out back. I had planted some collards. My sister-in-law says they're coming in nice. Ever been to L.A.?"

"No, sir."

"You should drive out there some time," he said. "That desert is something to see."

Roscoe's wife had told Mama that the doctor gave him nine months, and that was at the end of December. I realized then that dealing with dead people wasn't nearly as difficult as dealing with the ones who are dying. Maybe that part scared me most of all, not knowing how or when or what next.

"I think I like this one here," he said. "Me and my Sojourner. Riding to Old Hill in the back of that Cadillac."

He looked out the window to the garages, some of them open with the cars in plain view.

"Got a good mind to let you take me for a ride right now, up in the front seat with you. I can know what it's like, since I'm paying for it."

Roscoe let out a careful laugh, one that came from somebody who had gotten used to the pain, had learned how to work around it as best he could. He touched the head pillow, and ran his fingers across the stitches.

"You got yours picked out yet, youngblood?"

"Not something I'm ready to think about yet."

"I guess it might be hard to keep your mind off dying, being around it so much," he said. "I wish Nita didn't have to see it. She's my world."

He stared into the open lid of his casket and traced around the seal with his fingers. Through the window behind him, one of the rocking chairs rested against the glass.

It wouldn't be long until they were filled, the people coming by to pay respects to the late Roscoe Grayne.

"You got you a lady?" he asked me.

"Yes, sir."

"Who are her people?"

"Watters. Lorraine Watters."

"Shit, yeah, I know big-head Sonny. And ol' Rhonda, too. I haven't seen their daughter since she was 'bout yea tall," he said, holding his had two feet from the ground. "And here she is courting Randy's boy."

His voice sounded bigger then, like his body forgot he was sick long enough for him to get the words out.

"You love this girl, Roy Deacon?"

I hesitated for a moment. "Yeah, I love her."

"You told her as much?"

"Not yet."

"What's the holdup?"

"We won't be together much longer. She's leaving for school, and I am, too."

He nodded his head, eased one leg out of the footrest, and stretched it out a bit, just like we were in his living room just talking.

"Well, things work out how they're supposed to," he said. "Your daddy used to say that all the time."

"Still does."

He leaned back in his chair and sighed hard enough to hear the buried rattle in his lungs.

"You a religious man, youngblood?"

I didn't answer right off. As far as work went, it was easier to tell people what they wanted to hear. I had only known Mr. Grayne for an afternoon, but he didn't seem like the type to bullshit around.

"No, sir. I can't say that I'm much on church and whatnot."

"So when y'all turn my key and lock me in," he said, turning his hand like he was sealing himself in, "you think that's it?"

"I'm still trying to figure it out."

"You and me both."

He nodded his head and rubbed his hands in his lap, tracing back and forth along the seams of his slacks.

"I told my wife I love her, and I said sorry to most everybody I ever did wrong. Then I got right with God. If there is a heaven, maybe I got a shot." He knocked his signet ring hard against the side of the casket. "If it's all some bullshit, I won't know the difference. I'll be in my pine box."

"Cedar."

"Even better," he said. "Just like Daddy Rich said, 'Got to believe in something. Why not believe in me.'"

He managed a smile that wasn't clipped by a grimace or a cough. It just stretched across his face unencumbered.

Anita Grayne came out of the office with my parents. When Roscoe's wife put her hands on his shoulders, he raised himself a little higher. I wondered about what it took to love someone like that, take care of the details that came with dying. On those funeral Saturdays, we have to get in and out of churches quickly so they can get ready for the evening weddings. "Till death us do part" was just something to say for most folks. They probably never thought about seeing it through to our door.

"Youngblood," he said, close to a whisper. "You know Sonny Watters was the one pissed in the white folks' pool?"

I nodded.

"Tell him Scooter Grayne told you. I was supposed to take it to my grave, but I guess I'm close enough."

"Yes, sir. I'll tell him."

I've looked through my father's yearbook at the many candid photos of Roscoe "Scooter" Grayne. He had been a tall man who was thick around the shoulders. Though his arms were too weak by the time I met him, in the photos he talked with his hand, caught by the camera in midsentence.

After hearing the stories about Scooter, I was glad I got a chance to finally meet him. But knowing them always makes it that much harder when the time comes. Three weeks after his visit, I buried his body in the casket he had chosen. I wondered about the rest of him. Standing over his frail body, I wondered what became of the part that made him who he was—mind, spirit, soul—whatever the right word was. In case this world is not the end of things, I hope he was able to get over. He might have been right. Maybe we do have to believe in something.

Prom Night

The prom committee had plastered the theme along the walls of the Mobile Civic Center. "Endless Love: 1981 Murphy High School Prom." The background consisted of two sideways hearts joined to make an infinity symbol, but it looked more like a bow tie. Lionel Richie's face had been painted in one heart, and Diana Ross occupied the other. It looked ridiculous, but it was prom night, and ridiculousness was in the air as the Class of 1981 wore the finest formalwear money could rent.

The colors were louder than the voices. I saw tuxedos in shades that I didn't know existed. Buster Green wore baby blue with matching shoes. As Lorraine and I stood in front of the backdrop, waiting for the photographer to snap our picture, I watched the parade.

"It's like the circus came to town," I said.

"Be nice."

"If Buster says a word to me, I'm jankin' his ass."

"Then you can dance with Buster Green," she said through her clenched teeth as the photographer stood ready.

He told us to say cheese, we did, and that was that. A little keepsake of 1981, available in overpriced packages to be delivered in four to six weeks. People were taking their own pictures all around, snapping Polaroids of one another, so we could all see how bad we looked without having to wait.

Slim and Natasha stood a ways behind us in the picture line, and they got back to our table fifteen minutes after we did. Ruben and Kendra were already there. Both Slim and Ruben wore white dinner jackets just like mine. Ruben and I had ordered ours from the same place, but Slim had to get one from the big and tall store in Bel Air Mall.

The prom started at eight, and nobody wanted to be the first ones through the door. By the time we all sat down, it was around nine fifteen. Lorraine, Kendra, and Natasha went to take a picture together before the line got too long. No sooner had the girls had left than Buster Green came around, talking shit.

"Females got smart and left y'all sorry asses. 'Bout damn time."

"Don't come around here starting shit, tonight," I told him.

"I don't know why you came. Summer-school prom ain't till August."

"Aww, Ruben. That's why your lady's titties ain't real," he said. "I could hear that newspaper crunching when she walked past.' "

"Her titties as real as your mama's," Ruben said. "You might not remember how they taste, but I do."

"You're lucky I'm wearing rented shoes," he said. "Otherwise, I'd put this ten and a half dead in your narrow ass."

Ruben let Buster get away with the last word, and he shot us the bird as he scooted across the floor to his lady. When the girls came back, we opened the class gifts that were inside the school-colored boxes at each place setting. Inside were glass-encased desk clocks with digital faces. With the gift boxes, roses, and candlelight, the Civic Center looked nothing like the empty room where we would graduate in two weeks' time. The long blue curtains behind us hid the risers that would seat our parents and friends. The deejay spun the records on the same stage that we would cross to get our diplomas.

The last dance was "Endless Love," the extended version. The deejay had played it four times already. By the end of the night, some of the decorations had started to fall. A girl from the prom committee had already begun to fill a Glad bag with a twisted length of streamers. The prom night that we'd spent months saving for and talking about was down to its last spin on the turntable. While we danced, Lorraine had one hand along my neck while the other rubbed my arm, her fingers tight and tense along my elbow. It was uncomfortable, but I didn't say anything. Neither one of us did.

The house lights came up before the song ended, and the chalk-shaded faces of Lionel Richie and Diana Ross lost their luster beneath the fluorescent bulbs. Without the warm glow of the candles, we saw the Civic Center for what it was, concrete walls and a slate floor. As the deejay stopped his music, Lorraine and I let go and followed our friends back to the table. We took our Endless Love digital clocks, batteries not included, and headed for the exit doors.

Memorial Day was a welcome relief. We'd had little tastes of summer here and there for a couple of months, only to have the night chill come back when it had seemed gone for good. The uncertain spring had lingered too long, bringing rain showers and thunderstorms, those peculiar changes that were hard to predict. At least with the heat of summer, we knew what to expect. We started the long weekend on Friday with a cookout on Edgewater Beach. My father allowed himself a few afternoon hours away from the office. Maurice brought Jeanine, and Aunt Camille and Uncle Greg drove down from Detroit.

Paul and I helped Maurice carry the grill from the back of his El Camino. He had built it in our grandfather's garage, cutting a thirty-gallon drum lengthwise and welding hinges on one side and a handle on the other. The bright yellow drum looked like a metal Pac-Man, impossible to miss among the black hibachis up and down the beach. Once we dragged the grill to our spot, Paul dumped the charcoal in, and Maurice sloshed lighter fluid onto the briquettes.

"That's too much lighter fluid, Maurice," his father yelled over to him from his lawn chair.

"How about you come take care of this and I sit on my behind all day?"

"How about I take you back to the group home?"

"Youngbloods," Maurice said to Paul and me out of his father's earshot. "Tell my daddy I'm a grown-ass man, and I know what the hell I'm doing."

Jeanine walked over and stood by Maurice. With her arms folded, her chest looked like it grew another cup size. With the cocoa butter she'd rubbed on herself, I caught myself staring already. She was new to the family, and I didn't want to get off on the wrong foot. Everybody had taken a liking to her, and her only flaw was cheating at spades, but then again, so did Maurice.

"Your daddy's right," Jeanine said. "That's way too much."

"You're trying to get on his good side," he told her.

"I'm trying not to catch fire," she said. "It's hot enough as it is."

When she arrived in March, Jeanine had appreciated the break from the Detroit winter weather, but it was just Memorial Day and she was already tired of the heat. She kept fanning herself with a bridal magazine.

"Y'all can let your cousin burn you up if you want to," she told us. "I'm getting a pop."

"You mean a drink," Paul said. "We don't say pop. We say drink."

"Sweetheart, I say what I damn well please."

She popped her gum, winked.

"Baby," Maurice said, "bring me pop, too. Please."

Paul stared at him, but Maurice wouldn't raise his head.

"Pop," Paul said. "Got you whipped."

"You'll understand one day," he said. "Some woman will have you saying all kinds of thangs you thought you never would."

Jeanine walked down to the beach as Maurice struck the cluster of matches in his hand. Paul and I had already stepped back by the time the flame hit the lighter fluid, sending up a wall of fire right in front of Maurice.

"Boy's always been hardheaded," Uncle Greg said.

"I bet it won't go out," Maurice said.

Once the flames tapered off, the waves of heat rising from the grill distorted the view of the beach. A patchwork of families, umbrellas, and towels covered the thin stretch of sand. The beach people lit their grills, iced their sodas, and went about the hard work required for relaxation.

My grandfather sat in his lounge chair and drank off-brand ginger ale my mother bought for ten cents a can. He had on his swimming trunks and a cabana shirt. A pencil saved his place in the book of crossword puzzles that he'd set on the cooler. Except for the color of their hair, my grandfather and Uncle Greg looked just alike. My uncle sat on a lawn chair with a frayed seat that looked on the verge of coming loose. The beads of water from his High Life can dripped down on his clothes, a pair of slacks cut off at the knee and hemmed, and a family reunion T-shirt that was older than I was.

"Watch out for those fast women in New Orleans," Uncle Greg said. "They'll leave you used and confused."

"How would you know?" Aunt Camille said. "You'll have a wonderful time, Roy. Lots of culture in New Orleans."

"Lots of big-legged women, too," Greg said.

"You remember Dean and Ella Kirby?" my father asked Greg. "They have two mortuaries, doing real well over there. Ella's got a nephew in business school at Tulane. The boy is smart as a whip." My father shook his head. "They're grooming him. They said they wouldn't mind Roy doing a little work with them this fall."

It was the first I'd heard of it. Maurice looked at me as he stood over the grill flipping baby backs. He gave me that look he has, like I had farted in his car or something.

"That's good," Granddaddy said, lifting his hat long enough to wipe the sweat from his forehead. "He can see how other folks do business."

The grill sizzled as Maurice poured a can of beer over the meat, looking me dead in the eye as he dug his fork into the ribs. My father had a habit of talking about my time as if it were his own, but until I said otherwise, I suppose it really was his time. I planned to talk to him, but it would have to be later. I just bit my tongue and waited for the food that Maurice pulled off the grill.

After we ate, my parents played bid whist with Jeanine and Aunt Camille while Uncle Greg slept off his food under their beach umbrella.

"Wake my daddy up so we can play spades," Maurice said.

"Your daddy cheats worse than you do."

"He only cheats when he plays with your daddy," he said. "I know all the signs. If he scratches his face on the right side, that means play diamonds. He bites his lip, that's clubs."

"See. That's why I don't play with him," Paul said.

Behind us, three little girls walked from car to car tying slim yellow ribbons onto antennae. The two older girls wore bright red satchels filled with yellow leaflets. The smallest one, much younger than the others, ran to keep up, her flip-flops slapping the soles of her feet. She wore plastic sunglasses with flowers on each corner. She walked in our direction, handing out small flyers she carried in a Wonder Woman lunch box with "Danielle" written around the edges in permanent marker.

"Hey, Miss Deacon," she said, handing Mama a flyer. "I'm going to be at your school next year."

"I'll look forward to having you," Mama said.

"Enjoy your summer then, sweetheart," Uncle Greg said. "Mrs. Deacon will work you like a slave."

"Hush, Greg," Aunt Camille said.

"You-all tell your people I said hello," Mama said, as they made their way down the beach.

The girls were the granddaughters of Nancy Freed. She was heading up the march the NAACP chapter had scheduled during Jubilee Days, a downtown street festival held every year over Memorial Day weekend. On the flyer, the words REMEMBER MICHAEL DONALD ran across the top margin, RAIN OR SHINE across the bottom.

The speakers listed on the flyer were all local this time. By May, the known names had come and gone. They had fires to help put out in other places. I leaned over my mother's shoulder and read the details of the march itinerary: where to gather, when, the order of speakers, and the marching route.

"More marching," Camille said. "Seems like we've done enough to go around the world and back."

The march was scheduled for noon, on the same day the mayor was scheduled to break ground on the new convention center. The elected officials had been talking about it for years, how much it would cost, how many jobs, economic impact, and so on. Nancy Freed had figured that was the best time to get some attention. Politicians, in shining hard hats and golden shovels, might be uncomfortable enough to take notice.

The attention was necessary. It had been two months, and no one had been indicted. Sonny had told Paul that the delay must have been connected to conspiracy charges. He had said it took time to build a major case. A generous logic had taken hold—the more time they took, the stronger the case would be. Maybe the authorities were building their case against Bennie Jack Hays and as many others as they could connect up the Klan ladder. That seemed to be the only reasonable explanation for the delay.

The march was due diligence. A healthy dose of the Negro optimism. Keep Hope Alive. We Shall Overcome. Lift Every Voice. Nancy Freed was of the old school that believed enough marching would bring the good news we had patiently awaited from city hall. Any day now. It was just a matter of time.

While everybody else was playing cards, Paul and I took a walk down to the far end of Edgewater with our grandfather. In the summers, he would bring us over so we could learn to swim. He liked the waters as much as Paul did, still walking his miles up and down every morning. He would point out to us certain points—trees, light posts, docks—landmarks that had once parted the waters, separating the white beaches from the black ones. The only other job my grandfather had ever had was as an Edgewater lifeguard.

At the pier, my grandfather kept an old rescue boat that he'd salvaged. He refinished the wood and put an outboard motor on it, and we'd ride with him around the bay and up into the delta. When he thought we were ready for the deep water, he would take us out and drop anchor about fifty yards from the Edgewater pier.

"Swim to the pier and come back and touch the boat," he said.

It looked so much farther than it was.

"Strong strokes, Roy. Remember to breathe."

Learning to swim had not been easy in the thick bay water. I didn't like water that wouldn't let me see the bottom. I embellished the waterweeds and driftwood that brushed against me, scared of what I couldn't see below the waterline.

"Doesn't matter how deep the water is if you're up on the surface."

He kept a life preserver in his hand, but he had no intention of throwing it.

"Just keep on swimming."

His words carried across the water, making him sound closer than he actually was.

"That's it. Good, good."

If I ever got into trouble, Paul was a few strokes away. If I sank, his hands would find my stomach and lift me up toward the surface.

"Don't matter how deep the water is," Paul said. "If you can swim, you don't have to worry about the bottom."

The first time I made it to the boat, my grandfather

extended his hand and pulled me in while Paul stayed in the water, floating with his toes and face above water.

"See?" Paul said. "It's easy when you stop fighting it."

Later that afternoon, I stood on the end of the pier with Paul and all the other kids, waiting to jump. When it was our turn to jump, I froze.

"Stop being scared."

"I ain't scared."

"Then jump, fool."

"I ain't no fool."

I stood there looking down at the water, trying to make up my mind. Before I could, I felt the force of hands on my back, and then I was flying off the pier into the water. I had just enough time to take a breath before I hit the surface. The bay was about ten feet deep off the pier, and it didn't take long for my feet to hit the bottom and then push myself back up to the surface. The water was cool in some places, warm in others. It was just water, nothing for me to be scared of anymore. When I came up, Paul was in the water, laughing.

"See?" he said.

I suppose I should have been thankful. If he hadn't pushed me, I'd still be up there, scared of nothing at all. All the same, I hit him in the mouth on principle.

By 1981, the pier we used to jump from had fallen to pieces, mostly from Hurricane Camille. All that was left were the snaggled rows of beams that rose out of the water. They were just a place for anglers to cast their lines, looking for fish that gathered among the pillars.

The only remaining structure was a little church called Mt. Olive that was just off the beach road. My grandfather walked past it every morning. He said on a Sunday morning each spring, when the water was warm enough, all the members who joined in the winter were baptized at once. On a few Sunday afternoons I had seen them, children mostly, lined up to take their turns in the water. It was an experience few people had known, a saltwater baptismal. I always wondered if the brine burned their eyes like chlorine had burned mine.

"This is where I always turn around," Granddaddy said. "If I go any farther, I might get too tired to make it back."

We walked him back to where our family was sitting and helped them pack everything to leave. Before Paul and I headed home, we took the boat up into the delta. We had a chance to enjoy the early-summer days, when the afternoon sun was still comfortable. Paul sat facing me with his head against the bow and his legs over the front seat. With his mirrored sunglasses, I couldn't tell if he was awake until he started patting his stomach, having once again eaten way too much. While he relaxed, I wove through Polecat Bay and Coffee Bayou. Once we got to the river, we headed up toward the delta.

The sky had more birds than clouds. Ospreys nested on the utility towers, and the fish crows sat among the cypress trees. Their trunks were circled by waterlines, rings of algae that marked how high the water rose. Some of the low branches lay submerged when the tide was high. Fish swam through the same branches that carried birds at low tide.

We crossed from the savannah into the fresh water of the swamp, and I slowed the boat to a crawl and worked my way through the narrows. At a quiet place near Chickasaw I killed the motor, and Paul lay across the bow with his head and his legs dangling over the sides.

"You're asking for a gator to come around and snatch off a foot," I told him.

"These gators can kiss my ass."

"Dangle your ass in that water, and they might."

Paul was staring into the tall grass behind us when something started moving. Whatever it was—deer, nutria, squirrel—it moved in the other direction. The sound of its steps became faint. The swamp animals were more afraid of us than we were of them. With the sky open along the marshes, the animals were seen before they were heard. It was different in the swamp. With the trees all around us, the only signs of living things were the sounds of their hidden steps, their final noises when they disappeared into the waters.

"I hope I can be there," he said.

"Where?"

Paul sat up and faced me, with his back to the bow. He gripped the edges of the boat, steadying his body with the bend of his arms.

"In Atmore. When they strap them in that chair."

"They need to indict somebody first."

"It won't be much longer," he said.

The air was cooler there than it was on the beach, the city streets, most anywhere. That kind of cool only happened on the water. The sun filtered through the trees and flowed easy, giving us the right mix of light and shade. It was a popular place, just not for people. A three-foot alligator sunned itself on a log. The tributary we had entered narrowed until the tree trunks brushed against the hull on either side. It would have been nice if we could have stayed out there longer, but we'd gone as far as we could. We'd been out longer than we thought. The sun that had been overhead most of the day was now sinking out ahead.

"You ready?" I asked him.

He nodded. I reversed the motor while he pushed

against the tree trunks, backing us out of the narrow waters so we could make our way back to Edgewater. Before we took the boat in, I stopped so Paul could take one more swim. Years before I was able to brave those waters, I sat on that same seat beside my grandfather and watched my brother swim around the boat. When I was underwater, all I could think about was breathing again. But Paul loved it, said the water helped to clear his mind.

"You coming in?" he said.

"I don't want to come out smelling like mullet."

"Your feet smell like corn chips already."

He disappeared before I could say anything back. I looked at the spot where he went under, waiting for him to come up there. I was looking in the wrong place. He knocked hard on the bottom of the hull. He did it the week after we saw *Jaws,* and I almost pissed myself. He surface and threw a handful of mud into my face.

"Kiss my ass," I told him. "Get in so we can go."

Navigating the water was a lot easier than getting through the traffic on the roads home. It took us longer than usual to cross the bridge. Traffic was heavy on both sides of the highway, and the cars that cut over to the causeway found that it was just as slow. The vehicles were loaded down with luggage and children, and the drivers were in a hurry to start their summers. We were just trying to get home.

The signs of spring were gone from our block. The leaves were full-grown and thick. In the stretch of grass between our houses, Mr. Lockhart was asleep on a rusted patio chair. He had given up on his lava rocks and gone back to the store-brand charcoal that burned in his grill. He was sleeping hard, with his mouth wide open. His beer can had slipped from his fingers, and the Colt 45 mixed into the sandy patch of yard beneath him where his grass never grew. The sound of our music didn't wake him when we pulled into the driveway.

Paul said it was still too nice out to be in the house, so he sat on the porch for a minute. I smelled like barbecue and funk and decided to go in to take a shower. When I was on my way into the house, Ricky Boone rode by on his bike with the bag of rolled-up copies of the *Mobile Press*. When I came back outside, Paul was gone. All that was left on the stoop were the windblown pages—comics caught in the briars, classifieds stuck in the rails. The front page was still on the top step, where Paul must have been sitting when he read the evening news.

DONALD PROBE RENEWED;
ALL THREE SUSPECTS FREED

The drug-related crime theory had fallen apart, just like Mr. Watters had said. The boys they'd arrested were guilty of nothing but getting high. The police had no one lined up to take their places in the county jail. The Klansmen who lived on Herndon Avenue were still as free as the rest of us.

Paul's truck was gone, and the ax that hung between the rakes and shovels on the garage wall wasn't there anymore. I stood in the driveway, numb, as Ricky Boone came back around the cul-de-sac, throwing handfuls of bad news to the other side of the street.

I heard the ax before I saw it. The swings cut through the yelling and police radios. The ax did the job quickly. The first half a dozen or so licks were the high-pitched crack of the ax head on the bark, and then the sound got deeper, body blows on the tree's insides. I could smell the mothball odor of camphor oil, getting stronger as the trunk was chopped to pieces. As the wound in the tree got wider, the crowd cheered the punishment of that tree, the only accomplice they could get their hands on.

The small crowd that surrounded the tree got there before the police did. When the cops arrived, they sealed off the area with barricades at both ends of the street. The latecomers pressed against the barriers a good thirty, forty yards from the tree, but they closed the distance with their voices, talking back to that ax every time it landed.

Within the perimeter, three officers sat on their horses. A dozen others stood nearby in riot helmets, chin straps unbuckled. No demands for us to disperse. No sirens. Wilcox was there, talking into his radio. He didn't say anything to me when I passed him. The police seemed intent on letting things brew no further, but they had no desire to instigate, just let the crowd yell and holler until they were too worn out to do anything else. Like everyone else on either end of the street, they watched and listened to the hacking.

Paul sat on the curb in front of the fireplug, his shirt soaked through, peeling blistered skin off his palm. He stared across the street. It was the house lived in by Henry Hays, owned by his father Bennie Jack. The porch was empty, but three cars were in the driveway. There had to be two dozen police on that street that day, as many as the day they found the body, but nobody seemed too concerned about the Klansmen across the street. All eyes were on the tree, and the next man to take the ax.

The patch on his shirt said Norman. He knew what he was doing—his hands moving apart on the backswing, closing as he brought it around. The wood chips flew all over, settling in the cracks of the gutter, along the faded red curb near the fireplug. When he stopped chopping, he looked at something behind me. I turned around to see that the circle of people had turned into a line. I was next without intending to be. He held the ax by the head and extended the handle toward me.

"It's on you, brother," he said,

He handed me the ax that had come from my house. The oxblood handle had a hole my father had drilled through it, laced with a leather cord so it could hang on the wall. That ax was older than I was. We'd used it to chop away the trees that fell on our roof after Hurricane Camille, and my father had used it after all the storms that had come before, clearing all the rubbish that had to go before things could get back to normal.

"C'mon now," somebody said behind me.

I took my licks like the rest of them, but I didn't last for long. My hands were used to other things, and the blisters on my palms came up as fast as the sweat did. I looked behind me, and there was Pony. He didn't say a word, just shrugged his shoulders and reached for the ax. He was as big as Norman was, and the blows he made were loud and wild. Some landed in the wound, and others hit the bark above. Pony cut fish at the IGA, and he still had his uniform on. His strings were undone, and the front of his apron was halfway over his shoulder as he swung.

The line of folks behind him was loud but patient. The blows came quickly, as fresh hands took hold of the handle. The thin neck of trunk that remained carried too great a weight. It was just a matter of time.

A march had been carefully planned for the next Monday. The marching had become nostalgic over the years, lest-we-forget affairs. But things had changed. The jail was empty, and the people gathered along Herndon couldn't wait for Monday. We needed to see something happen.

I looked back, and Paul was gone. I saw him jumping the fence that separated the vacant lot from the field of weeds and flowers. He left before the inevitable, the first hesitant cracks of the tree as it began to break free of its base. Then came the swell of voices. The crowd grew loud on both ends of the street and urged Pony not to stop. He cried like a child. His nose ran, and the snot mixed with the tears and sweat, a mess that the bits of dust clung to.

I knew why the police had been so calm. The rest of the people gathered weren't on Herndon Avenue that Saturday morning when Michael's body was found, so they might not have realized. On either side of the red-painted curb, fifty feet apart, there were two camphor trees. The hanging tree was protected by the blue barriers on each side. Paul had started to cut the only tree he could get close to. As for the other one, two officers stood beneath its shade just in case anybody got too close. The tree we had surrounded was just a proxy, its trunk all but severed. Cued by the fatal cracks of the timber, the crowd erupted as the wide crown of the camphor crashed to the street.

I sat in my car and watched them as they made short work of its remains. The men in the tan coveralls took their chain saws to the fifteen-foot camphor. They rode in the truck that came on Thursdays, picking up bags of grass clippings, bundles of twigs. After storms, they collected the dangerous branches, tangled in power lines, blocking the streets. The large sections of trunk were thrown in the payload. The limbs were fed to the chipper and turned to dust. They shaved the stump down as close to the ground as they could. One of the men brought over a push broom and swept the dust into the gutter. Then they were gone.

It was like nothing had happened there. No hanging. No protest. Just another quiet evening in the city under the trees. Then I looked down at my clothes. My sweat gave the dust something to stick to, and it was all over my face, hands, and T-shirt. Everyone who swung that ax left as filthy as I was, covered in the stubborn bits we carried away.

I thought that Paul might have gone over to Sonny's,

but his truck wasn't there when I pulled into the driveway. I thought Sonny's light might be on and his war room filled, but the front of the house was dark. Lorraine saw me coming up the driveway and had the kitchen door open before I rang the bell.

"Your mother called here looking for you," she said looking over my shoulder, up the street. "Said your dad drove over to Herndon to see if you two were still there."

"It was the wrong tree," I told her. "All that, and it was the wrong one."

"I wish I knew what to tell you." She held a dish towel under the faucet, the cold tap running along with just enough of the hot. She wrung it tight and gave it to me. "It'd be nice if things just happened like they're supposed to for once."

When I wiped my face, the dirt and flecks of wood stained the green and blue flowers stitched on the cloth.

"I'm glad you're all right," she said. "Anything's liable to happen tonight."

"Where's everybody?"

"Mama's at mass, praying like it'll do any good. Daddy's outside."

Lorraine took the dish towel and rinsed it in the sink. She looked out onto the patio, where her father sat in a lounge chair with his back to us.

"How long's he been out there?"

"Since he got off the phone with Uncle Lyle," she said.

Next to Sonny's chair, there was a plastic cup of ice, most of it melted, and a bottle of Johnnie Walker Black three-quarters full.

"They might have been better off twenty years ago, when they knew to expect the worst."

I opened the sliding door, and Mr. Watters didn't even look up. Three legs of his chair were on the brick patio, and one of the back legs had sunk a few inches into the compost that covered the flower bed.

"Took the afternoon off to cut the grass. First time in I don't know how long," he said. "Then come this shit."

Sonny had mowed in circles around the birdbath. The rest he'd cut up and down. Lines of clippings marked his rows along the yard, up to the place where he had stopped.

"Those three they had in jail had nothing to do with it. Building a conspiracy case, my ass."

The mower was still out there, in the stretch of long grass and weeds between the garden and the shed.

"They wanted Lyle and me to come down for a press conference. Said we need to help keep folks cool." He dumped the water out of his glass, his fingers stretched across the lip to catch the little bit of ice he had left. "I told them I wasn't helping do shit."

He fixed himself another drink.

"Help keep folks cool. Fuck being cool. If it burns, it burns."

When he motioned for me to sit down, he looked at my clothes.

"You went over there, I see."

"Don't know what good it did."

"I know the feeling."

He held up his cup, ran his thumb across the sweat that clouded the plastic.

"I usually drink Seagram's. This here's my good-time liquor," he said, grabbing the top of the Johnnie Walker bottle. "I'm drinking it anyway."

"They have to arrest somebody."

"I deal with those people every day, Roy. They don't have to do a goddamn thing."

As he held that cup against his stomach, water dripped along his shirt, MOBILE COUNTY TRAINING SCHOOL in faded red letters.

"You need to get on home before it gets too late," he told me. "We got murderers on the loose."

"Yes, sir."

"We'll still be marching on Monday," he said. "Rain or shine."

Lorraine was standing with me by my car when the bug truck came down their street. They always came at night and left mist that turned yellow in the wake of the streetlights, where the insects gathered, swarmed in the poison. There was a hint of something sweet in that chemical smell, meant to put us at ease about what we were breathing. That truck, the low drone of the misting pumps, was one of the surest signs that summer had come. One of the slow-moving trucks of summer. Ice cream and mosquitoes.

When I had turned into their driveway, my headlights shone through the window of the darkened study. With his office empty, the only sounds of Sonny's work came from the backyard. The John Deere engine started on the second pull, and the top of Sonny's head began to move down and back along the top edge of bricks. He was pushing his mower again, along the stretch of yard between the garden and the wall.

Let us March.
Let us not forget.
This Memorial Day,
Let us remember Michael Donald.

The flyers were all around, even on blocks emptied by the holidays, with no one there to read them. They detailed the intended march route, a triangle of wishful thinking. From the crime scene to the courthouse to the jail. The original plan, however, had been changed. The police department amended the march permit. Because of what happened on Friday, public demonstrations on Herndon Avenue would no longer be allowed. Safety precautions. The march would instead go from the Afro-American Archive building to the courthouse and back again. Undaunted, Nancy Freed stood in front of the archive in a Free Mandela T-shirt and a pair of orthopedic shoes. She held a megaphone, ready to dispatch orders when the time came.

Sonny sat on the steps nearby in a pair of run-over work boots and overalls it looked like he'd slept in. Paul sat beside him. Sonny talked every now and then, and Paul just kind of nodded. I was too far away to hear what they were saying. I was in the parking lot, helping Lorraine. She sat on the ground, a ten-foot length of paper unrolled beside her, filling in the letters of the marching banner. The colors were black and green.

"Your daddy doing any better?" I asked her.

She shook her head. "Still trying to figure out something that doesn't make any sense. On top of all that, he spent half the night at the hospital. They took Council to South Alabama last night."

"How bad is he?"

"They don't know yet," she said. "But he's been in and out so much."

The letters spelling out MICHAEL'S MARCH FOR JUSTICE had been penciled on the paper to make sure they fit. Lorraine had outlined each letter in black, and we had all set to filling them out with the shoe box of green paint markers. She instructed the children on the other end to stay inside the lines.

"How's your brother?" she asked.

"He didn't want to talk about it."

"Be nice if not talking about it made it go away."

"He'll be all right," I told her. "This'll work out some kind of way."

She didn't answer right off, just kept on painting,

making quick work of the unpainted letters, careful not to smudge the rest. "We'll see."

Mrs. Freed held up her megaphone and asked for a moment of prayer for Council Ferguson. The people that had been milling around got close enough to join hands as a preacher from Eight Mile led a prayer for Council: "Look in on Council Ferguson, our good shepherd for all these years." Maybe he realized that his words were starting to sound like a eulogy, so he upped his tempo, delivered the common prologue to such marches: *wings of eagles, run and not be weary, promised land, path of righteousness*. Once he had said his piece, he ended with amen. "And amen again." For good measure.

The people who had prayed for sunshine didn't realize what they were asking for. The glare was blinding against the bright white of the archive. The weather wasn't fit for marching. It was already 80 degrees. Some of the old folks had turned out overdressed, hard-soled shoes and their best clothes. The planned route was three miles. I wondered if they'd be able to make it.

Nancy held the megaphone to her mouth once more to yell instructions, the most important of which was to say nothing from beginning to end. A silent march. No songs, and no chanting. "Silence" was the last word she yelled into the megaphone before we lined up and began to march.

The parade route went right through the middle of the Jubilee Fest. As soon as we walked over to Government Street, the quiet faded fast. The silent spectacle we were meant to create had to compete with the sights and sounds of the festivities—the generators that powered the vending trailers, the cover band on the Bienville Square stage. We were a few blocks or so removed from the Civic Center parking lot, where the bright carriages of the Ferris wheel rose above the rooftops. The screams of the riders carried down the side streets and drowned out our steps.

During the Jubilee Festivals that fell on election years, the politicians rode around in convertibles like they were beauty queens. The day of the march, all the politicians were at the waterfront, "breaking new ground," like all the posters said. Plans for the new Convention Center had been unveiled. We marched by one of the billboards that featured a rendering of the proposed development. It was quite a picture, a structure of glass and steel rivaled only by the other amenities that would share the waterfront property—a cruise ship terminal, a minor league baseball stadium, a riverside amphitheater. It would be an amazing future. Airbrushed trees and people, and not a cloud in the sky. On the top and bottom, WATERFRONT MOBILE: PORTAL TO THE NEW SOUTH.

We walked by one of those billboards in our old-time pose—holding hands, arms crossed in front, a posture much harder than it looks in the pictures. Can't get anywhere fast walking like that. Singing might have made the blocks go by a little easier, given some harmony to our steps. By the time I got the hang of it, we had turned the corner on the way back to where we started, from Government Street and the square back toward the Avenue and the archive building. A small crowd waited there, eager to hear the speeches. Some stood up when we rounded the corner, while others remained seated near the empty microphone, waiting to hear what came next.

Council Ferguson died on the second Monday in June. It was Lyle who made the phone call early that morning. I knew what had happened the minute I heard his voice. What started with the phone call that Monday ended a few days later, on a sad Saturday morning at New Emmanuel Baptist Church. The sanctuary was new and barely finished, but it was twice the size of their old building. Even that wasn't big enough to hold everyone who felt compelled to come, pay their respects to L. Council Ferguson.

There wasn't room enough for all of the flowers that had come for him. The family had decided to display just one, a wreath of red and white roses at the foot of the casket. The lid was open, and the bottom half was draped with the flag. Some of the veterans that had served with him lined several of the front rows on the right side of the church.

By noon, the church was filled, and others waited out-side on either side of the steps. It seemed like everyone who had ever known him came. The people he'd helped to orga-nize, longshoremen and mill workers, the porters who were still alive. Others came as well. Local dignitaries. Politicians doing their civic duty. The mayor. City council. County com-mission. When someone died, everybody wanted to do the right thing, and they wanted to be seen doing it.

The Ferguson family lined the front pews—Lyle's wife, Anna, their three children, and his brothers and sisters, their kids. All of those listed in the lengthy obituaries that ran in the local papers were gathered. Everyone was there except for Lyle. My father and I stood with Reverend Bell at the mouth of the hallway that led to the sanctuary. Lyle was going to deliver his father's eulogy, but first he'd asked for a few minutes to himself and gone into the pastor's study. His voice was hoarse, and his eyes made him look as tired as he sounded. I had disturbed him just long enough to give him the glass of water he had asked for.

"They wanted me to see if you needed anything else," I said, setting the glass on the table near his chair.

"Thank you, Roy," he said.

I'd learned that it is best to give people their space when they ask for it, but when I turned to walk away, he stopped me.

"I just needed a minute to get myself right," he said. "You just get to your wit's end, and then you think there's not any further you can go. Then you lose your best friend."

I felt for Lyle. All of those people outside were waiting for his eulogy, and the little bit of uplift it could give them. He just wanted to grieve. His father's funeral could not have been a private affair, because there were too many people who needed to say good-bye. Council Ferguson belonged to everyone, and by extension so did Lyle.

"I see all those people out there that he helped," he said. "All it does is make me think about the one I couldn't."

For people like Council Ferguson and Nancy Freed, and later Sonny and Lyle, Mobile had been a place of quiet victories. But it had been two weeks since the suspects were released, and no one else had been arrested. The only punishment rendered had been doled out at the root of that camphor tree. A month or so after Michael's body was found, Council had said on television, "If we cannot get justice for Michael Donald, then all of my work has been in vain." Those ended up being the last words he said in public. Once they took him to the hospital just before Memorial Day, he never came home.

"It all took its toll on him," he said. "Trying to make the world do right. Taking everything to heart."

People assume I am stronger than I really am. They confide things, regrets mostly. Things that they didn't have a chance to say to their departed before it was too late. As unsettling as the candor was, I did my best to listen.

"One of the things I always admired about your people," he said, "is that you always know the right thing to say."

"It's difficult sometimes," I told him. "A lot of time there is no right thing."

He nodded, gripping the rolled funeral program that listed the order of service, the regimen we would follow as we delivered Council to Old Hill. The picture on the cover had been taken in those robust years, before Lyle's father succumbed to one illness after another.

"If it were up to me, I'd just tell what I feel," he said. "We're all just going uphill until we die. The hill might not be as steep as it used to be, but we're still walking."

He looked so much like Council. The bones of his face, so many things.

"He called the office first thing every morning when he was able," Lyle told me. "Always wanted to know what I was working on. When your brother answered the phone, he always talked to him. My father admired him for what he did for us, all that work to help his friend."

His voice changed then. Tighter and some anger with the words. "I wish we had something to show for it."

"Maybe things will turn around," I told him, not knowing what else to say.

He smiled at me the way people smile at children, their naive questions.

"We went to the U.S. attorney last week," he said. "They don't like to intervene in local matters. States' rights."

Reverend Bell had four or five soft chairs in his study, but Lyle was sitting on one of the pews that had been salvaged from the old sanctuary.

"Your brother asked me if I had any hope," Lyle said. "I finally had to tell him no."

The pew looked uncomfortable. Stern and rigid, creaking with the shifting of his weight. It was cut from the sort of wood that was unyielding.

"This case is dead," he told me, in the tone that carried in it resignation, fatigue. "Civil case can't get far without a criminal prosecution. We know who killed Emmett Till. Medgar. All the others. Michael's name goes on that roll. All these years I've been trying to strike names off."

He placed his rolled-up program on the seat beside

him. The pew he sat on had been on the front row of the old church. A little shelf under the seat carried books, Bibles and hymnals that had been well worn. Lyle took one of the books, a hard surface to write on, as he added notes to the eulogy he'd written on the back of the program.

"I've been trying to figure out what to say about my father. Then I thought about one of the things they wrote about him in the paper this week. People called him a titan," he said. "We both know what happened to the Titans in the end."

A grandfather clock was hidden in the corner of Reverend Bell's study. I hadn't noticed it until it tolled the quarter hour. The funeral was scheduled to start in fifteen minutes.

"Just five more minutes, and I'll come on," he said. "I'll get myself together. I guess I have no choice."

He looked down at his program. Smoothed it out and stared at the picture of his father, the same one we'd used as a guide when we worked on Council's face.

"You all did a wonderful job with him," he said. "He looks like everyone remembered."

I gave Lyle his five minutes, stood waiting for him in the short hallway that connected the pastor's chamber and the sanctuary. My father and Reverend Bell were waiting. My father nodded to me, talking without talking. He used those little gestures and eyes to direct me during the services. He was asking if Lyle was all right. I nodded that he'd be out directly.

The door of the sanctuary was opened just enough for me to see the pallbearers, sitting on the first row of side pews, dressed in their dark suits and white gloves, each with a small lily pinned to his lapel. Reverend Bell pulled the door closed and looked at the notes he held in his hand, the brief remarks he would make before Lyle would speak.

I stood at the door, making sure he had his last five minutes alone. The little hallway was the last unfinished part of Emmanuel. They had completed the parts that were in plain view, but a few others still needed work. I stood on the naked side of the wet wall, where the PVC piping snaked into the baptismal on the other side of the cinder blocks. On the other side of the hall, the light filtered through the window. Those who wanted to honor Council Ferguson kept coming in a steady stream, the silhouettes passing on the etched glass and their shadows falling across the wall.

A different Lyle came out of that room. The other one, tired and confused, was gone, and everyone saw the Lyle Ferguson they expected. The one they needed to say something to make sense of this latest loss. When he walked into the pulpit, he didn't have the paper in his hand. He clutched both sides of the lectern, and delivered his father's eulogy.

Lyle spoke about one of his earliest memories of his father—sitting on Council's lap, listening to Joe Louis defend his title. A fitting tribute, because Joe Louis had died a few months before. Lyle spoke of following his two favorite champions. He talked of how champions were measured and tested, defeated and redeemed. "Council Ferguson was a champion, yours and ours." The grievers in the audience agreed; their amens moved in waves to the front of the church, where Council lay before them, surrounded by the flag and just enough flowers. The dignitaries nodded along with the mourners.

"You know Council Ferguson was a titan. He had an old Bell telephone in the office I shared with him. One at home, too. Lots of you all called him on it—at all hours." Lyle smiled when he said this, a light moment, giving those in the audience permission to laugh with him. "When that Bell tele-phone rang this time, it was the Lord calling him on home." More amens. Lyle got quiet for a little while. "Over these years, we've buried the men and women who helped to right our past." He paused for a moment, looking down on the pulpit, the color-draped casket below him. "It saddens me, it saddened my father, when we are forced to bury the ones who could have shaped our future. Sometimes in our haste to move past tragedy—conflict—the truth gets left in that dust pile. Only if we let it."

The dignitaries weren't as quick to nod then. But there were amens behind them and all around. Lyle had always been discreet, giving an economy to his words that was pre-cise, efficient. He didn't have to be explicit. Everyone in the room knew who he was talking about. The murder of Michael Donald was still in the air, just as foul as it had been. *Amen.* And then it was over. All that remained was putting Council in the ground.

As we prepared to leave the church, a gospel quartet rose along with the pallbearers, sang from the time my fa-ther closed the casket until the men reached the door. Their voices were old, and some of the notes weren't as precise as they once had been. But they felt what they were singing, and I suppose the people around them did, too. It won't be very long, they sang.

I walked in front of the pallbearers, keeping the aisle clear so they could walk unobstructed. It was hard, though. People reaching out and touching the casket, making the trip to the door a cumbersome walk for the men. Eight hands on the casket rails, eight sets of feet trying to move as one. De-spite the crowd, they moved patiently until they got Council's body to the hearse. And then it was my turn. I pulled out of the Emmanuel parking lot and led the line of cars, too long to see in the rearview, as we moved to Old Hill.

Interments are always smaller than funerals. It's hard enough for some people to make it to the church, let alone the cemetery. They would rather say their good-byes in the Lord's house, not stand there in the middle of the grass and stones. But Council's crowd was still large. Even the grave-diggers standing ready wore dress shirts and fresh pairs of pressed work pants, free of the red dust and mud that in their work was inevitable.

Sonny and Rhonda Watters stood at the graveside with Lorraine and Corey. I hadn't seen Sonny dressed in years. Even when they went to mass, he was casual, a little rumpled at times. He kept a suit in the downtown office to change into when he had to go to court. His clothes looked rigid around him, seemed like they had him boxed in.

My brother stood behind Sonny, and Paul looked just as empty. He wore his best clothes, the serious attire my father had splurged on. He put them on every afternoon to go to the job that had become everything to him.

"Lyle and Sonny told me they'll find some other things for me to work on," he had said. "I had forgotten there was anything else."

The uplifting words of the eulogy had run their course. All that was left were those ecclesiastical notes. The rites. The veterans folded Council's flag, and Reverend Bell spoke of ashes and dust. The quartet sang Taps—"Love, good night. Must thou go, when the day, and the night, need thee so?" I had only heard the trumpets and bugles, but never before the words. Once they finished singing, everyone was silent, and all that was left was the soft sound of the cranking as we lowered L. Council Ferguson into the ground.

Paul waited with me as the others went away. His truck was parked at the far end of the cemetery road. He'd been at the end of the procession. I suppose he'd taken a minute to decide if he wanted to come here and follow. Maybe he'd missed the procession altogether. Some people take their time, navigating the streets without the traffic stopping for them. A lot of folks are in no rush to get to those grounds.

The spring pollen was gone, but the summer heat brought the dust that was just as bad. When too much time passed between the rains, the dirt got loose and even a moderate wind would blow it into everything, coating our good clothes or clouding the finish of the cars it was my job to keep sparkling.

"After everything he did in this world," Paul said, "this is what happens. We put him in a hole and look down on him."

"Well, he's in a better place," I told him.

"Don't sell it if you don't believe it."

"What am I supposed to say?" I told him.

"Wish I knew."

Once the mourners threw their flowers and fistfuls of dirt, it was time for the others to come and finish. The grave-diggers stepped into their coveralls, took up their shovels, and walked toward Council Ferguson's grave. We watched them in silence for the first few minutes, hearing the sound their shovels made when they struck the rocks hidden in the pile.

"You think they're gone?" Paul asked me.

"Who?"

"Any of them," he said, nodding toward the lines of headstones, some carrying our name.

The Ferguson family plot was not too far from our own. It had once seemed so distant, but I thought about it more than I wanted to. We were all destined for Old Hill. No matter what we did between the present and the end, that part of it had been settled before we were even born.

"When you have them on the table," he said, "you ever think they're still here?"

"I don't know," I told him.

"Jesus walked around for forty days. I wonder how long it'll take the rest of us."

"It's easier for me not to wonder."

"I wish I didn't have to," he said.

At the head of Council's grave lay a simple stone. It carried his name and the years he spent in the world. Perhaps something more ornate would follow. Sometimes people add stones that list the handles they used to remember the departed. Champion. Titan. I remembered what Lyle had said. The Titans. I had studied them in school just like he had. They were as much human as they were god. In the end, they died like the rest of us.

Take a ride with me," Paul said.

"Where?"

"I just want you to see something."

We parked at the corner and watched them. The boys who lived in the house on Herndon were up early, ready to get their Fourth of July off to a good start. They had company, too. I counted seven in all. Four men and three women. The Dodge in the driveway had its trunk open, and they were loading cases of Old Milwaukee. A couple of the men had already started drinking.

"That's them," Paul said. "You'd think they'd be old men or something."

Not a one of those men looked older than thirty. One even looked like he was our age.

"I always imagine them wearing hoods," Paul said. "No need to hide your face when nobody's looking."

Seven thirty on a holiday morning, and the house on Herndon was alive with activity. Two men brought out coolers, one plastic and the other one Styrofoam. Another man and two women carried out bags of groceries, Lay's potato chips and hot-dog buns. They had boxes, too. A case of frozen meat patties, a cardboard box of fireworks.

"I suppose they have a lot to celebrate."

They were boisterous. Oblivious to anything going on outside that yard, including us. I might expect them to be inconspicuous. Laying low for a while. But watching them, they didn't seem the cautious type. No need to look over their shoulders. They'd killed a body across the street and just gone on about their business. Like hanging a body was the most natural thing in the world.

"Seems like the police or somebody could do something," I said.

"If they wanted to do something, they'd have done it already."

The folks in that house on Herndon loaded everything into the Chevy truck with a small rebel flag in the back window. Four people, two men and two women, loaded into the Dodge Wildcat in the driveway. Another man—his gut made him look ten years older—got in the driver's seat of the truck. A woman in a bikini top and a T-shirt over her shoulder came out of the house and locked the door behind her.

She took some sparklers from the box of fireworks and lit one with her cigarette. The glow was dulled by the daylight. From where we sat, the crackle and pop were impossible to hear. I'm sure she was looking forward to that evening, when the big shows would explode over the towns up and down the bay. She got in the car when the sparkler went out, and the last one they waited for stood by the garbage can that was still on the curb.

The boy who looked to be our age stood near the street, dumping the ashes from the grill into the trash. He'd brought the garden hose out with him. Once he'd finished cleaning the basin, he went to work on the metal grate. He squeezed the spray trigger full blast, sending the watered-down grime cascading toward the sewer.

"They barbecue in the yard most days when it's nice," Paul said. He dug his fingers into one of the holes in the seat vinyl, tearing away foam and dropping it to the floor with the other pieces.

"How long you been coming over here?"

The piece of foam that he dropped from his fingers settled on the floorboards with the rest.

"Long enough."

"You need to stop coming round here."

"Doesn't matter where I am. I can still see it," Paul told me. "It's like I see them doing what they did to him."

There were stubborn places on the grate that needed more than water. The boy took out his pocketknife and used the blunt edge to scrape off the grime. Once he finished, he loaded the grill into the back of the truck. As both vehicles backed out of the driveway, their radios blasted the same song, an upbeat song I'd never heard before, playing on a station I had no reason to listen to. They sped toward Springhill, rattling the loose manhole cover at the end of the street. The woman in the bikini had lit a second sparkler, dropped it in the street when the flame got too close to her fingers. On the Fourth of July morning, that sparkler burned against the asphalt for a few seconds more. And then it was just us, the burned-out sparklers, and the latest addition to the roll of infamous trees.

In the City Under the Trees, many had become infamous for one reason or another. We had read a story in the paper the week before about a peculiar tree in Needham, about a hundred miles north of Mobile. "The Tree That Really Cries," the headline had said. The wailing had been described as something between a brass and a wind. Softer than a hum, but louder than a whisper. It had attracted thousands of people, from holy rollers to botanists.

The experts had offered their explanations—sap rising from the roots, a chemical reaction from the soil, minerals in the water. Bodies were the same way. Sometimes they did strange things when they were on the table, made noises. Sometimes it was the gases leaving, or the effects the chemi cals had, blood running out and fluids running in. There were all sorts of reasons, but none of them mystical. Unless you choose to believe in such things.

But whatever anyone thought of it, phenomenon or miracle, they could all agree on one thing. The sound was dying. The estimate was that in a few days more, that thirty-foot pecan tree in Choctaw County would be dead silent like the others. Beside the picture of the tree, the newspaper printed a map of how to get there, but I had no reason to go. I had seen my fill of infamous trees. As I sat in my brother's truck, one was right outside the window.

When we were younger, Paul and I had hiked through the acres of anonymous woods with the rest of Mr. Davie's scouts. The trees we learned had names that read like stories. Grandfather's beard. Devil's walking stick. Hercules's club. Goldenrain. Burning bush. Tree of heaven. Mr. Davie made pieces of cardboard with numbers painted on them, tied them to the branches in the old-growth woods. For our merit badges, we matched the numbers to the name in English and Latin. *Magnolia grandiflora*. *Gingko biloba*. *Pinus palustris*.

Among the trees we learned was the camphor laurel. *Cinnamomum camphora*. The smell of the leaves was familiar. On the embalming table, I sometimes smelled camphor oil from the liniments on old people brought from the nursing homes. The infirm used the vapors to increase the circulation, facilitate blood flow through ailing bodies. I'm sure Michael's killers didn't have a clue, but the tree they chose was a tree meant for healing.

One grew in a schoolyard in Baldwin County, not too far from the Little Bethel Cemetery. A sign near its base marked it as a Champion Tree of Alabama, the biggest of the species. Dark green stars peppered the hiking maps, marking their whereabouts. We had done most of our hiking in Mobile and Baldwin Counties, between them home to nearly forty of those trees.

The Champions were identified by their plaques, but there were no markers to give away the infamous one on Herndon Avenue. The blue barricades had been taken away, and the homemade memorials were gone. Except for a dingy bit of yellow tape caught in the sewer grate, all signs of a crime scene were gone, either by the elements or by design.

The Fourth of July was an empty holiday. Aunt Camille and Uncle Greg didn't come down. Maurice and Jeanine had gone back to Michigan. The Fourth fell on a Saturday that year, but my parents let me take the day off while they handled the day's services. So it was just me, Paul, and our grandfather on Edgewater Beach.

When we caught up with him, Granddaddy had already started making the boil. Charcoal and twigs of driftwood lined the bottom of the shallow hole he'd dug. He scooped out a trench so the fire could breathe. Once the wood burned down to embers, we covered the pit with a grate and a twenty-gallon pot. After the sweet corn and potatoes had cooked, we dropped the shrimp, crawfish, and sausage in for the last few minutes. At just about sunset, we ate and waited for the fireworks.

"You boys remember when I taught you to swim right out there?" my grandfather said. He pointed toward the pier, squinting like he could see himself out there, correcting our strokes.

"Yes, sir," Paul said. "We remember."

"Your grandmother and I used to bring Randall and Greg down here in the summertime."

He told the same stories every time. Perhaps it was nostalgia, old age, or a little of both. Double-checking the memories to make sure they were still there. As we walked down the empty stretch, he pointed out where things used to be. Changing houses, guard towers, concession stands. They had been replaced by then with a line of green and gold port-o-potties and a signpost listing the prohibitions. No dumping. No diving. No lifeguard on duty.

When Paul and I got in the water, my grandfather didn't follow us in. He just stood there on the beach, hands clasped behind him, waiting for the fireworks. The water was nearly empty by then as the last of the swimmers came ashore and waited for the festivities to begin. The show that had been planned for that year would be bigger than usual on account of the bicentennial year. In 1781, Cornwallis surrendered at Yorktown, kicking off two hundred years of liberty. The first explosive whistled into the sky, exploded in red, white, and blue. "The Battle Hymn of the Republic" played over the loudspeakers, underscored by the applause from the gathered.

Paul and I watched from the water. I dipped under and looked up at the starbursts distorted by the waves. While the water played with the light, it magnified the sounds. The whistles and booms were sharp beneath the waves. Paul was a little farther out, treading with clean, slow strokes that kept his head well above the surface. During the thirty-minute show, the Eastern Shore fireboats shot their water cannons in the air. The lights on their decks had colored filters, tinting the arcs of water with the red, white, and blue.

When the fireworks ended, people gathered their belongings and packed their cars. Once the sky was dark again, and the last color on the beach was the red glow of taillights as vehicles passed, my grandfather doused the fire and threw the sand over the hole, leaving it like he found it.

"You boys ready?"

By then I had already gotten out of the water. When I picked up our shirts and shook off the sand, Paul stood in the shallow water, looking down the beach. Little starbursts dotted the shoreline, where beachgoers continued their own fire shows, with Roman candles and bottle rockets. I thought about the people we'd seen that morning on Herndon Avenue. Maybe they were back on their street lighting sparklers, finishing the celebration they had started. They could have been somewhere near, for all we knew. It was a free country, after all. They were free to go where they pleased.

"Let's go," I said, but Paul hadn't moved. He stood there, slow to leave the ankle-deep water, waiting for a Jubilee that would never come.

Jubilee

July 15 fell on a Wednesday that year. Paul and I had planned to go to the Eastern Shore the night before like we always did, hang out at Edgewater until midnight. My father had told me that I could have the day off if things weren't too busy, but we got three bodies, and I ended up having to work. I had to go to the same nursing home twice in one day.

I tried to think about the only bright side I could find. In four weeks, I'd be gone, and it would be somebody else's run to make. On the way home from the second pickup, I saw the approaching weather out the window. Sunny days in July were nothing remarkable, but that Tuesday's overcast gave me something to look forward to. The first Jubilee of the season looked like it was only a few hours away. It gave me a distraction, at least. Every few minutes I looked out the hall window to make sure the clouds were still there.

There had been close calls all summer. The conditions looked right, and then the balance would fall apart. The cloud cover passed over, or the rains came. The wind could blow too quickly, or succumb to the humidity and not blow at all. When I left the funeral home at nine o'clock that evening, the air felt like it was supposed to. I went home to change clothes, and then I made my way across the bridge.

Paul had left for Edgewater before I did. Whenever he got there early, he would go for a swim. The bay waters felt different on those nights, patches of cold and warm, some parts thick and others swift moving. While I spent a lot of those hours asleep in the back of my brother's truck or walking the beach, Paul spent much of that time in the water. He liked the water most of all on those nights. Said the waters eased his mind.

His truck was parked on the side of the beach road, near the remains of the pier. I parked right behind him. The buckets and stakes were still in the payload. He left them in there all summer, just in case. I called Paul's name, expecting to hear him call back from the water, the beach, somewhere, but there was nothing there but the east-blowing wind that rattled the hooks and shackles of the sailboats down the beach.

A pack of cigarettes sat on his dashboard, but when I opened the box, there was only one left. I couldn't smoke his last one. Maybe when he came out of the water, we'd run to the Shell station up on Highway 98 and get a carton. Paul had thrown his shirt across the seat, and his shoes were on the floorboard. I called for him again. I thought that maybe he was too far out to hear me yelling against the wind. I just stood there on the beach and waited.

Paul had always liked the bay, said the waters eased his mind. But those waters can be tricky even for the best swimmers. The currents were familiar there in the water we'd learned to swim in, but sometimes the rules would change on you. Hidden things along the bottom, some that have been there forever and others just carried down from the river. So many things to be careful of, rips and breaks, water moving fast along the jetties. All kinds of water moving in and out all at once. It's easy to get turned around, disoriented. Even for the strongest of us.

I took the floodlight from my brother's toolbox. I found the old lifeboat anchored about a hundred yards out. I called out to him again. Maybe he was out there, just beyond where the light faded. So I waited.

The medical examiner said that it was an accident, but I can't help but wonder. I wonder about a lot of things. How it might have been different if he'd still been here. If he had never stopped on the way home and found Michael's body. If he hadn't gone in the water without me.

I never made it to New Orleans. After my brother passed, it was no time for me to leave. I went to college in Mobile. In the back of my mind, I kept saying that I might eventually leave, but I never did. I couldn't do that to my parents. Instead, I just stayed and worked as hard as I could. I did my part and tried my best to keep moving.

EPILOGUE

In the months and years after Michael Donald was killed, nobody forgot what happened even if they wanted to. But there seemed to be a collective resignation for most people. Some believed that justice would never come. I'm sorry to say I felt the same.

But then in the fall of 1983, Lyle Ferguson was appointed the assistant U.S. attorney for Mobile. His first order of business was going after the people who killed Michael Donald. He had the FBI question a nineteen-year-old Klansman by the name of James "Tiger" Knowles. It didn't take long for Knowles to roll over. He confessed to killing Michael Donald, and he also told the FBI who was with him. Henry Hays, the son of the man who had ordered the murder, Bennie Jack Hays. It was no surprise. They were the ones everybody had always suspected.

Justice came in pieces. Trials and mistrials. I went to as many of the trials as I could. The one I remember most was the first of them, the murder trial of Henry Hays. It started just before Christmas in 1983. Lorraine was home on her winter break, and she sat beside me in the courthouse as we listened to Tiger Knowles tell what they did to Michael Donald on that night almost three years before.

Bennie Jack Hays was upset over the mistrial of Josephus Anderson, who had killed a white police officer in Birmingham. Hays decided that action was required. He sent his son Henry and Knowles to find a black man to kill. Missionary work was what they called it. They set out with a box cutter, a gun, and a borrowed rope. Tiger made the noose, thirteen coils, then burned both ends of the rope so it wouldn't fray.

As they were riding around looking for a victim, Michael was watching the UAB game at his sister's house. When it was over, he set out for home. By 11:00 P.M., Henry and Tiger had been riding up and down King Avenue and St. Stephens Road for forty minutes. They were about to call it a night, but then they saw him. Michael had stopped for cigarettes at the corner gas station when they found him. They used his kindness against him, asked for directions to a downtown bar. "Hey, buddy. You know where we can find Powers?"

Henry spoke low so Michael would come closer to hear him.

"Where?"

"Powers Lounge. Know where that is?"

"Oh. Hang a right at the stop sign, three lights down."

When Michael pointed out the way, he turned his head. He didn't see Hays pull the gun. He didn't hear Tiger open his door and come around behind him with the box cutter. Knowles forced Michael into the backseat and set off over the causeway. "Do what we say, and we won't kill you. We just want your money." When the scattered lights from the gas stations came into the car, Michael looked down and saw the noose Tiger had hidden between his feet. "No, please don't kill me. You know, you can do whatever you want to, beat me or anything else. But just don't kill me."

Lyle: "When you got over to Baldwin County, did he ever try to fight back?"

Tiger: "Yes, he did. He attacked both of us, Henry and myself, and he fought like a madman."

They stopped near one of the marshes north of the causeway. As soon as Tiger opened the door, Michael went for the gun. It fired once, hitting nothing, and fell to the ground. Michael had gotten free of Tiger, but by then Henry Hays knocked him to the ground with a tree branch. Knowles straddled him, while Hayes went back to the truck for the rope.

Tiger: "Between the both of us, we got the rope around his neck . . ."

The boot print on the side of Michael's face belonged to Henry. He held his foot there while the two of them pulled the rope as tight as they could get it. Then Henry picked up the branch and started beating.

Lyle: "Where was Henry hitting him?"

Tiger: "In the head. Anywhere."

Lyle: "Was Michael on the ground?"

Tiger: "He kept getting up and falling back down."

Michael managed to catch the branch to stop Henry from swinging. That's when Henry got the box cutter and started slashing.

Lyle: "What happened after Henry slashed him with the knife?"

Tiger: "He just fell. And then Henry rushed over to the

other end of the rope and grabbed the rope and started pulling. It was like he was enjoying this. Then he was pulling it, and then finally I said, 'Well, he's dead.' "

Some of the people in the courtroom lowered their heads. Others just rocked. There were tears in the jury box. The people in those first rows knew Michael, and others just knew him from that story, and from the pieces that filled evidence bags on a nearby table. The yellow rope. A dark blue pair of Levi's. A leather wallet with money still inside. A silver belt buckle. A plaid shirt. A gray pullover sweater. All with splotches of old blood. The toes of the Converse sneakers were scraped where they'd dragged Michael's body across the street.

Lyle: "What time did y'all hang the body?"

Tiger: "About five thirty."

My brother got off work at six that morning and stopped for the doughnuts. It took ten minutes to get to Springhill, if that. Paul bought the same thing every Saturday morning from the Krispy Kreme—three crullers, three chocolate iced rings, half a dozen glazed. He'd left the truck running because he'd just be in and out. That time of morning there was never a line. Down the street, Tiger and Henry sat in the living room with the windows open. They wanted to hear the commotion when the body was found. It didn't take long. Forty-five minutes after they put Michael's body in the camphor tree, they heard Paul screaming.

Lorraine squeezed my hand, held it tight. She was there with me when I had to bury my brother. When Lorraine first left for school, she called me all the time, wrote me just as much. She always wanted to make sure I was all right. Eventually, we put more space between the phone calls and letters, and prepared to go our ways. But that December we sat there together and listened to those difficult words from the men who had killed Michael Donald and affected all of us.

"I used to watch Lyle and my father in court all the time," Lorraine said, as we stood in front of the courthouse. "I was always bored. Some things I couldn't really appreciate until I was old enough."

The civil trial started on Valentine's Day in 1987. That was the one that everybody remembers. Sonny was one of the lawyers who tried the civil case against the United Klan of America, Inc. The Donald family won a $7 million verdict that the Klan never paid. Bankrupting them was as close to justice as the family would get.

I was at that trial as well, but Lorraine wasn't sitting beside me. She was sitting in the first row behind the lawyers. She had taken a leave from law school to help with the trial. When it was over, Lorraine went back to Tuscaloosa to finish, and then she came back to Mobile. As much as we both talked about leaving for good, here we are.

A few more cars come down the beach road, but most of the people don't venture this far down. A trip across the sand with full baskets is a long enough walk as it is. I don't mind it so much. It's the price I pay for a little peace. The voices are so far away the words can't reach me. The noises don't last long enough to be a bother. Tires on the road shells. The last bit of radio before the engine's turned off. The slam of a car door. After those moments, it is quiet. Or it was quiet, at least. I forgot that I left my phone on. The ringer is so loud it nearly scares me. HOME flashes in the display. Lorraine is calling.

"Happy Birthday."

"Not for another nine and a half minutes."

"Your watch is slow. Forty's nothing to be scared of."

"How would you know?"

"I've heard rumors," she tells me. "The weather holding up all right?"

"Looks like it."

I can hear the girls in the background. They just turned six in April.

"The ladies have a surprise for you."

When they sing "Happy Birthday" into the phone, Nia sings a little bit louder. Karen sounds halfway asleep. They sing three verses—*Happy Birthday to you / How old are you / May the good Lord bless you*—and would have sung more if they knew any.

"Did you get our crabs yet?" Nia is talking over her sister, who's awake now and still singing.

"Not yet," I tell them. "Go on to bed, and I might have some in the morning. Okay?"

"Okay."

They are a handful. Well-intentioned and overwhelming at the same time. They covered the back of the truck with their mother's bumper stickers: "Re-elect Lorraine Deacon Circuit Judge." I had to peel half of them off to get the tailgate open.

"They'll be up half the night," I tell Lorraine.

"If I didn't let them call, I'd hear about it. You know how they are about their daddy."

"Jack didn't want to sing to me, I guess."

"My father had him out there cutting his yard this afternoon. He's upstairs, knocked out," she tells me. "He can sing at the surprise party you found out about."

"You know your daddy can't keep a secret. Don't tell him I ratted him out."

"Oh, so I'm supposed to keep a secret about the secret he let slip?"

"Something like that."

She laughs for a moment, and then we're both quiet. I had tried to sound cheerful, but when I'm out here, it gets hard.

"You okay?"

"Yes and no. You know."

"Yeah. I know."

She has let me have these nights to myself, no matter how hard they can be sometimes. Jubilees are like those drifting holidays, movable feasts they're called, that come according to a formula few of us really understand. I've stopped trying to understand why. I just come here to make my own peace.

Paul stands in the ankle-high water, looking at the sky. The clouds look like they might be thinning. The matches down the beach are flickering again. Even to the most optimistic of the watchers, it isn't a good sign. Things can go either way.

"The weather might break," I tell Paul.

"It won't be long," Paul tells me. "Have a little faith."

The tide is coming in a little farther now. The edge of the wet sand gets a little closer each time. His feet are in the water, and he's looking at the clouds.

"It'll hold," he says. No doubt in his mind.

I remember what Sonny said in his closing at the civil trial. It sounded like a eulogy. *There's no logic in this. There's no reason in this. There's no rhyme to it.* I think about that when I'm here with the peace I've tried to make with things I can't explain. I think about it when I'm at Old Hill, where Paul is buried in the plot with our namesakes.

"It'll be here after while," he says. "I wish I could wait here with you, but—"

"I know."

I stayed in Mobile to do the only work I've ever known. I still stand in those churches on Saturdays, listening to the same scriptures I hear repeated on Sunday mornings. We care for the bodies of the dead. The rest of them—I don't know. I have more questions than I have faith. A mustard seed, they say. Maybe that's enough. One day I'll know. We all will.

"For the brothers who ain't here."

I take a drink, and I pour a swallow on the sand. I look down at the ground as the bit of Crown I poured wets the driftwood, soaks into the sand.

"For the brothers who ain't here."

Author's Note

Some background information on the Jubilee phenomenon came from the city of Daphne website: www.daphneal.com. Additional information on the Mobile area was found on the city of Mobile website: www.cityofmobile.org.

The court transcript from the *Beulah Mae Donald v. United Klans of America, Inc.* civil trial was provided by the Southern Poverty Law Center, with the aid of the Honorable Vanzetta McPherson.

Mortuary science consultation was provided by Bernard Howard, of Christian Benevolent Funeral Home, Mobile, Alabama. Forensic science consultation was provided by Dr. Roger Mitchell Jr., a fellow at the Office of the Chief Medical Examiner, New York, New York.

Information on the history of Mobile's black community was collected at the National African-American

Archives-Museum, 564 Martin Luther King Jr. Drive, Mobile, AL 36603.

Champion tree information was obtained from the booklet entitled *Champion Trees of Alabama*, published by the Alabama Forestry Commission and available online at www .forestry.state.al.us.

While this work is fictional, several sources were reviewed during the completion of this novel. Many of the articles listed below were found in the local history collection at the Mobile Public Library:

"Ex-Klansman Hays gets June 6 execution date" (staff and wire reports). *Mobile Register*, May 2, 1997.

"Mother of slain black son takes possession of KKK building won in lawsuit." *Jet*, June 8, 1987, p. 72.

"Paying for racism." *Time*, February 23, 1987, p. 129.

Associated Press. "Blacks criticize handling of Alabama Klan case." Special to the *New York Times*, June 20, 1983.

Busby, Renee. "Knowles tells of murdering Donald." *Mobile Press*, February 5, 1988.

———. "Knowles testifies he was ordered to kill." *Mobile Register*, February 5, 1988.

———. "Donald's brother: Hays must 'deal with the Lord now.'" *Mobile Register*, August 9, 1993.

———. "Hays house historic?" *Mobile Press-Register*, November 22, 1995.

Donelson, Cathy. "Seven-million-dollar award against KKK sends a message about racism." *Montgomery Advertiser*, February 15, 1987.

Drago Jr., Arthur. "KKK official, wife charged with fraud." *Mobile Register*, September 14, 1984.

Drago, Chip. "Black officers call for reprimand." *Mobile Register*, March 24, 1981.

———. "Two held in '81 murder." *Mobile Register*, June 17, 1983.

Durrett, Mary Alma. "A turning point case." *Azalea City News & Review*, April 11, 1985.

Herndon, Mike. "Spanish Fort to take over Meaher Park?" *Mobile Press-Register*, November 18, 1995.

Ivins, Molly. "Beulah Mae Donald: Ms. Magazine woman of the year." *Ms. Magazine*, January, 16, 1988.

Jennings, Tom. "Reward offered in teen's death." *Mobile Press*, March 23, 1981.

———. "Three charged with murder in Mobile hanging case." *Mobile Press*, March 25, 1981.

———. "Three men remain in custody as slaying motive sought." *Mobile Press*, March 26, 1981.

Johnson, Vi. "Former Klansman 'guilty' in Michael Donald slaying." *Inner City News*, May 27, 1989.

Jordan, Herb. "SCLC chief Jackson to lead protest march." *Mobile Press*, April 2, 1981.

———. "Klan said operated like military." *Mobile Register*, February 11, 1987.

———. "Jury rules against Klansmen." *Mobile Register*, February 13, 1987.

———. "Hay's hearing postponed." *Mobile Register*, May 13, 1989.

———. "Ex-Klansman: Cox said black should be hanged." *Mobile Register*, May 17, 1989.

Jordan, Herb, and Kathy Jumper. "Figures tells blacks here to be cool, cautious." *Mobile Register*, March 24, 1981.

Jumper, Kathy. "Police ask for help in death probe." *Mobile Register*, March 23, 1981.

———. "Hays indicted for Donald murder." *Mobile Register*, June 23, 1983.

———. "Klansman pleads innocent to capital murder charge." *Mobile Register*, July 9, 1983.

———. "Hays said looking for a black." *Mobile Register*, December 7, 1983.

———. "Details of killing related by Knowles." *Mobile Register*, December 8, 1983.

———. "Hays' ex-wife testifies in Donald murder case." *Mobile Press*, December 9, 1983.

———. "Hays trial proceedings tense." *Mobile Register*, December 9, 1983.

———. "Hays found guilty of capital murder." *Mobile Press-Register*, December 11, 1983.

———. "Knowles testifies against Cox." *Mobile Register*, March 13, 1985.

———. "Former area Klansman testifies against Cox; Galanos rests case." *Mobile Register*, March 14, 1985.

———. "Mother sought reasons not revenge, for killing." *Mobile Press-Register*, December 20, 1987.

Jumper, Kathy, and Eddie Menton. "Three charged in Donald murder." *Mobile Register*, March 26, 1981.

Kenney, Nancy. "Body of 21st Youth Found." *Mobile Press* (Associated Press), March 31, 1981.

Kornbluth, Jesse. "The woman who beat the Klan." *New York Times Magazine*, November 1, 1987, p. 136.

Kunen, James S. "Seeking justice for her lynched son, an Alabama mother ruins the Klan that killed him." *People Weekly*, June 8, 1987, p. 27.

Langford, David. "Police doubt hanging a racial incident." *Mobile Register* (Associated Press), March 27, 1981.

Mason, Tom. "The tree that really cries." *Mobile Press*, April 28, 1981.

McFadyen, Chris. "Attorneys set sights on Klan assets." *National Law Journal*, March 2, 1987, p. 9.

Menton, Eddie, and Herb Jordan. "Man found hanged on city street." *Mobile Press-Register*, March 22, 1981.

Mitchell, Cynthia D. "God will give the courage" (letter to the editor). *Mobile Press-Register*, June 24, 1989.

Mitchell, Garry. "Civil rights leaders hail KKK verdict." *Mobile Press-Register*, February 14, 1987.

Moore, Trudy S. "Black lawyer forces KKK to pay $7 million for lynching black, 19." *Jet*, March 9, 1987.

Poore, Ralph. "Boyington Oak a local legend." *Mobile Press*, May 1, 1989.

Press, Aric. "Going after the Klan; a $7 million verdict imperils a hate group." *Newsweek*, February 23, 1987.

Reeks, Anne. "$250,000 bonds are set in Mobile hanging case." *Mobile Press*, March 27, 1981.

———. "Bail set for men charged in Donald slaying." *Mobile Press-Mobile Register Weekend*, March 28, 1981.

———. "Murder suspects bound over." *Mobile Press*, April 16, 1981.

———. "Bail for three men accused in Donald Case is reduced." *Mobile Register*, May 9, 1981.

———. "Alleged perjurer in Donald case held." *Mobile Register*, June 12, 1981.

———. "Donald probe renewed; all three suspects freed." *Mobile Press-Register*, June 14, 1981.

Reifenberg, Michael P., and the Associated Press. "Convict in Mobile lynching among those freed by board." *Mobile Register*, September 11, 2000.

Smith, Buddy. "Nature factor in eliminating obscure legend from Baldwin." *Mobile Press-Register*, March 22, 1981.

Sweatt, Earl. "Three deny guilt in Donald murder." *Mobile Register*, April 1, 1981.

Werneth, George. "All-white jury to hear Klan trial." *Mobile Register*, February 10, 1987.

Wilson, Michael. "New trial for Hays denied." *Mobile Register*, March 7, 1995.

———. "Execution of a Klansman: Michael didn't come home." *Mobile Register*, June 1, 1997.

———. "Execution of a Klansman: Raised in hate." *Mobile Register*, June 2, 1997.

———. "Execution of a Klansman: Bennie Jack's Klan." *Mobile Register*, June 3, 1997.

———. "Execution of a Klansman: Cases closed." *Mobile Register*, June 4, 1997.

———. "Execution of a Klansman: The final hours." *Mobile Register*, June 5, 1997.

———. "Execution of a Klansman: Hays put to death." *Mobile Register*, June 6, 1997.

———. "Klansman's death row appeal rejected by circuit court." *Mobile Press-Register*, June 8, 1996.

———. "Witness to the execution." *Mobile Press-Register*, June 10, 1997.

———. "Hays made confession to minister." *Mobile Register*, July 8, 1997.

Reading Group Guide

Many people in today's America assume that the horror of lynching is a thing of the past. But Ravi Howard's eloquent first novel describes a lynching that happened just in 1981, in a middle-class neighborhood in Mobile, Alabama. In elegant prose, Howard lays out not only the grotesque murder itself, but also the consequences that spread necessarily from it, like ripples from a rock thrown into a pond. Based on a true story, the novel engages powerful questions of racism, identity, family, and memory, with originality and subtlety. The story of Roy Deacon and his brother Paul, and their intricate negotiations with family, death, tradition, and religion, is told with marvelous attention to the smallest details of everyday life. It is through these details and images that Roy and Paul's world moves in each of us, and Howard understands the relationship between great and small in a way that illuminates every page. The pain of any death, but especially that of a crime as hideous as lynching, can never be forgotten.

QUESTIONS FOR DISCUSSION

1. In what ways does this novel reveal the differences between racism as it was practiced in the civil rights era and as it exists more recently?

2. Religion and the church have played a crucial role in African-American history. How does Howard show the strengths and possible weaknesses of this tradition through his characters?

3. This story is, among many other things, an exploration of the power of memory. How did the end of the novel change your perception of the Prologue, and of Roy Deacon's character?

4. The ties, joys, and obligations of family is another major theme of Howard's novel. How would you describe the difference between Roy's father and Lorraine's father, and the effects that these fathers have on their children?

5. Do you think the author demonstrates a difference in the ways that men and women respond to death?

6. How did you feel about Roy's final decision to accept his role in the family business, in spite of his youthful determination to escape it? How does familial obligation shape our lives?

7. Is it a simple thing to assign blame in this tragic story? Are the police portrayed as enemies?

8. What are some of the meanings of "Jubilee" in this novel, and especially to the character of Roy?

9. In what ways does Howard explore the idea of identity? What is the importance of identity, to anyone of any culture, in today's world?

10. Think about the ways in which racism exists not only in America, but also in the world today. How has it impacted your life?

QUESTIONS FOR THE AUTHOR

1. What does the title of this novel mean to you?

The title of Like Trees, Walking *comes from a Bible verse, Mark 8:24. In the parable, Jesus heals a blind man by rubbing clay across his eyes. Jesus does the action once, and asks the man what he sees. The man says that he can see, but men appear to be like trees walking. Then Jesus repeats the action, and the man can see clearly. For me, the title was an acknowledgment that there are often intermediate steps involved in change or progress. During that process, we become aware of the changes as well as the challenges still ahead.*

2. How do you view the role of identity in African-American culture today? Do you see this role changing from what it was in the early sixties and before?

Since so many African-Americans have Southern roots, I think there is a multilayered relationship with that legacy. Through the 1960s, many were leaving Jim Crow and racism but holding on to the family bonds. In recent years, there seems to be a sense of rediscovery of Southern history, both the bitter and the sweet, which can be found throughout black literature. For reasons of family, cost of living, and professional opportunity, more blacks are returning to the South. I think it's important for many blacks to embrace and confront elements of our history in America.

3. Were the characters in this novel, especially in their family relations, in any way based on your own experience?

Growing up in Montgomery, Alabama, I had the chance to meet many people who had firsthand experience with the civil rights movement. The stories they told were much richer than the sanitized versions of history that are often presented. That experience inspired me to write a more street-level view of historical fiction. It's been my experience that people are sometimes reluctant participants in historical events. Things happen around them and they adapt. That happened in Montgomery, Mobile, and in other places. I wanted to write a story that reflected that idea, how Roy, Paul, Lorraine, and their families adjust to this murder and its aftermath.

4. Your narrative style is precise, perceptive, and also compassionate. How do you work with anger in relation to the frustrating slowness with which our culture seems to change?

I am not sure if it is a question of anger or frustration, but I think it is more a question of seeing the details necessary to draw our own conclusions about the world. I think there is power in being able to find our own answers, instead of waiting for others to point them out. That is why writing is empowering, whether it is fiction or nonfiction, because writers have to do for themselves.

5. What do you see as the role of fiction, as opposed to nonfiction, in addressing change and reaching the hearts of people who are inflexible in their beliefs?

There is a term used to describe science fiction, calling it speculative fiction. I think the term speculative fiction can also be applied to historical fiction. We can never really know what historical figures were thinking in those quiet, private moments. I think fiction allows us to say, "What if?" Historical fiction gives us a chance to think about the interior humanity of real and imagined characters during pivotal eras.

5/23

LAURA ONGIRI

RAVI HOWARD received the 2001 Zora Neale Hurston/ Richard Wright Award for College Writers for his short story "Like Trees, Walking." After graduating from Howard University, he received his MFA from the University of Virginia. His writing has also appeared in *The Massachusetts Review* and *Callaloo*. *Like Trees, Walking* is his first novel. A native of Montgomery, Alabama, Howard lives in Mobile.